SOUTHERN BACK ROADS

M. Edward Warner

Contents

Acknowledgement

F or the dads...

Who at their best ushered us into manhood. And who at their worst taught us what we didn't want to be.

Preface

The Atheists have won. The last vestige of religion has surrendered to the army of knowledge. With the fall of the Catholic Church, the last stronghold of the world's religions, the religious wars are over! As the Roman Catholic Church was emptied of its instruments of superstition, Dr. Wolfe shouted his keynote phrase to the jeering army, "Science is the new religion, and *Star Trek* is the future!" We are free!

Almost...

Welcome to the future. The Eyebits Corporation is dedicated to making the future the best it can be for you and those closest to you. Together, we can make this world one free of disease, poverty, starvation, religion, want, failed marriages, poor health, untimely death, abuse, and neglect. By staying connected, you contribute to the most peaceful time in Earth's history.

By being connected, you conform, and conforming keeps you safe.

Soon, you will no longer have to disconnect. The bit corps of engineers is hard at work developing the permanent, non-removable Eyebits. Once engaged, these self-adhesive contact bits never have to be removed. Even your dreams will consist of the same peaceful environment you enjoy in the waking world.

Private dreams are dangerous.

We are tirelessly working to keep the world as it is. Conformity is the number one core value of the Eyebits Corporation. You are encouraged to grant us complete access to your Eyebits. Complete access allows the corporation to monitor all aspects of your life anywhere and anytime you are connected.

Let us care for you.

Thought equals suffering. Let us take away your suffering. Complete access allows your personal Eyebit to select for you exactly what you need. Complete access will allow us to choose your perfect lifelong mate, the perfect diet, and even the best fashion for your bit-suit to display. We know what you want before you want it.

Submission is perfection.

Today is the future, and the future is a great place to be if you let us make it that way for you. ~Bitcorp

Introduction

J ack stood before the car holding his granddaughter's hand. Even though he had spent his entire adult life in this automobile's presence, it still impressed him. The Vista-Blue paint sparkled in the museum light, and he wondered if it always looked *that* good or if it was mostly the lighting.

"Papaw Jack, it's your car, the one you got from your Grandpa Pops," his granddaughter stated matter-of-factly as she pointed at the antique vehicle.

"That's right, sweetie. The one I helped him restore in the old house when I was a young man."

"Sir?" A voice called from the left of where they were standing. "Oh my, it is you!" a museum tour guide said as he approached Jack. "They told us you liked to drop by randomly, but I didn't think it would be on my shift." The guide stood in awe for a moment before regaining his composure. "Sir, can I please shake your hand?"

"Of course," Jack said as he thrust his hand out.

"It's an honor to meet you. I've read all about your exploits," the guide said.

The two men finished shaking hands, and Jack looked back at the car. "Is it all right if I sit in her?"

The tour guide seemed confused for a moment before he realized Jack wasn't just being polite but was trying to observe the museum rules. "Oh, yes, sir. The way I see it, this is your Mustang anyway. We're just parking it for you."

Jack had just eased into the driver's seat when his granddaughter asked, "Can I drive?"

"Well, of course you can," Jack said as he helped her climb into the car. She sat down on his lap and immediately started making *vroom vroom* noises and trying to turn the wheel. Jack joined in the fun and gave out commands. "Red light. Green light."

The two carried on this way for a few minutes before Jack's legs began to hurt and he had to get out of the car. He left his granddaughter in the driver's seat and delighted in watching her explore the car. The museum guide had come to stand beside him.

"Sir, may I ask you a question?" the guide said.

"Of course you can, young man."

"Is it true you were once addicted to an Eyebit?"

"Didn't you say you read all my exploits?"

"Oh, yes, sir. But most of them talk about the later years. I'm interested in how you managed to get free of it to begin with. How did you first see the addiction? Like, how did it start?" the guide clarified.

"Oh, you mean how did I get free from the Eyebits that were later proven to be designed to be addictive? But that story isn't as exciting as the others."

"I still would like to hear it if you don't mind."

"Okay, young man. She's occupied for the moment, so I suppose I can tell you." Jack pointed at his granddaughter, cleared his throat, and began. "So, most people know of how Pops and I worked on this car, which led to the change. But it was my dad, Kyle, who kickstarted the whole thing. See, Dad grew up without Eyebits, but I didn't. He knew something was wrong. He just didn't know what to do about it..."

CHAPTER ONE

Eyebit Immersion 100%

Years had passed since Kyle last visited his father's house. *Place still looks pretty good. Dad really kept it up,* Kyle thought as he examined the landscape. As he stood in the street in front of the house, his Eyebit provided a steady stream of information. When he directed his pupils to the yard, information appeared on the screen.

- ***Grass manicured approx. 5 days ago.***

Looking at the shrubs led his Eyebit to provide a detailed history and analysis.

- ***Pruned approx. 45 days ago. Soil acidic. Recommend base supplements.***

Kyle looked over to the vegetable garden, and a picture of a healthy, mature example of what was growing was displayed on the left side of the screen. On the right was a picture of the garden's current state. Across the bottom of the screen streamed an analysis of its current condition and recommendations for optimization.

- *Yellow Squash. For optimal flavor, pick 5 days from now.*

- *Tomatoes. Deceased. Uproot and replant from seed in spring.*

- *Green bell peppers. Pick in 24 hours.*

- *Peanuts. Ready for picking.*

- *Basil. Ready for picking.*

Returning his attention to the front door, Kyle approached. He recalled the last time he and his father had exchanged words. *In anger,* Kyle thought. The fight they had had was small enough that they avoided coming to blows but big enough to keep him away.

Kyle noticed a parcel sitting to the left of the front door. When he examined the package, Kyle's Eyebit detected the airway bill. Upon scanning the barcode, the package's history was displayed.

- *Robox Drone #190345767 performed a pickup for Order #07 at antique parts*

- *Robox Drone #898736435 processed shipment at facility*

- *Robox Drone #635464750 loaded shipment. Freighter #876456 moved to CLT*

- ***Robox Drone #343740403 processed shipment for delivery***

- ***Robox Drone #562398463 delivered shipment (left at door)***

Tucking the shipment under his arm, Kyle knocked on his father's front door. Surprisingly, the door was ajar and opened with the force of his first knock.

"Dad?" he called out. As Kyle entered the house, his Eyebit offered no information. **Privacy block in place!** blinked across the screen over and over.

Having never seen that error before, Kyle queried, "Define 'privacy block." Then he called out "Dad?" once more.

Privacy Block. Address is in the shower and is indecent. When bathing is complete, connection will be established.

"Address? What? Dad! Are you here!?" Kyle called out again.

"Back here! In the garage." Pops's voice echoed through the house.

Kyle followed the familiar sound of a ratchet cranking as it reverberated through the house. Once he entered the garage, his breath was taken away. Suspended approximately five feet in the air was an antique automobile. A real, dyed-in-the-wool, internal combustion engine car!

Kyle had not seen a car anywhere other than a museum since he was a kid. "Dad! Wow! Where did you get *that*?" he asked, astonishment overcoming his face. Without waiting for an answer, Kyle walked to the front of the car and looked at the grille. "Is that? That's a Mustang! Dad... how did you...?"

The sound of the ratchet that had been in the background since Kyle stumbled in stopped, and Pops stepped out from under the elevated car.

Kyle stared at his father. Pops didn't look as big as he once had, dressed only in mechanic's coveralls, his hair significantly thinned out and completely gray. Still no facial hair though. Even at his age, he still managed to stay clean-shaven.

"Son," Pops said, his tone defensive, "what ya got there?"

Following his gaze, Kyle looked under his arm. He had forgotten about the package he was carrying. "Oh right, sorry. According to the history this was..." Kyle looked at the air waybill to repeat the history and stopped as his Eyebit reported, ***Privacy block in place!***

"That's weird. It worked a minute ago," Kyle said. "Anyway. Robox dropped this off for you." He handed Pops the package.

Pops huffed. "Robox... Jeez, freakin' drones. Back in my day packages were delivered by people."

"Yeah, Dad, we know... but the efficiency of machines versus people is incalculable."

"Whatever, boy. It was good enough to put you through college," Pops retorted as tension mounted.

After a moment of awkward silence, Kyle decided not to argue with his father.

Pops spoke. "So, why are you here?"

Kyle stuttered as he replied. "I... I sent you an email. I can't believe you still use email."

"Yeah... I have an email." Pops huffed sarcastically as he all but pointed out the outdated incandescent Christmas lights strung across the garage, the antique Mustang, and the twice-recycled car lift.

Kyle decided to launch into his purpose for reaching out to his dad after all these years. "It's Jack," Kyle said heavily.

"What about him?"

"Well, he..."

"Look, son, you wanna talk to me like a man, take those goddamn things off your face!"

Rolling his eyes at his father, Kyle pushed a button on the left arm of his Eyebit. Instantly, the lenses separated from the bridge and folded straight up. When the lenses opened, a bright white flash emitted from the glasses.

Almost like a light bomb, Pops thought as he watched Kyle grab the bridge of his nose and close his eyes.

"Boy? What's the matter?" Pops asked as he watched Kyle stumble.

"Nothing, Dad, I just haven't unplugged since last night. Usually, I don't take this off until bedtime," Kyle answered wearily.

"Oh yeah? What happens when you drink too much and pass out?"

"Well, it has a program that monitors your intake and cuts you off from the bar automatically."

Pops rolled his eyes and reached for his moonshine bottle. "Here, see if this helps," he said as he handed Kyle the glass jar.

With his eyes closed, Kyle, assuming Pops was giving him water or cola, took a healthy gulp. Kyle immediately launched into a cough and stood straight up.

"Damn... Dad!" he exclaimed between coughs. "What do you call that?" He gasped for breath.

"Knock 'em stiff," Pops said with a smile.

"Knock 'em stiff?" After a moment's reflection, Kyle reconnected with a childhood memory, one of a much younger Pops bearing down on him the importance of "our" history.

Almost all of our modern problems can be answered or explained away by respecting and remembering our history, boy. Pops's voice replayed in Kyle's head over and over.

"Isn't that what Civil War soldiers used to make in camp when their whiskey ran out?" Kyle barely managed to cough out the sentence coherently.

"Well, how 'bout that. I did manage to teach you something." Pops beamed. "Cigarette?" He extended a hand-rolled cigarette to Kyle.

"What? No! How do you have those? Isn't that illeg—never mind." Upon regaining his composure, Kyle pinched both sides of the Eyebit's arms, pulled them off his face, and began to speak again. "Like I was saying... Jack... I'm worried about him." Kyle spoke in the way people did when they were uncomfortable. He was attempting to articulate his concerns about his son but doing so in a way that would spare his feelings if he were actually in the room.

Pops was not moved by Kyle's speech but instead was convinced that Kyle was having trouble conveying his thoughts because he wasn't wearing his Eyebit.

As Kyle continued to speak, Pops said, "So what I'm hearing is you're having trouble relating to your son."

CHAPTER TWO

Eyebit Immersion 99%

CHECK YOUR CONNECTION.

"Yes, exactly!" Kyle exclaimed. "He just seems so distant, and I don't know how to reach him. I'm watching him near the end of his teenage years, and he just seems so... blank." Kyle looked at his father.

"Well... whaddya want me to do about it?" Pops said, confused.

"Well, Dad, I thought you could talk to him. Maybe relate to him and help him out of his shell." Kyle's tone was pleading.

"Relate to him!? Are you crazy? I have nothing in common with someone from his generation. Boy, look around yourself!" Pops was almost shouting. "There is nothing in this garage, or this house for that matter, a boy his age would be interested in being exposed to.

Especially nowadays. Kids today—and their parents—are so mindless, so lazy, that if it doesn't come outta them stupid goggles, they don't give a shit! Tell me, boy, how much does he wear that thing?"

Kyle, unable to offer a counterargument, unclenched his jaw and responded, "Um, all day."

"Okay, so your kid has his head hijacked by a voluntary sensory input device all day and here you stand wondering why he is 'so distant' and 'blank.' Well, son, voilà! I've figured out your problem."

Pops had turned his attention back to his Mustang and left Kyle standing where he was, wearing a look of disdain. Employing an anger-management technique, Kyle inhaled three deep breaths through the nose and exhaled out the mouth. Clenching his fist and jaw, Kyle refocused his objectives, took another swig of knock 'em stiff, and counted to ten.

Stupid old man. I'm not going to walk away this time, Kyle told himself as he turned to face his father.

"Dad!" With confidence in his voice, Kyle commanded his father's attention. "Listen, you may not be up on the times and all that, but I need your help. Your grandson is at a critical stage right now, and I don't know what to do."

As the two men stared each other down, Pops spoke. "How old is he now? Eighteen?"

"Yes."

Pops turned away from him. Facing his workbench and fiddling with what looked like ancient car parts, he spoke to his son but looked at the wall. "So, your adult son doesn't know what it is to be a man. What rites of passage have you taken him through?"

Confused by the question, Kyle said, "Rites of passage... I don't understand."

"Jesus, boy!" Pops said, disappointment clear in his voice. "What have you taught him how to do? Shave, mow the yard, grill, tie a necktie? Any of that stuff?"

Fearing what Pops's response was going to be, Kyle answered truthfully, nonetheless. "Well, none of that. The Eyebit does all that stuff... It's automatic."

Pops gritted his teeth in anger. "How does that stupid-looking thing you wear keep you from having to shave your face?"

Surprised that his father wasn't yelling, Kyle was excited to answer his question. "Well, it's really very simple. You select what kind of look you want, and the bit tells your brain which hair follicles to stimulate or suppress."

With a wide-eyed, scared look on his face, Pops took a step back from his son. "How does *that* work?"

Kyle, surprised by his father's reaction, dialed down the enthusiasm. "It's hormonal... I guess... I don't know."

Taking a deep breath, Pops asked, "This thing can change your body... and you 'don't know' how it works?"

Unable to meet his father's gaze, Kyle only stared at the floor and, with a hint of shame in his voice, offered a halfhearted counterpoint. "Look, Dad, it's safe, otherwise they wouldn't let people use them."

Pops, no longer interested in being disappointed by his child, said, "Sure, son. Keep telling yourself that." With a roll of his eyes, he turned his attention away. With his head up and shoulders back in a defiant posture, he marched to the passenger-side front tire, picked up the impact wrench, and started to loosen the lugs holding the tire in place.

Kyle's frustration was reaching the breaking point. As he stood watching his father work on this *ancient piece of shit,* he could only think to himself obvious questions in anger. *Why does he always have to be right? Why can't he just do something he is asked to do? Why does he have to be such a jerk? Why does he hate me?* Amid all those questions, Kyle was struck with an epiphany. *Always be right... hate me.*

As the answer washed over him, Kyle smiled to himself. He knew what to do. "Okay, Dad, you're disappointed in me, and I don't care anymore," he said, the words dripping with disdain. "I've spent years pondering why I'm not the way you wanted me to be or why I wasn't good enough for you, but now I'm over it. I came here today to extend you an olive branch, but you're too fucking close-minded to see it." Having gained his father's undivided attention, Kyle closed the distance between them.

"You're such a miserable, self-absorbed, alienating, egotistical bastard, that you don't even realize you have no one in this world that gives a shit about you. No one, that is, except me. You do understand that, right? You think you're so much better than everybody; there isn't a single soul that will even have a conversation with you. Tell me, jerk-off, have you thought about what will happen when you die? That's right, one day you'll be gone, and guess what... You've set yourself up to be remembered by only me! Trust your memory, your legacy, to me, do you? 'Your disappointment.'"

Standing only two feet from him, Kyle stared his father dead in the eye. Kyle's words struck such a nerve with his father that this time he was the one to look away in near-shame and self-realization. When he returned his son's eye contact, Kyle continued. "Let me spell it out for you... I want to allow you to make an impression on your grandson and forego my memories of you being your mark on the world. You have a chance, one last chance, to influence how history will remember you."

As Pops absorbed what Kyle said, he couldn't help but notice the changes in his son's facial expressions. *Interesting,* Pops thought to himself as he watched Kyle waiting for him to respond. *I like him*

better without that face thing and with the booze. Is it the bit or the booze?
He is really mad at me. He's right, though.

Accepting he was faced with the truth, Pops could only muster an "Okay, you can bring him by."

Kyle blinked in disbelief. "Okay... Good. Thank you." Upon realizing he had won—and not having fully expected to—Kyle backed off from his father and turned to leave. As he walked for the door, he told his father, "I'll bring him round tomorrow and leave him for awhile."

Unbeknownst to Kyle, the look on his father's face had changed from defeat to surprise. "Leave him? Wait... you're not going to be here? I'm gonna be alone with him?" Pops asked with alarm in his voice.

Not stopping his stride, Kyle said, "Yeah, Dad, it's about him getting to know you. I don't need to be here for that. Besides, I've got a lot going on at work. You two will be fine."

Pops, who was now trailing after his son, began to protest in earnest. "But what am I gonna do with him? What will we talk about?"

Ceasing his walk, Kyle turned to face his father. "I don't know, Dad. Tell him about your life! Talk about this car!" Kyle shouted as he flung his arms in the direction of the Mustang.

Now realizing that what he was about to undertake would leave him completely exposed, Pops wore an expression of near panic as he faced his son. Recognizing the fear, Kyle attempted to put him at ease.

"Dad, relax. It's just your grandson. Try and have some fun." A smile crept across his face, and he once again turned toward the door but stopped halfway. "Oh, Dad, one more thing. If there is anything else illegal in this house, like fireworks, pornography, or guns, do not expose Jack to it. I mean it."

Pops didn't say anything, only nodded. Still smiling, Kyle turned back toward the door.

"Ahhh, okay, I'll see you kids tomorrow," Pops called after his son, who had since disappeared into the house. Turning back to his car, Pops resumed work on the passenger front tire.

Staring off into space, he began to contemplate the events of the following day. He found himself wondering what his grandson would look like as a grown man. As his thoughts turned toward Kyle's concerns, he found himself snapped back to reality by a dull ache in his left arm.

As he gently massaged his arm, he dismissed the pain as strain from the wheel and returned his thoughts back to his conversation with Kyle.

"Finally," Pops whispered to himself as picked the wrench back up and went to work. "Finally."

As Kyle stood once again at the threshold of his father's front door, the feelings of dread and anger were gone. Even as he reflected on the last time he'd stood in that exact position after their big fight, he could not overcome the feeling of satisfaction and victory.

Missing the steady stream of information from his Eyebit, Kyle reached for his jacket pocket. As he did so, he happened to glance over at the shrubbery. When his hand didn't find his pocket, he looked back down, guided his hand in, and found his Eyebit. Once he had a secure hand on it, he turned his attention back to the shrubs.

Kyle had to blink a few times to ensure that he wasn't seeing things. As he approached the shrubbery, he was in awe. His dad had shaped the bushes into a splendid array of animals, which included an elephant, giraffe, lion, and monkey. As he moved in for a closer examination, he was amazed at the detail and accuracy of the designs.

These must have taken years to sculpt, Kyle thought as he reached out to touch the neck of the giraffe.

Still holding his Eyebit in his other hand, Kyle began to question himself. "I looked right at these shrubs earlier. How did I not notice this?" Keeping his gaze on the giraffe, Kyle put his Eyebit on and pressed the button on the arm to activate it. The instant he pushed the power button, Kyle was wearing a helmet made of light. There was a quick flash, and the light helmet was gone. Kyle was now reconnected to the Eyebit.

Retaining his thoughts, Kyle stared at the shrub. The animal shape was still there... along with all the other information that was provided, including the stock photograph of what the shrub *should* look like. Straining to identify the giraffe through the barrage of imagery, he began to become distracted by the other alerts.

1. *34 new messages.*

2. *Evening meal T minus 30 minutes.*

3. *Current Location: "Dad's Neighborhood."*

4. *Checking Vitals... Checking Vitals... Checking Vitals...*

WARNING. WARNING All the other images had disappeared from Kyle's vision. The entire field of view had gone black, and the word *WARNING* was flashing in red letters. After displaying the warning four times, Kyle's Eyebit explained.

1. *Alcohol in system.*

2. *Origin unknown.*

3. *Elevated amounts being absorbed into the blood.*

Kyle's Eyebit streamed the short burst of information across the display. *I didn't drink that much,* Kyle thought as he stood up.

Initiating purge procedures... Initiating purge procedures.

Being unfamiliar with purge procedures, Kyle started to question his Eyebit, but he was interrupted by a flashing strobe light. The black and white flashing made it completely impossible for Kyle to see beyond the Eyebit's lenses.

Even though the lenses were clear, the strobe prevented his eyes from adjusting. Before Kyle was able to stop the process or even understand what was happening, he started to vomit.

On his knees in front of the shrubs, Kyle convulsed uncontrollably. His Eyebit continued to assault his vision with strobing lights. As Kyle emptied the contents of his stomach onto his father's shrubs, he had a sudden understanding of what "purge procedures" meant.

Reduced to dry heaving, Kyle was about to remove his Eyebit when the strobing stopped.

Purge Complete. Purge complete. Purge complete. Have a nice day.

Groggy, Kyle got to his feet and started toward his transport. By the time he had turned around and taken the first two steps toward it, his Eyebit had returned to normal operating mode. As he centered his Eyebit on his transport, Kyle ticked his eye to the ***ACTIVATE*** icon, and the transport sparked to life.

Being connected to the Eyebit, the transport anticipated his needs. The door opened automatically at just the right time, the seat adjusted to a reclining position, and a glass of water was provided. "Please specify destination," a computerized voice said.

As Kyle eased back into his seat, he said, "Home." *Ahhh, perfect. Just what I need,* Kyle thought as he sipped the ice-cold water. As the door closed, Kyle could have sworn he heard cackling coming from his dad's house. For a brief second, he wondered if Pops had intentionally given him the moonshine, knowing the Eyebit would make him throw it up when he put it back on. *Wouldn't surprise me.*

Shifting his body to see out the last crack before the door closed, Kyle caught a glimpse of the silhouette of his father. Before he could examine the laughter further, Kyle's attention was diverted. A blue light began to flash across the bottom of his right lens.

Ping. Ping. Ping.

His wife was calling. "Answer," Kyle said as he returned to a reclining position.

"Hi, Kyle," she said casually. "How did it go with your father?"

CHAPTER THREE

Eyebit Immersion 98%

DISCONNECT, AND RE-CONNECT.

*B*ing... *Bing... Bing...* Kyle's Eyebit had been trying to wake him for the last few minutes. Lying in bed, he was weighing his options. Next to him was his wife, Claire. She was a petite brunette with deep, soulful brown eyes. To Kyle, she was everything he could ever want in a wife. His *perfect match* according to his Eyebit, and he had come to believe it.

Outside of bed was everything else he had to do today. Chores, transport service, grocery shopping, and taking Jack to his dad's. *Or I can stay here and...* Allowing his mind to wander to various thoughts of sexual depravity, Kyle decided to proposition his wife. But either way, he had to put on his Eyebit to get started.

Once he got connected, Kyle pinged his wife with a sex request. When the denial message was returned, he rolled over to inquire personally. Claire was sitting upright, leaning against the headboard with a pillow supporting her back. *Probably been that way all night.*

Reaching over and touching her inner thigh, Kyle began to make his move. Claire was nonresponsive. Working his way up her thigh just a little higher, Kyle was interrupted by an incoming message from Claire. ***Sorry honey, I'm not in the mood. I've been testing the new dream bit for the transition. Maybe later.*** Kyle didn't know it, but Claire had a Delay Mating option on her Eyebit that allowed the user to authorize a preselected mate's Eyebit to release just enough oxytocin to make the person lose interest in sex.

Now that Kyle was being artificially satisfied, his thoughts returned to the list of items that had to be accomplished that day. Ticking his eye to the shower, he decided that's where he would start. As he approached it, the water was already warm, and he stepped straight in.

Once he crossed the threshold, his Eyebit alerted him to a water shortage and a government-mandated ration. ***Body cleanliness 50%, 4 gallons hot water, 1 gallon cold water approved for bathing.***

Better hurry, Kyle thought as he reached for the pre-lathered wash-cloth.

Starting with his hair, Kyle quickly worked his way down. Even though he hated it, washing soap off his feet with cold water was better than using it for his face or chest. As the hot water supply began to taper off, Kyle not only could see the warning in his Eyebit but could feel it.

He was on the last gallon and wasn't able to finish washing between his toes but contented himself to let frigid water run over them. Using the last spurts of water dripping from the shower head, Kyle cupped his hands and managed to pool enough water to dash the top of his head.

Almost made it this time, Kyle thought as he emerged from the shower. *I really should find out why the government is limiting water. What's changed from when I was a kid?* Kyle's thought was quickly forgotten as he had an idea. *I wonder if there is a bit that will adjust my body temperature so the cold water wouldn't feel as cold.*

Exploiting the fact that his wife worked for the bit corps of engineers, Kyle emerged from the bathroom looking for Claire. She was in the exact spot he had last seen her in. "Honey, is there a bit that will make the last gallon not seem so cold?" Kyle asked as he finished drying his hair with his bath towel.

"No, all new ideas or customer requests are on hold until after the transition," she answered plainly.

Standing in his closet, Kyle examined his appearance in his Eyebit. His outfit was perfectly matched, and he was now approved to display himself in public. *Ahh, real clothes. Nothing better than that,* Kyle thought as he finished tying his shoes. *I guess I'm just old-fashioned that way.*

As he was dressing, Kyle's Eyebit had organized the most optimal way for him to execute his errands. Waiting for his bit to provide him with the next step in his day, he worried how it would go with Jack and his dad.

Drop off Jack.

Upon reading the first instruction, Kyle exited his closet and walked down the hall to Jack's room. Kyle found Jack's bedroom door closed.

Even though he was irritated by his son's self-imposed exile, Kyle still mustered the patience to ping Jack's bit. No response. Kyle pinged a second time. No response. Kyle banged on the door. "I'm coming in!" he shouted as he pushed open the door.

Kyle's bit was assaulted with a barrage of imagery—pictures, celebrity quotes, five viewscreens playing movies, and somewhere in the background, music. They all flooded Kyle's sensory input. He couldn't help but think that this was a typical teenager's room. He found it somewhat like the way his bedroom had been at that age.

The major difference was, of course, that Kyle's teenage room was full of tangible objects. The posters on his walls were real posters he'd tacked up. His movies played on television sets. He had a stereo.

Nowadays kids' rooms were mostly plain. All the decorations were done through the Eyebit and projected outward. Like a webpage you wore on your face. You didn't see it unless you were looking at it. Kyle waded in and found Jack lying on his bed staring at the ceiling. "Son, you're drooling," Kyle said with disgust.

Jack didn't respond.

"Son! Hey!" Kyle shouted.

When that didn't work, Kyle took a more extreme approach. Ticking his eye to the home menu, he accessed the ***Owner's Control Panel***. Followed by ***Jack's Room*** *and* ***Off***. With that simple eye stroke, Jack's room was no longer active.

When Jack's display went blank, he began to blink and look around. Realizing he was drooling, Jack wiped it away. "What did you do that for!?" he demanded angrily.

Frustrated, Kyle chose not to answer his question. "It's time to go. We're gonna be late. Your granddad is waiting for us."

Having forgotten about the date, Jack whined, "Awww, is that today? Do I have to?"

Kyle squinted at his son. "Yes, you've known about it all week."

Jack exhaled heavily but didn't move.

Kyle prodded him. "Let's go!"

"Kyle, I would rather not," Jack said.

"Son, it is important that you get to know your grandfather. He may not have much time left for this world, and you should be there. I was like you once. I didn't want to be around my grandparents either. Now they're gone, and to this day, I regret not knowing them," Kyle said, his tone sympathetic.

"Well, that's your problem, Kyle, not mine," Jack retorted.

Realizing sympathy wasn't going to work, Kyle became angry. "Okay, get your ass up now, and come with me! If you don't, I'll leave your room off indefinitely!"

"Fine! Leave it off. I'll leave!"

Jack had called his bluff. "Okay, smart-ass, the transports are going for service today. Do you want to spend your dollar-bits on a taxi?"

Jack, unable to offer a counterargument, sat in silence.

"Okay, then. You ready to go?" Kyle asked.

"All right. Fine. Whatever. Let's get this over with." Jack stormed out of his room with Kyle in tow.

As the transport glided to a stop in front of Pops's house, Kyle broke the silence that had been present since the two had left their home. "Jack, listen, there's some things you need to know before you see Pops. Your granddad is... different. He's not like other people's granddads."

Jack wasn't listening. It hadn't dawned on Kyle that he'd switched off Jack's room, not Jack's Eyebit. Once Jack had left the confines of his bedroom, his Eyebit reengaged. Realizing Jack wasn't going to respond to verbal communication, Kyle looked beyond his screen prompts and watched his son's face.

What Kyle saw was a reminder of yesteryear's drug addicts. Blank, lost, and the occasional lip curl. The one difference was the eyes. They were moving so rapidly from side to side, up and down, in all directions that someone might suspect a medical condition. But it was just Jack being fully engaged in the bit world. *That's why we're here,* Kyle reassured himself as he pinged Jack's Eyebit. **We're here.**

After emerging from the transport, the two made their way to the front door. Kyle spied another Robox delivery and picked it up. Shaking his head with a slight smile, Kyle tucked the package under his arm.

As it had been on his last visit, the front door was unsecured and swung open with a gentle push. Kyle entered first. When Jack crossed the threshold, he immediately stopped.

"Privacy block? Kyle, my Eyebit says that there is a privacy block in place. I don't understand."

Having watched him enter, and more curious about his son's reaction than he was willing to warn him, Kyle was already facing Jack. After a prolonged moment of silence between the two, Kyle remarked, "So, you *can* speak."

Jack had not budged from the entryway just past the threshold. "Kyle, what's going on? Why can't I see?" Jack asked, near panic.

Kyle disengaged his Eyebit and paused for a moment to orient himself. "Son, this is what I have been trying to explain to you. Your Eyebit isn't going to work much here. Your Granddad is a bit... old-fashioned."

"Old-fashioned? I don't take your meaning."

Kyle could only smile. "Come on, use your eyes, not your Eyebit."

Kyle began to lead the way toward the garage, Jack stumbling behind. "Wait!" Jack protested. "I can't see... I don't know..."

Before Kyle could turn around and take Jack by the hand, he heard a crash. Jack had bumped into an end table and knocked over a glass bowl.

A shout came from out of the blackness. "Back here."

Both Jack and Kyle looked toward the garage. "Come on, son," Kyle said, leading Jack toward the garage door. Entering the garage, Kyle spotted Pops right off and gave him a slight nod as if to say, "We're here. Hope you're ready."

Kyle broke his father's gaze and immediately stepped aside to allow Jack to come in. Jack's body was rigid as he approached the garage entryway. As he crossed the threshold of the garage, he failed to realize that there was a six-inch drop in the pavement. As he stumbled forward, he felt a hand grab his arm. Kyle had been watching Jack in anticipation of... anything.

"Careful, son, these old houses are a little different than the ones you're used to," Kyle said as he released Jack's arm. "Jack, this is your grandfather. You haven't seen him since you were a baby."

Kyle had directed Jack's attention to the man now standing before him. Jack, with a confused look on his face, turned to Kyle. "Kyle, my Eyebit isn't working. I can't see his profile." Redirecting his attention to Pops, Jack asked, "What do I call you?"

"Kyle?" Pops smirked. "Your son calls you by your first name? Seriously?"

Kyle gave Pops a sidelong glance and began to explain. "Yeah, all the kids do that nowadays. The Eyebits don't display nicknames in profile information, just proper names." Pops didn't break his stare, which Kyle interpreted as wanting more information, so he continued. "See, when you look at someone, the Eyebit displays a profile with all their personal information—name, age, et cetera—but nicknames like Dad or Mom don't apply."

Pops rolled his eyes. "Okay, but babies have to learn to talk. Did you read him your profile information or what?"

Kyle, knowing that his father was not going to like his answer, paused a moment and considered lying. "Ah, well... Dad... Umm, okay, the truth is parents put on an Infa-bit and it teaches them to—"

Pops interrupted him. "Stop talking," he demanded as he squinted, his eyes becoming thin slits.

Kyle found himself relieved that his scolding wasn't more severe and took the opportunity to allow Pops to focus his attention on Jack. Jack didn't take his gaze from Pops.

"I haven't met anyone without a profile before," Jack said.

Pops delivered his response without feeling. "Oh. Well, I'm sorry for you."

Jack was taken aback by Pops's lack of interest in being at all modern. "What do you... do? How do you buy stuff?"

Pops, not even remotely interested in this line of questioning, returned his energies to the car. Jack followed him, watching his every move suspiciously. He was searching for a word to describe what an Eyebit-less person was. Without the instantly available information of who, what, why, where, and when, all Jack could muster was a single word for Pops. *Stranger.* This both scared and excited him.

"I don't even know your name," Jack said, perplexed.

The phrase carried the force of a sucker punch to the gut, and Pops suddenly found himself saddened almost to tears. Regaining his composure, he set down the passenger door he was attempting to re-attach. "Okay, boy. You wanna know about me? Fine, but there is one thing that must happen first."

Jack didn't answer. He just looked at Pops.

"You have to take that thing off."

Jack, looking confused, simply asked, "What thing?"

Pops didn't speak his response. He merely pointed with his right index finger at Jack's eye. Jack, mirroring Pops's motion, reached up and touched his Eyebit. Only after his hand came into contact with it did Jack understand what Pops meant had to be taken off.

Jack, frightened at the prospect of being without an Eyebit connection, backed away from Pops. "No."

Pops didn't speak; nor did he back down. He stood in place waiting for compliance. After a moment of silence, Jack felt compelled to continue. "Why?" he asked, unease lacing his voice.

Pops tried to bite back his anger in his response but didn't succeed very well. "Manners, boy! It's rude to not give your undivided attention to someone you're having a conversation with."

Jack looked truly perplexed. "Why don't you just put one on and we won't have to talk? Then I can learn everything about you."

Frustration mounting, Pops turned to where Kyle had been standing. "Son, help me out here." To Pops's surprise, at some point in his conversation with Jack, Kyle had managed to slip out the door, leaving the two alone.

Pops realized he was going to have to deal with this situation on his own. He released an exasperated sigh. "Okay. Boy, you have two options. You didn't notice, but your dad left, and he won't be back for a while." Jack looked around in disbelief as Pops continued. "So you can either take that thing off or you can sit here in the corner."

Jack didn't respond, so Pops went on. "Look, I know that the 'privacy block' message is going to get annoying soon, and I'm here to tell you I have mountains of patience. When I was your age, we didn't have unlimited-battery-life Eyebits. We had cellphones, and they had a limited power supply, so when they ran out of juice, we had to wait for a recharge."

Jack, not seeing any other alternative, simply stated, "I'll wait for Kyle to return."

Pops, not at all surprised by Jack's answer, said, "Want a chair?" Pops sidestepped over to his workbench, retrieved a folding chair, opened it, and handed it to Jack. As Jack attempted to comfort himself in the rusted chair, Pops pulled up his cushioned stool.

Sitting down facing Jack, Pops took a glance at his watch. He pictured in his mind's eye what Jack was seeing. ***Privacy block in place. Privacy block in place. Privacy block in place.*** *God, how annoying,* Pops thought as he wondered how long this kid could hold out.

Pops's mind was flooded with panicky thoughts. He had no idea how he was going to handle this should Jack actually decide to participate. *What am I doing? What do I do if he decides to interact with me? What if he asks something I don't want to answer? He looks like his grandmother.* Pops's train of thought was suddenly interrupted.

"Okay, I'll take it off," Jack said, almost desperately.

"Wow! Thirty-seven seconds... Hope nobody calls the Department of Human Services on me," Pops said.

Even though he had agreed to remove his Eyebit, Jack was still unsure if he could. He could scarcely recall any memories where he didn't have it on. It took him several tries to work up the courage to push the release button. Pops just sat and watched in worried fascination.

"Your arm gettin' tired boy?" Pops asked with a crooked smile.

After Jack made a few more attempts to push the release button, Pops saw an opportunity to continue to prod. "Come on now... Just go fast, like a Band-Aid."

A few more moments passed, and Pops said. "Jesus, boy, you're reminding me of a teenage girl trying to pierce her own ears."

Jack made a sudden jerk and whacked the release button with lightning speed. He quickly forgot about trying to figure out what a Band-Aid was. "Ugh, whoa." Jack swayed back and forth on the rickety old chair while pinching the bridge of his nose. "I'm going to be sick."

Pops watched for a second to see if the boy was going to throw up or not before he reached for the bottle, the same one he had given Kyle the night before.

"Here, drink this," Pops said as he handed him the bottle.

Eyebit Immersion 96%

DISCONNECT, AND RECONNECT.

"Okay, now pull the slide back, and look down into the chamber," Pops said.

Jack handled the antique firearm with a steady hand.

"That's where the bullet about to be fired goes," Pops said.

Jack looked down into the chamber. "It's empty," he said, his speech slightly slurred.

Pops, with a half-crooked smile, casually said, "Yeah... You ain't gettin' those yet. Now with this kind of gun, once you release the slide, it will spring into place. Be sure the safety is off, and you're ready to go."

Holding the old weapon in his hand, Jack felt... powerful. He knew what the gun did from his history classes. He also understood its implications, which he found seductive. Just the idea of getting in trouble made his heart beat fast. This brush with misbehaving, doing something with questionable legality, was something he hadn't ever experienced.

A familiar voice came from inside the house. Kyle had returned from his errands. "You guys back here?" Kyle called out.

As soon as Kyle entered the garage door, Jack got up to meet him. Extending his hand as he approached Kyle, Jack began to speak. "Kyle, look at this old—"

Kyle looked down to see a gun pointed at him, and he reacted without thinking. With his right palm, Kyle smacked the gun from Jack's hand. The gun skidded across the garage floor and came to rest under an antique refrigerator. Kyle then mustered even more force and backhanded Jack across the face, knocking him to the floor.

Looking up at Kyle, a wounded Jack attempted to speak through unfamiliar sensations of pain. "Phuuuck you, Kyle."

Kyle, eyes alive with anger, turned to Pops. "Is he drunk?"

"Well... I had to give it to him, son. The gun made him nervous," Pops said as he made his way to retrieve his weapon.

Pops's humor did not alleviate Kyle's anger. In fact, it seemed to have made it worse. "So, you got him drunk, allowed swearing, and exposed him to deadly weapons." Kyle's gaze was fixed on Pops. "Good! Fucking! Job! Dad!"

Pops said flatly, "Oh, you're disappointed? Well, I told you I didn't think it was a good idea for you to bring him here."

Now even angrier at Pops, Kyle started toward him. He began with his hands at his sides, but by the time he was within striking distance, his arms were extended out from his torso. Part of Kyle's Eyebit program was designed to manage his anger, but since he wasn't wearing it in Pops's house, the rage flowed as it had in the old days.

Pops picked up on Kyle's visual clues and sensed the immediate danger. When Kyle was within reaching distance, Pops whipped his right hand out from behind his back, and Kyle found himself at the business end of an aluminum baseball bat.

Kyle could feel the cold steel through his shirt but didn't take his eyes off Pops. Returning an icy stare, Pops spoke. "I'm too old to be fighting with you, boy! The last time you came at me like that I lost two teeth." He rotated his wrist, twisting the bat into Kyle's chest. "The gun I showed Jack wasn't loaded. Now, I warned you before you brought him here, and you wouldn't listen. Pick your son up, and get out of my house," he said coolly.

Kyle pushed the rage down inside himself and stepped backward, not taking his eyes off Pops. Only when he reached Jack did he break eye contact. "Come on, Jack. It's time to go," he said as he helped Jack to his feet.

Once vertical, Jack spoke with slurred speech. "You tawk funny, Paaapss. I like your car. It's a pwetty rainbow."

Pops couldn't help but crack a smile. Kyle, however, rolled his eyes and put Jack's arm over his shoulder for support as the two headed for the door. When they reached it, Pops put the bat tip down on the floor and leaned on it like it was a cane. Letting out a long exhale, Pops noticed a dull ache in his arm and subconsciously started rubbing.

"Shit!" Pops cussed out loud as he heard the transport pull away.

Jack had never felt anything like this before, a sudden pain in his stomach followed by an intense burning in his throat and the horrible taste of acid-soaked food. He crouched in front of the toilet, vomiting uncontrollably. He remained Eyebit-less.

It would just make him throw up the moonshine anyway, just like it did me, Kyle thought, standing above his son, attempting to offer comfort. As he watched Jack throw up for the first time in his life, he couldn't help but marvel at how wonderful today's technology was.

Even an illness from a foreign germ invader was detected by the Eyebit early enough to mitigate any symptoms. *People just don't get sick anymore,* Kyle thought to himself as he handed Jack a wet washcloth to wipe away the sweat, spit, tears, and food.

Once the spasms had subsided and there was nothing left in Jack's stomach to expel, Kyle bent over and put his forearms under Jack's arms to lift him. "Wait! Wait!" Jack said before Kyle could bring him to his feet. Jack put his hands back on the underside of the toilet and gently ran his hands along the base of the bowl. "It's so cold and smooth. How have I not noticed this before?"

Kyle rolled his eyes. "Of course you have, you just never paid attention. Your Eyebit keeps you from noticing it." Assuming that Jack was still feeling the effects of the moonshine, Kyle smiled and said, "Okay, Helen Keller, come on, let's go."

Kyle heaved Jack up to the sink and instructed his son to "Brush your teeth, but not your entire tongue. Just the front, otherwise you'll gag." Then he ushered Jack to bed. "Okay, son, get some sleep, and hopefully you'll feel better tomorrow. I'm going to leave your Eyebit right here." Kyle put the Eyebit on the bedside table and left Jack's room. Fighting the instinct to leave the door cracked, he told himself, *No, he is an adult, not a child,* and pulled the door all the way closed.

As the light faded and darkness washed over Jack, two images refused to vacate his mind—the gun and the car. As he drifted toward sleep, he began to fantasize about not just using those two items but possessing them. The feelings of want and desire and curiosity and rebellion sparked in his mind as sleep took him.

Pops examined the cemetery's landscape. The upkeep had been minimal. The abandonment of the church had taken its toll. "Why did you want to be buried at a church, sweetie?" Pops said as he pruned the flowers around his wife's grave. He couldn't help noticing how overgrown the rest of the cemetery was. *How sad,* Pops thought.

Ever since this denomination went bankrupt, all their churches were simply abandoned overnight. When the money went, the ability to maintain the grounds went as well. Some private citizens had managed to donate money to keep the areas up, but eventually that stopped too.

Pops had come to believe that like most other things in this day and age, people just quit caring. "Honey, I tried to get this church added to the 'historical preservation society's museum division,' but nobody much goes to museums anymore. City council told me that there was no need to allocate funds for something the people could get from the comfort of their homes."

Pops finished manicuring his wife's grave and rose to leave. After one last long pause, he came out with what he had really come to tell her. "I'm so sorry, sweetie. If I had known, if *we* had known it would turn out this way, I never would have fought in that fucking army."

Pops retraced the history of events in his mind. Once religion fell to science, technology became the new god, which turned out to be even more powerful than money. The people gave what little remained of their souls over to it and lost themselves. *And here we are,* Pops thought as he moved on in conversation with his wife's gravestone.

"I blew it with Kyle again. I'm so sorry. He came to me with an offer and a second chance, and I spit it right back in his face." Pops choked back tears as he continued to apologize. "I'm sorry I wasn't a better father, I'm sorry that he has come to hate me, and I'm sorry I broke my promise to you." Pops wiped the tears away and cleared his throat but continued his own character assassination.

"Why am I so fucking stubborn? Why do I alienate every single person in my life? Why can't I just be normal?" Standing rigid, Pops bit his lower lip too hard and gained his own attention. "Okay, honey, I'll see you soon." As Pops turned to begin his four-mile walk home, a single word kept repeating itself in his head: change. *Just change. Just do it. It's that simple.*

Before he was out of visual range of his wife's grave, Pops turned to take one final look. As his eyes trailed away from her gravesite, they scanned across another, this one belonging to the dilapidated church building itself.

As Pops took in the rotting shell of omnipresence, he basked in the memory of her formal glory. She had been magnificent and assured, her stained-glass windows displaying every color of the spectrum, her majestic organ pipes ringing out in harmony with the voice of a people divinely inspired. But that's all it would ever be, a memory.

As the image faded and reality returned, Pops's smile faded away from his face, and he examined her broken corpse. Her stained-glass window had been smashed years ago. The roof had caved in, and her organ pipes had corroded beyond repair.

A simple but profound truth suddenly presented itself to Pops: the church always reflects the state of the religion.

"Hollow and empty," Pops said aloud as he stepped outside the boundaries of what he still recognized as hallowed ground. Putting his hat back on as he turned to leave, he muttered to himself, "Just like everything else."

CHAPTER FIVE

Eyebit Immersion 95%

RUNNING DIAGNOSTICS...

It was the throbbing in his head that woke Jack, not the sun pouring in from the window adjacent to his bed. As he slowly opened his eyes, the pounding intensified. Once his eyes adjusted to the sheer brightness of his room, Jack looked around, confused.

There were no posters, no movies, no view screens, only stark white walls. It took him a moment to realize he didn't have his Eyebit on. Only when he spied it sitting on his bedside table did he understand why his room looked the way it did.

As he reached for his Eyebit, his hand carried a noticeable tremble. "What the hell?" Jack exclaimed as he steadied one hand with the other. Clasping his hands together, Jack decided to seek counsel and exited his room, looking for his parents. He left his Eyebit on the bedside table.

Jack called out for his mother. "Claire?" No response. "Claire?" Still no response. He wandered about the house until he entered the kitchen. Claire was standing in front of the stove leaning on an island countertop. She was watching the stove. "Hey, what are you doing?" Jack asked, even though he knew the answer.

"I'm fixing breakfast," Claire said without breaking her gaze. Claire's Eyebit was connected to the stove, which was completely automated for breakfast preparation. Cooking breakfast and managing nine other tasks at the same time, Claire did not realize Jack had continued speaking to her.

Turning her attention to Jack, Claire was shocked to find her child was not connected. "Where's your Eyebit?" she asked, almost accusatorily.

Jack was awash in the plainness of the kitchen, which contained no color, just white walls and whitewashed appliances. He wasn't going back to his room for his Eyebit. Jack didn't realize it, but not having his Eyebit on was causing him to feel the symptoms of withdrawal, and he snipped at his mother.

"Look, just verbally tell me about last night," Jack said with an irritated sigh. Claire didn't respond. "Helllooo!" Jack said in an aggressive tone.

Claire, not breaking her gaze from the stove, said, "Put your bit on and have it check your attitude. Then I'll communicate with you."

Jack was not swayed and left the kitchen in a huff.

Sitting on the edge of his bed, Jack held his Eyebit, contemplating putting it on. He couldn't escape one thought. *Why? Why was Claire sooo insistent that I have this on? Why is Pops sooo insistent that I not wear it around him?* Either way, the subject of the strife was the Eyebit. In the end, familiarity won out, and Jack put it on.

As it was programmed to do, the Eyebit immediately displayed Jack's room the way he had decorated it. With a single swipe of his eye, his room condensed into a single icon at the bottom of his view.

"Contact Kyle." A symbol that Jack had always wondered about appeared in his view, accompanied by a ringing sound. As he waited for Kyle to answer, Jack wondered about the symbol before him. *What is that? It's weird looking... Why not display the face or profile of the person being contacted?*

Kyle answered the call, and Jack's questions were forgotten. "How you feeling?" Kyle asked.

"My head hurts."

"Well, keep your Eyebit on. It will get better."

After a moment of silence, Kyle spoke. "Jack... I'm very busy. Was there something else you needed?"

Without even thinking, Jack said, "Yes, I wanna use the transport."

"Okay, make sure Claire doesn't need it. I'll dial her in." In an instant, Claire's face entered Jack's field of view alongside Kyle's. "Jack wants to use the transport. Do you need it today?"

Claire didn't answer the question right away. Instead, she commented on Jack's connection. "Oh, decided to join the rest of the world, did you?"

Jack didn't respond but sat in silence, waiting for the verdict.

"Where do you want to go?" Kyle asked.

Jack answered with a touch of assertiveness in his voice. "To see Pops."

Having gained the undivided attention of both Kyle and Claire, Jack suddenly felt uncomfortable. "Ummm, okay," Kyle said. "After last night, I didn't think you would want to go back."

"Why?" Claire asked. "You just put your Eyebit back on, and you haven't been offline that long... ever. Your grandfather won't let you wear it around him. Don't you want to feel better?" In what seemed like a single breath to Jack, Claire continued. "Your headache is gone now, isn't it? The Eyebit is good for you. We are encouraged to avoid situations that require us to remove it."

Kyle interrupted. "Guys, I am very busy. I don't have a problem with Jack using the transport to see Pops, Claire, do you?"

Bothered by becoming the center of attention, Claire let her dissatisfaction be known by the tone of her voice. "Fine! Whatever! Just don't come crying to me when you feel like shit! Be home in time for dinner."

With approval granted, Jack ended the communication before goodbyes could be exchanged and left the house.

————————————

The transport glided to a stop and powered down just as Jack stepped out and the auto door closed behind him. Jack stood in the street looking at the house before he decided to continue through the yard. Anticipating Pops's request, Jack decided to remove the Eyebit before entering the house.

Jack's eyes hurt as the full power of the sun beat down upon them for what he thought may well have been the first time. As he stood before the door, Jack realized he didn't know how to proceed. How was he supposed to get the attention of the occupants?

Every house he had ever been to had been connected to the Eyebit, through which his presence was announced, and then the person inside opened the door. Thinking back on the night before, Jack recalled that Kyle had made a fist and then beat it against the door.

Jack did as such. Unfamiliar with how much force to use, Jack was able to knock three times before pain shot through his knuckles. As he looked down to examine his hand, the door cracked open, and he was met with just a head sticking out between the door and the frame.

Pops recognized Jack immediately and opened the door the rest of the way. Jack's attention was drawn to Pops's right hand. In it was the same handgun Jack had been shown the night before. Pops clicked the safety back on and put the gun in his pocket.

"Come in, boy. You're letting the flies in," Pops said as he put his left hand on Jack's shoulder and guided him in. Having just returned from the cemetery, Pops's mind still rang with the single thought he couldn't escape. *Change.*

Closing the door and fastening the dead bolt, Pops began to speak. "What brings you by?"

"I wanted to talk to you," Jack said halfheartedly.

Pops couldn't help but smile. "Okay, well, I'm working in the garage. Come on."

Pops led the way, and as Jack followed, he took in his surroundings. Most places didn't have physical decorations anymore. Jack stopped when he encountered a picture of a young woman. "Who's that?"

"That's your grandmother."

Pops's answer surprised Jack. "Really?"

As he took in her features, he was surprised at how pretty she was. She had long hair and blue eyes and was tall for a woman. What struck Jack the most was her smile. She seemed to radiate... something. As Pops watched Jack examine the portrait, he was reminded that Jack had never really met his grandmother.

"She was a hell of a lady," Pops said as he continued to watch Jack. "The kind of person that when they walk into a room, it gets brighter, you know?" Pops had come to stand beside Jack, and the two faced the portrait.

"She doesn't look like you," Jack said.

Pops was confused. "Like me? What? You mean old?"

Jack, realizing that he may have insulted Pops, began to backpedal. "No. I mean, wait."

Pops interrupted him. "It's okay. She wasn't born a grandmother, just like I wasn't born a grandfather. We were young once too. See that baby she's holding? That's your dad."

Jack had been so engrossed he hadn't noticed the baby. The realization that his grandfather had once been the same age as himself had a profound effect on Jack, and he suddenly found himself at ease. He'd had the vague understanding that old people had once been young, sure, but he didn't know any personally, so the concept had always been sort of abstract to him.

Entering the garage, Jack launched into questions. "What's 'dad'? I've heard Kyle call you that. Why doesn't he call you... Well... what's your first name? Is it 'Pops'? And if Kyle calls you Dad, why would you say that Kyle is my dad?"

Pops looked at Jack with raised eyebrows. "Finished?"

Jack nodded.

"Here, have a seat, and I'll tell you." Pops kicked a stool on wheels in Jack's direction. Jack, unsure if the ancient stool would support his weight, gently eased onto the seat. When he fully released his legs, the stool creaked ever so slightly but held up.

"I'm glad you're here," Pops said as he looked at Jack. "Come on over here. I could use some help. Hand me that screwdriver."

CHAPTER SIX

Eyebit Immersion 94%

RUNNING DIAGNOSTICS...

"Okay, now hold the flashlight right there, and don't move it." Pops released his hand from Jack's wrist. As soon as he did, Pops couldn't help but notice that the boy's arm became overly rigid, and he fought the temptation to smack his elbow, just to see if he would move. "Good," Pops said with a bit of surprise in his voice. "Okay, where were we?"

"Dad," Jack answered.

"Right. Yes. To answer your question, I must first ask you a question," Pops said then waited for Jack to respond.

Jack's answer came after a moment of silence passed between the two. "Okay."

"Why do you call Kyle 'Kyle'?" Pops asked. Letting Jack ponder for a moment, Pops wiped his hands with an already-soiled rag.

Jack began to speak with hesitation, as if the question was a trick. "It's what I've always known."

Pops shook his head. "Okay, but... why?"

Jack, clearly confused, stammered in his answer. "It's... what I see when I look at him. It's the first piece of information that appears in his profile."

Pops tossed the rag down and pointed at Jack with his index finger. "Exactly!"

Jack smiled, relieved that he had been right in his guess.

Pops continued, "Have you ever tried to update your profile information? Somebody else's or even yours?"

Jack was more confident in his answer this time, mostly because he had tried to update his profile information. "It won't let you."

Pops, with an almost playful look on his face, asked, "Why not?"

Jack, confident, answered, "It's locked."

Pops, capitalizing on the art of conversation, took a passive-aggressive posture. "Oh, I see... Well, that's good I suppose. Don't want anybody messing with it." Pops scratched his head. "But it's yours, right? I mean, you pay for it. You own the rights to your information. But you can't alter it?"

Jack, holding firm, said, "It's locked."

Pops smiled. "Even to its owner? That's kind of odd, don't you think? What if I wanted to change my name to 'Bumblefuck'?"

Jack had no response.

"Think about it, boy. I want the world to refer to me as Bumblefuck. How do I change that?"

Jack was dumbfounded. "I don't know." He mumbled, "I don't think you can."

Pops was clearly in charge of the conversation. "Don't fret about it, boy. It's permanently recorded once your parents name you. You gotta go through a legal name change to update that information."

Upon realizing that an option—any option—had been removed from his sphere of self-definition, Jack felt a growing pit in his stomach that he couldn't explain. It welled from his bowels, up through his chest, and into his lungs. He breathed deeper and found that his fists were beginning to clench.

Pops, recognizing the manifestation of adolescent anger, was pleased with himself. *Let's see if I can get a few sparks of rebellion going,* he thought as he redirected his attention to the car. "Okay, move the flashlight over here."

Jack was still processing the knowledge bestowed by Pops and continued to ask questions. "Okay, but Dad is not a bad name, so why doesn't it show up when I look at Kyle? Initial profiles are created by your parents, so why wouldn't they put in there the title dad?"

Pops was pleased with how fast Jack arrived exactly where he wanted him to be with his questioning of his reality. "Well, the answer to your question is the Lewinsky Laws," Pops said flatly as if it was common knowledge. It wasn't common knowledge to Jack.

"And those are?" he asked with raised eyebrows.

Pops could anticipate the order of questions Jack was going to have and immediately answered him. "Monica Lewinsky is a kind of patron saint for those who suffered from any kind of online harassment. The laws are named for her."

"What's a patron saint?" Jack asked.

Pops let out a sigh at Jack's question. He had anticipated this one as well but was hoping, maybe, Jack wouldn't ask it. The sigh was passionless. Not a frustrated sigh, but instead it was a broken and defeated one. "Folk hero is a better way to say it. Basically, instead of being beaten by the thing, she was able to overcome it and, in so doing, inspired others who might have fallen to the same fate."

"What happened to her?"

"She was a young woman who had an affair with the then President of the United States. The story got out, and the sordid details were specific, and intimate, and private, and inescapable. As a result, she became a target, *the* target, for every cyberbully, comedian, talk show host, and preacher alive." Pops paused and then expounded on the situation with more passion in his voice than before.

"A lesser person would have killed themselves, and many who suffered the way she did chose that route. However, Monica was able to rebrand herself and became a kind of inspiration for those who were ever victimized by online harassment. She transcended and helped countless others do the same."

"That's good, I guess. But why did there need to be laws to support that?" Jack asked.

"Believe it or not, boy, there was a time when there was no internet, no Eyebits, no profiles. Those things were all built in the computer age. Freedom of speech was very much alive and well during that time, and with that came posted cruelty, entire websites dedicated to hate, and ongoing chats or forums of pure meanness." Pops paused and looked up at Jack. He was pleased to see him listening intently.

"While interpreting his view of the Constitution, Supreme Court Justice Thurgood Marshall famously said that 'the right to swing your arm stops when the other man's nose comes into jeopardy.' Framers of the Lewinsky Laws seized on that ruling and ultimately won the right to prosecute those who were deemed 'cyberbullies.'"

Pausing again, just to check, Pops saw that Jack was enthralled by what he was saying. "Almost overnight, people complied with the law. Suicide rates declined, and the internet became a friendlier place.

Name-calling all together was eventually outlawed. So, the reason that you call Kyle by his name is because the Eyebit is compliant with the letter of the law, and nicknames like Dad or Mom are categorized as name-calling or cyberbullying and technically illegal."

"But I don't understand. We still have freedom of speech. They teach us that in school," Jack said in a confused tone.

"Well, technically, you do. But where people lose it is right there, spelled out in black and white, in the terms and conditions of all Eyebit products. Nestled neatly between the lines is a section where you agree to give up that right, and only then do you get to use their shit."

Jack was irritated, borderline mad, but not surprised by what he had learned. "That makes sense, I guess. It seems like it has to be all or nothing."

Pops was slightly disappointed at Jack's lackadaisical acceptance of the facts. "Well, I find it very offensive! In my day it was considered rude to call your parents by their first names. My daddy would have backhanded me if I ever called him Jack."

Upon hearing that he had been named after his great-grandfather, Jack perked up. "Your father's name was Jack too?"

"Yeah, it was. But I called him Dad, like any kid would," Pops said coolly.

Pops allowed Jack to process the idea of referring to someone by something other than their first name. The two worked mostly in silence, except for the occasional flashlight direction and tool explanation. Jack had begun to allow his eyes to wander when he happened upon a strange symbol.

"What's chev-roll-at." Jack pronounced the first sound with a hard "che."

Pops stopped what he was working on and looked at Jack. "What?"

"This symbol reads 'chev-roll-at' underneath it, and it's shaped like the state of Tennessee."

Pops could not fathom what the hell the boy was talking about and repositioned himself to see what Jack was seeing. "Oh... Chevrolet. Chevrolet is another car manufacturer."

Jack was confused. Why was a piece from a different manufacturer on Pops's car? "Kyle told me this was a Ford... Mustang. Why is there a Chevrolet part on a Ford?"

Pops cocked an eyebrow at the boy. "First, just say Chevy. It sounds cooler. Second, because it fits the space."

That explanation allowed Jack to make other assumptions about the state of the vehicle. "So, is that why it's all different colors?" While asking the question, Jack reached out to touch the red driver's-side door, then the Vista-Blue quarter panel. As his eyes trailed to the kelly-green hood, Pops began to speak.

"That's right. See, nobody makes these parts anymore, so I've had to piece them together."

Still not fully comprehending the logistics of how Pops assembled his car, Jack asked, "Okay... but from where? Where did you get this stuff?"

With a twinkle in his eye, Pops faced Jack and made air quotes with his hands while he said, "I 'liberate' them." Then he turned toward his toolbox.

"Liberate?" Jack repeated as he stared at the back of Pops's head.

"Means to set free," Pops explained as he located the tool he had been searching for and turned back to the car.

A confused Jack only questioned further. "But... you didn't free them. You took them."

Pops slumped his shoulders and looked up at Jack disapprovingly. "Not much for reading between the lines, are you? Another side effect of having matter-of-fact information streamed directly to your face, I guess. Yes, I stole them. But my intentions were honorable, so I 'liberated' them from their previous owners," Pops said as he made air quotes again.

To win sympathy and justify his actions—not only to himself—Pops continued to explain. "See, they were just going to rot where they were left, but I intervened and gave them a new life, new purpose. I delivered them from certain death, and by doing so, my actions could be called righteous!"

Jack had never heard such talk. His entire life he had been taught, told, force-fed, and had it browbeaten into him that stealing was bad. All forms of theft were to be regarded as criminal, and punishment was always to be expected. *Eyebits will anticipate your needs* was broadcast to the world. *Eliminates crime,* they said, and the world went along.

As Jack pondered the world as he had known it, along with his place in it, a new concept began to form in his mind. *Folk hero.* This phrase was new. It held power and potential. It was a pathway to something else. *Was that what Pops was trying to be?* Jack wondered all this as he looked at his cantankerous grandfather.

Standing before him was someone who just didn't conform. Someone who simply ignored the principles that the rest of society adhered to. The most astonishing aspect of this realization was the inescapable fact that nothing, no punishment, had been delivered to Pops because of his "liberations." *How?* Jack had to know.

CHAPTER SEVEN

Eyebit Immersion 93%

RESTART DEVICE...

As Jack pondered his next line of questioning, he watched Pops work on his car. Examining Pops's movements, Jack longed to know what Pops knew. In front of Jack was a pile of... well, *junk*. Despite that, Pops was operating with a seemingly intimate knowledge of a machine Jack had never had the opportunity to touch before.

Jack watched Pops's movements in awe. He would grab an old tool, dive back under the hood, then spring up as if he were a swimmer needing air. Occasionally he would swear. Sometimes he would pull a twisted piece of metal from the engine, examine it, shrug, and toss it aside.

Jack broke the silence. "Okay. How do you know what you're doing? You look like you've been doing this forever."

Pops didn't look up from the engine. He merely turned his head and reached for the workbench, grabbed his well-worn copy of *Auto-*

mobiles A to Zoom, and handed it to Jack. "All the technical stuff I get from that. The rest your great-granddad showed me."

Jack examined the book, a real book. The pages were worn and stained with years of grease. It smelled. It was coarse and tattered. Nevertheless, it felt good in his hands. As Jack examined the book, he read the chapter titles aloud. Instead of reading them as statements, in his ignorance, he had to read them like questions. "Auto Body? Axle? Bumper? Driveshaft?"

Suddenly feeling self-conscious, Jack stopped reading aloud. He contented himself to quietly sit and examine the book while Pops worked in the background. When he was satisfied, he attempted to incorporate himself into what Pops was doing. "Can I help?" Jack asked eagerly.

Before Pops could answer, Jack spouted off another question. "What's that?"

Pops smiled to himself. "A timing belt, and before you ask me what it does, look it up. Timing belt."

As Jack thumbed through the automotive book, Pops propped himself up on his elbows and watched the boy, waiting.

"Umm, okay, a timing belt is…

"'A timing belt, timing chain, or cam belt is a part of an internal combustion engine that synchronizes the rotation of the crankshaft and the camshaft(s) so that the engine's valves open and close at the proper times during each cylinder's intake and exhaust strokes. In an interference engine, the timing belt or chain is also critical to preventing the piston from striking the valves. A timing belt is a belt that usually features teeth on the inside surface, while a timing chain is a roller chain.'"

Jack finished reading the definition of a timing belt and contemplated its meaning. After reading the definition to himself a second time, he paused, still not understanding.

"Hmmm, crankshaft," Jack muttered to himself and flipped to the section titled Crankshaft.

As Pops watched Jack seek out the answers on his own, he was overcome with a sense of paternal pride and began to smile. "Come here, boy. That book is good and all, but sometimes you just have to get dirty," Pops said as he motioned for Jack to come stand beside him. "This is the timing chain; see how it's connected to these two wheel-looking things?" Pops pointed out the parts he was referring to.

The conversation carried on this way for hours. Jack and Pops discussed parts and their individual functions. There was no order or structure, just an exchange of knowledge and experience. As the hours waned on, Jack came to see Pops's passion for what he was doing. Pops seemed vibrant to Jack, as if what he was building was not just a relic, but a machine that was keeping him alive somehow.

Finally, Pops broke up their conversation by asking Jack, "What time's your dad coming to get you?"

"He's not. I came by myself."

Pops's eyes bugged out of his head. "What? You came here in a transport?" he asked excitedly.

Jack, startled, was hesitant to answer. "Y-Yes."

Pops sprang up from his roller-stool so fast the backs of his knees struck the cushion and sent it sailing to the other side of the garage. "Why didn't you say so, boy," he said as he grabbed Jack by both arms. He was smiling. "We don't have a lot of time. We gotta go!" Pops released Jack, and upon doing so he felt a dull ache in his left arm and began to massage it slowly.

Paying the pain little mind, he quickly moved on to the next item of importance. "Where's my list?"

Jack watched Pops's rapid movement with worried surprise. He had never seen someone that old move that quickly. "Boy, where's my list?" Pops called out again.

Jack had no idea what list Pops was referring to but offered to assist, nonetheless.

"Umm, okay, what's on it?" he asked.

Pops, with his head buried deep in an old wooden filing cabinet, shouted, "Car parts!"

Jack looked around and spotted a piece of paper separate from all the others. He shouted back at Pops, "What's this, on top of this box called a CD player?" Jack picked up the paper, which had items listed on it, even if he didn't know what those items were.

As he turned back toward Pops, he began to mutter to himself, "What's a CD player?"

Pops rushed forward to meet Jack. "That's it! That's it! Good job. Let's go," he said as he clasped the paper and took it out of Jack's hands.

Standing in front of the transport, Jack was unsure about applying his Eyebit, considering Pops's distaste of the technology.

"Go ahead, boy. It won't run without it, and we gotta get moving," Pops said.

Jack put his Eyebit on, and the transport sparked to life. The driver-side door opened, and Jack jumped into the seat. It took him a moment to realize that Pops wasn't wearing an Eyebit and the transport wouldn't let him in.

Jack ticked his eyes to the door controls and opened the passenger door. Bending over to hear and be heard but still hiding his face behind his hat, Pops waited for Jack to speak.

"You're not wearing an Eyebit, so it won't deploy you a seat," Jack said to the top of Pops's cowboy hat.

Pops, undeterred, gave Jack instructions. "Flick to the transport icon."

"Okay." Jack did as he said.

"Now, flick to 'Occupancy.' Okay, in the bottom right you should see MI. That stands for manual interface. Tick that."

Before Jack's eyes, schematics of the transport appeared.

Pops continued with his instructions. "Now, if you flick to the spot for passenger seating, it should give the options of what it can do. Tick Deployment."

In an instant, the passenger seat glided into position, and Pops sat down. Careful to avoid eye contact, Pops kept the brim of his hat covering his eyes, but he could still see Jack's nose and below. Jack's mouth was open in the classic expression of amazement.

"Close your mouth, boy. You look like a doofus."

Jack did not move.

"Here, let me help you." Pops reached over, made a plank with his hand, placed it under Jack's chin, and ever so gently closed his mouth.

Jack broke out of his trance. "How... How? You hate these things. How did you know how to do that? I didn't even know that."

Pops finished adjusting himself as best he could. "Well, now you do. Know your enemy, boy. Know your enemy."

As the transport sliced through the early evening air along its virtual guide track, Pops sat completely still, holding himself. To Jack, he appeared to be paler than normal. When the transport reached their destination, Pops leaped from it before the door had completely opened.

Once free, Pops began to dust himself off and shake as if he had been exposed to a contagion of some kind. Jack just watched his grandfather dance, one eyebrow raised.

"Don't look at me like that. These things make me feel icky," Pops said as he readjusted his coat.

Jack, still wearing his Eyebit, examined his surroundings. "Where are we?" he asked as Pops quietly slipped around the transport to come up behind him. As Jack looked at each building, his Eyebit displayed *No Trespassing. **DO NOT ENTER.***

"All these buildings are..." Before Jack could finish, he felt a hand push his head forward so he was facing the ground, then he saw the flash of his Eyebit disengaging. "Ugh," he said.

The nausea associated with disengagement lessened the more he did it. Nevertheless, Jack was still perturbed at the rudeness of the action. He turned to find Pops standing behind him with both hands raised as if he had a weapon pointed at him.

"Sorry, boy, but every time you disengage those things the last image and sounds are preserved. And I can't have that."

Jack was still a little miffed. "Yeah, how about you tell me that stuff while I already have it off, like in your garage... when we aren't talking about your car."

Pops, realizing that Jack was correct but still unwilling to show it, offered no sympathy. "Hmph, whoops... my bad."

Jack rolled his eyes at his grandfather's remark, turned away, and started examining the landscape again. "What is this place. Where are we?"

Pops walked toward the chain-link fence that surrounded what used to be the front door. "End of the line... for you anyway." He pointed at the transport as if to indicate that Jack needed to stay there.

"Bullshit!" Jack fired back. "I'm not staying here!"

Pops's face lost all expression. "Boy, you don't want to go in there. Once you do, there's no turning back." Pops continued as he approached Jack. "Inside that building, you will encounter wonders that will change how you see your world, and you may not like it. In that 'old building' rests the potential to reshape your perception and make you question things. And the answers will only lead to more questions."

Pops changed his tone to sound more buddy-like and less grim. "Your world is easier to stay in. Stay in there. You can be happy. I can't take you into that building and remain guiltless. There ain't no reason whatsoever for you to delve into youthful curiosity."

Jack looked at Pops skeptically. "What could possibly be in this old building that could do that?"

Pops offered no explanation and shrugged.

"I'm going in there with you. So you might as well tell me."

Pops breathed deeply. "It's where the physical embodiment of America's passion for the road ended up. All its wonder and dreams and adventure and freedom were lost and sent here to die."

Jack was the first to move, and he marched toward the fence. As he approached the building, he looked above the entrance at the giant letters that used to spell out what the place had been named.

FO . D MO . . R COMPAN . MAN.F.CT . . ING .LANT

Pops followed Jack, smiled to himself, and thought, *That's more like it.* He was pleased that Jack was showing a sense of adventure. Upon reaching the fence, Pops lifted a corner of the chain link and allowed Jack to go in first. "After you," he said.

Once on the other side, Jack held the same fencing up for Pops. After snaking their way through, the two men started for the gaping wound that had once been the front door and disappeared into the darkness.

CHAPTER EIGHT

Eyebit Immersion 92%

RESTART DEVICE...

J ack and Pops were enveloped in darkness.

"Watch your step. These buildings aren't maintained like they used to be," Pops said.

Jack, snickering at the absurdness of 'watching' anything, only muttered, "Watch what? I can't see anything!"

Pops, realizing that Jack was right, reached into his pocket and produced a Zippo lighter. Unable to walk and reach into his pocket at the same time, he'd paused long enough for Jack to bump into him.

"Careful, boy! You can get hurt running into brick shithouses like that!" Pops said jovially. He wasn't surprised when Jack didn't laugh. He knew as soon as he said it that Jack wouldn't get it.

Flipping the top off his Zippo, Pops took a moment to be comforted by the *chink* it made. Then, with three flicks of the flint wheel, fire sprang from the wick, and the darkness was vanquished.

Pops quickly took stock of his surroundings. Even though he was familiar with the location, it had been a while since his last visit. Then, examining Jack, he noticed that his hands were trembling.

"What's wrong?" Pops asked as he moved the lighter toward Jack's hands to illuminate them.

Jack had no idea what was happening. "I don't know. They've been doing that since we came in. I ca-ca-can't make it stop."

Pops knew exactly what was happening but put up a charade, nonetheless. "Let me have a look." He clasped Jack's hand. He then pinched his wrist with his middle and index finger. "Yep," he said then moved the flame next to his face. "Oh jeez," Pops gasped.

That only added to Jack's nervousness. "What? What is it?" Jack said, almost in a panic.

Pops raised an eyebrow and shot sarcasm at the boy. "Easy. In your condition, those eyes'll pop out if you're not careful." Lastly Pops put two fingers on Jack's neck then counted to five. "Yep, just as I thought..." Pops held his breath to build suspense. Then he whispered his diagnosis to Jack. "By George, you're *alive*!"

With slight relief and some annoyance, Jack cut his eyes at Pops. "Yes, I know I'm alive! What's wrong with me?"

Pops smiled. "Nothing is. Not anymore anyway." Based on Jack's look of confusion, Pops could tell he wasn't getting through to him. "Let me rephrase. You're *living*! What you're feeling is adrenaline. It's induced by your actions; you're feeling it now because you're not wearing your zombie maker."

"Will it stop?" Jack asked with a twinge of fear in his voice.

Pops shook his head. "Yes, it will pass, but ask yourself this question... Do you really want it to?" Pops let the experience sink in for a moment before adding, "I told you there was no going back."

Refocusing on what they were there to do, Pops turned back toward the hallway. "Come on, Frankenstein, this lighter is getting hot. Reclamation is this way."

Jack clenched his fist, thrust his arm down, and flared his hand open in an attempt to lose the shakes. He breathed deeply and asked, "What are we looking for?"

Pops didn't turn around, just kept moving forward. "It's a who, and his name is Bones."

This was just one more of the things Pops said that Jack didn't understand. Finally resolving to not be ignorant, he decided to keep asking questions. "Bones? What bones?"

Pops, still facing forward, responded, "Every hospital has one."

That didn't answer Jack's question. "What bones? What hospital? What are you talking about?"

Even though Jack couldn't see it, Pops rolled his eyes. "I forget your dad doesn't have any interest in family history. Your great-grandmother was an emergency room nurse my entire life. Her hospital had a Bones. 'Every hospital has one,' she used to say to me." Pops looked down, kicked a tin can farther into the hallway, and returned to his explanation.

"Bones is a term of endearment applied to a person who is intimate with a building... or starship. In a hospital, it was usually a wise doctor or pharmacist or sometimes a medical examiner in the morgue." Pops kicked the can again. "The nickname Bones carries a certain distinction and respect but not the same distinction and respect as a dean of medicine or a captain because they run a building or a ship. But a Bones keeps the whole thing alive, and a Bones always knows all the tricks."

For the first time in his life, Jack thought a nickname could be a good thing.

Tink.

Pops had snapped the Zippo shut. "There," he said.

It took a moment for Jack's eyes to readjust to the darkness. Although it wasn't completely dark, there was a faint orange glow up ahead and to the right.

"Follow the light, and watch your step," Pops said.

Jack did as Pops said, following in his footsteps. Jack couldn't see where Pops was leading, just his tall, lanky, wide-brim hat-wearing silhouette. Pops stopped suddenly. This time, Jack stopped as well.

"Watch this," Pops whispered to Jack. "Hey, Bones!" Pops shouted.

Jack couldn't see but heard a loud clank followed by a muffled scream.

"Tee-hee-hee. Makes him jump every time." As Pops chuckled to himself, he waited for Bones to make Pops's favorite arm movement, which was to disengage his Eyebit. Once he was sure that was completed, he said to Jack, "Come on, boy."

Pops stepped aside, and Jack was allowed to take in the full view of where he was. It was astonishing; Jack's breath was taken away at what he saw. Row after row of smashed cars lined either side of a giant circular vat of glowing orange liquid. Above the vat was a huge claw that had in its grasp a car that looked like Pops's car, only ever so slightly different.

"Pops," Jack said, calling his attention to what he was looking at. "That one looks like yours, but different. It's got something written on the back... What's Shelby?"

As Pops looked up, the claw released the car, and Pops's eyes watched its plunge into the molten abyss. As it struck the surface, the car's cold metal let out a hiss, and smoke began to rise from the body. Slowly, as the car sank deeper, the hissing became louder and louder, more desperate, until it was gone.

To Pops, it seemed like a scream. He didn't provide Jack with a clear answer and only said, "Another dead dream." Pops snaked his way around the destroyed and smashed cars, working his way to where Bones was standing.

"I thought I told you not to come in that entrance," Bones said to Pops sternly.

"Apologies." Pops tipped his cowboy hat toward Bones.

Bones smiled and shook his head. "I haven't seen you in a while," he said as if he were asking why Pops had waited so long to visit.

"Yeah, I've been busy. I trust you still have my list. Any luck?"

Bones smiled. "For you? Of course. And what about mine?"

"I wouldn't be here if I couldn't pay you," Pops said. Jack was surprised as Bones's smile got even bigger.

"Okay, wait here. I'll get 'em," Bones said, and Pops nodded.

After Bones was out of sight, Pops leaned over to Jack and said, slightly above a whisper, "Your eyes are sharper than mine, so keep a lookout for a non-smashed passenger-side Mustang door."

Jack had to think about what the door Pops already had looked like. Then he had to envision it as the opposite to fit on the other side. Once Jack had an image in his mind, he wondered why Pops wouldn't just ask Bones for it.

"In case you're wondering why I didn't ask Bones for it," Pops said as if he was reading Jack's mind, "I have, and he can't seem to produce it. I think it's because he doesn't know what to look for, exactly."

Jack, still curious, asked, "Why don't you just go look for it yourself?"

Pops quickly answered, "'Cause, that's rude, boy! This is his place, we are guests, he is helping us, and we will show him some respect. Having said that, should you spot it, I'll point it out in a way as to not hurt his feelings. It's how men used to interact with each other, understand?"

Jack only nodded.

While the two waited for Bones to return, Jack thought about the nickname Bones and how Pops had described it. As best Jack could figure, it didn't apply to where they were. "Why do you call him Bones?" Jack asked.

Pops tore his eyes from the claw that had just dropped the Shelby and faced Jack. "Why? Isn't it obvious?" he exclaimed.

Jack, unsure of Pops's meaning, was hesitant to respond. "Well, this isn't a hospital. Nothing is living here." He made a gesture with his hand as if to showcase the twisted pieces of metal.

"Oh, I see," Pops said. "Again with reading between the lines. What's the definition of life?"

Jack was completely sure of his answer and recited what he had learned. "Oh, well, my Eyebit says that life is anything that consumes and repurposes energy, breathes oxygen, responds to stimuli, and produces offspring."

Pops almost jumped when he heard Jack's definition. "Yes! Exactly! Think about a car itself. It runs on an internal combustion engine, which requires oxygen. You drive it by turning the wheel, so it responds to stimuli. It consumes and repurposes energy via the type of fuel used. Tee-hee-hee. And it produces offspring." Pops chuckled.

"And how does it produce offspring?" Jack asked.

"Via the backseat, boy, and I am *not* having that conversation with you." Pops stared at Jack as if daring him to respond.

"I don't see how that fits," Jack said, not fully understanding what Pops meant.

"Of course you don't. Okay, then," Pops continued, "by your definition of life, fire itself fits, but you wouldn't count fire as a valid argument either, would you?"

Jack shook his head and said, "You can't talk to a car or fire."

Pops smiled. "Good point. So, your view of alive is flesh, blood, and something you can carry on a conversation with?"

"Yeah, they have to be aware of what's going on and talk to you," Jack said, most assuredly.

Pops had once again trapped Jack in a critical thinking exercise and intended to make him squirm. "Okay, well, I feel sorry for your dog."

Jack was dumbfounded. He had never considered the possibility that someone might not consider his dog alive. *Animals count,* he thought to himself. *They have feelings. Don't they?*

Pops could tell by Jack's facial expressions and furrowed brow that he had gotten through to him. "Don't fret about it, boy. We could philosophize about the definition of life all day long. It's as simple as this: at some point it will come down to what you believe."

Jack made eye contact with Pops, and as he began to speak, Pops could tell it was from his soul. "I-I never thought about..."

Before he could finish, Pops cut him off. "No one with an Eyebit does! I told you there was no going—" Pops was interrupted by a loud crash, and he turned to see Bones pushing a wheeled cart toward them.

CHAPTER NINE

Eyebit Immersion 91%

ERROR... RESTART DEVICE... ERROR

Both Pops and Jack directed their attention toward Bones, who was approaching them with a grin that seemed to stretch from ear to ear. He walked directly up to Pops, and Pops immediately started picking up the parts and examining them. Bones glanced over at Jack, who was simply standing there.

Jack made brief eye contact and offered a slight smile before looking away.

Bones resumed watching Pops for only a moment, then he said, "Do you mind if I check out what you brought me for all this?"

Pops didn't look up to meet his eyes, just reached into his pocket and handed him a small vial. "Sure. Just don't face me when you do."

Bones took the vial greedily and turned away muttering, "Sure, sure."

Jack watched as Bones reengaged his Eyebit and looked down at his cupped hands. "Okay, okay, good, good. I'll call you back." Bones then disengaged his Eyebit and turned back around to face Pops. "Okay, this is good stuff, ninety-eight percent pure! I've got five interested buyers already. In another thirty seconds, I'll have fifteen."

Jack was watching the exchange between the two men when he heard a clang like something hitting the floor. When he looked over, he noticed a small corridor where spare parts were housed. Jack looked back at Pops and Bones, who were engaged in heavy conversation about car parts. Instead of interrupting them, Jack decided to do a bit of exploring.

Out of the corner of his eye, Pops noticed Jack slipping away. He was pleased to see him going off on his own but knew that Bones wouldn't be. So Pops made an extra effort to distract Bones.

Jack rounded the corner and found the corridor went on farther. He was tempted to turn back but had spied what he thought were Mustang parts scattered about. So he breathed deeply, attempted to steady his hands, and proceeded.

Even though there was enough light to see his way back, he still worried he would get lost, so he memorized the writing on one of the cars at the corner. "Escape," he repeated to himself as he walked forward. Then he spied it—the door Pops had been looking for.

Jack knelt in front of the half-protruding door. He put his hands on it and realized he would have to forcibly remove it. He looked up at the mound of scrap metal on top of it and realized extracting it would be no easy task. "Okay, whatever," Jack muttered to himself. "Here lies Jack, crushed to death by falling car parts."

Jack gave the piece a good tug, but it didn't budge. He tried again; this time he redoubled his efforts only to have the piece barely slip out an inch. Determined not to give up, he sat on the ground, put his feet on either side of the piece, and pulled with his hand while pushing with his legs.

Jack breathed in, held his breath, and tugged with every ounce of his strength. The piece slipped ever so slightly and was beginning to give way when he felt a hand clasp his shoulder, followed by a voice.

"Boy! What are you doing?" Pops had managed to come up behind Jack completely unbeknownst to him and startle him.

Jack had been so frightened he'd let go of what he was holding onto and fell back onto the frigid concrete. "Why did you do that?" Jack exclaimed as he jumped up.

Pops, unmoved by the boy's reaction, offered no consolation. "Scare you?" Pops asked with not even a hint of surprise in his voice. He could tell that Jack was agitated. Noticing Jack's hands had started to tremble, Pops sought to use that energy.

"Okay, you're mad. That adrenaline in your veins will make you stronger. Use it to pull that door out."

The two men stared at each other for a moment before Pops grabbed him by the shoulders and shouted directly in Jack's face. "Not me, boy! That!" He turned Jack back to face the pile of discarded metal.

Jack set to it immediately. Not thinking, just feeling. Pops, knowing that Jack's upper body was severely underdeveloped, sought to encourage him and keep the supply of adrenaline flowing. "Come on, boy! Get some!" Pops continued to prod him as the door inched its way toward freedom.

"That's it! You got it!" When the door was nearly free, Jack began to groan as he gulped for breath. Pops's shouting became louder to counter Jack's noises. "Come on, boy. Hulk out on that shit!"

Jack let out a yell, and the bonds that held the door broke free. Jack collapsed to his knees, still clutching the passenger-side door.

Pops knelt beside him, swelling with pride as only a grandparent could. Pops kept his words short and to the point. "Good job, boy! I'm proud of you." As quickly as he said it, Pops turned his attention to the prize.

The word "proud" had awestruck Jack. Kyle had said that to him before, but it was different. It had never come from Jack exerting himself in any fashion, almost like Kyle had said it out of obligation. As he sat there catching his breath, Jack felt that Pops had meant it.

Jack looked back at the hole that was left from where the door had been. He was transfixed as he watched a piece of metal slowly bend and the hole close. Jack reasoned it was due to the enormous weight of the pile of metal.

"Oh wow! This is perfect! Do you have any idea how long I've been searching for this?" Pops was giddy. Smiling, Pops asked, "How did you find this?"

Jack made a motion with his hand as if to point toward something.

Before Jack could answer, Bones came running from around the corner. "What's going on over here? What are you two doing?"

Neither had to answer, because Bones trailed his eyes to the door at his feet and answered his own questions. "Oh."

Jack watched Pops rise to his feet, square his shoulders, and face Bones directly.

"We'll take that too," Pops said very matter-of-factly.

Bones looked at the door then back at Pops. "Yeah, I don't know. You've already got everything else on your list."

Pops cocked an eyebrow at Bones. "Is that so? Well then, we better reexamine our situation. How many buyers do you have for what I gave you? And we both know I gave you a bit more than I usually do."

Bones, unable to form words, could only mutter.

Pops's negotiation was strategic. He put on the friendliest smile he could muster. "Come on, Bones, it's been five minutes. You must have at least eighty buyers by now."

Bones, unaware of what Pops was doing to him, corrected the number without even considering what he was revealing. "Eighty-seven," he said, almost proudly.

Pops arched his body and exclaimed even louder, "Eighty-seven! Wow, you'll be able to pit them against each other and make double the credits!"

Bones smiled back at Pops.

Pops let a moment of silence grow between them as he eased closer to Bones. Confident that the idea of double credits was cemented in Bones's mind, Pops moved in for the kill. "It would be a shame to have to withdraw the sale over a piece of scrap metal no one cares about."

Bones was visibly wounded by the idea of no credits. Pops, now playing the nice guy, put his arm around his shoulder and lowered his tone. "Bonesy, I like you. I wanna buy from you. But it's all or nothing." Pops then drew his arm tight, pulling Bones's ear closer to his mouth. "You're not the only reclamation center in town." Pops's voice was nearly a whisper, but Jack could still make out what he was saying.

Bones did not respond to Pops except to nod.

Pops smiled. "Pleasure doing business with you," he said and extended his hand. The two clasped hands and shook.

Jack watched this exchange and remembered Kyle trying to convey the meaning of a handshake. At the time Jack had dismissed it, thinking, "When will I ever need to do that?"

Bones turned away from the two men, reengaged his Eyebit, and said as he walked away, "I gotta get back to work. Show yourselves out."

Jack, still on the floor, watched as Pops approached him with a plain look of seriousness on his face.

Upon reaching him, Pops knelt, slapped Jack on the knee, and extended his hand to help him to his feet. "Come on, son. We gotta go," he said as he straightened his wide-brimmed antique cowboy hat.

Pops picked up the door and led the way back toward the spot Bones had initially left them waiting before Jack wandered off. As the two gathered up all the parts that were on the list, it quickly became apparent that they weren't going to be able to handle everything without some sort of help.

Bones was nowhere to be found, and Pops was not about to borrow his cart without asking. He quickly worked the problem out and asked Jack a question. "You're wearing a Z-face uniform. Do you wear socks with your boots?"

It took Jack a moment to understand what Pops meant by "Z-face uniform." Once he figured out that he meant his image-projection clothes suit, he answered, "I wear socks."

Pops smiled. "Oh, how lucky."

Pops dropped his arms, and the parts he had been holding hit the floor with a loud crash. He approached Jack and knelt at his feet. Pops started with his left leg. Taking Jack's foot, he lifted the pants leg, located his sock, and started to shove his suit pant leg into the sock.

When Pops let go, Jack rebalanced himself before Pops moved to the next foot. "Loosen your collar," Pops said as he finished tucking Jack's other pant leg into his sock.

Jack did as he was told, all the while wondering, *What now?*

Pops stood up and faced Jack. "Pull your collar a little wider. Okay, don't move." He eyed Jack and then eyed the parts. "Here we go," he said as he started to drop and shove parts down Jack's suit.

"What... What the hell!" Jack exclaimed.

Pops didn't stop, just continued to shove in parts. "You got a better idea?"

Jack, fighting hard to stay still but failing, nearly shouted, "Yeah! We make multiple trips!"

Pops had already considered that, but this would be funnier. "Not enough time, boy. We gotta get." He shoved the last of the parts into Jack's suit and refastened his collar.

"You look great," Pops said with a smirk. "Here." He handed Jack the door.

Jack couldn't help but notice Pops's hands were empty. "And you're carrying... what?" he asked as he took a survey of the fact there was nothing left for Pops to bring out.

Pops thought quickly. "Ummm... I'm going to catch whatever falls out of your cheap socks."

Jack rolled his eyes and headed for the door.

Pops stayed back a few feet to be entertained by the sight of Jack hobbling toward the entrance. The combination of Jack trying to walk without bending his knees and the oddly shaped bulges in the suit caused Jack to have a slight bounce in his step.

From Pops's perspective, he looked like an overweight show dog trotting along whose fur moved a split second after its body. Pops couldn't help but stop and laugh out loud, so much so that he clapped his hands as he brought them to his knees.

Jack heard Pops laughing but didn't stop trotting. After a few moments, even Jack thought about how ridiculously funny he must have looked and smiled to himself.

Pops's laughter was interrupted by a sharp shooting pain in his arm. He straightened his body as he massaged it. He dismissed the pain. *Shouldn't have dropped those parts on the floor and picked 'em up like that.* Refocusing on Jack, Pops got serious and followed him back into the darkness from which they had come.

Jack had never been as happy to see a transport as he was then. The thought of rusty old metal rubbing against his skin was starting to bother him. Something wet leaked from the part resting on his hip. The unknown fluid was now at his knee. Being optimistic about his situation, Jack told himself, "Well, at least it didn't go down my crack."

Desperate to unload the material, Jack began to think about throwing off some of the car parts. Before reaching the passenger side of the transport, he chucked the Mustang door at it. He'd overestimated the distance, so the door struck the transport with a clang then made a thud as it hit the ground. "Damn," Jack said as he took stock of the damage to the transport.

"Don't sweat that," Pops said, catching up to Jack. "All these crap cans you drive have self-healing bodies."

Jack wasn't aware that the transport would repair itself. *Oh good*, he thought and proceeded to pull parts out of his suit and dump them on the ground next to the door.

"Put your Z-face on, and open the door," Pops said as he watched Jack nearly throw parts off of himself. "Slow down, boy. Let's do this smart," Pops said, and Jack stopped unloading parts.

Once the door was open, Pops took the Mustang door and laid it on top of where the passenger seat would be. He then climbed into the transport and squatted in front of the door. "Now, start handing me parts." As Jack handed Pops parts, he stacked them just so.

When Pops finished loading the transport, he gave the Mustang door a gentle shake. The pile shifted slightly but held. "Okay, good to go," he said.

Jack, recalling how Pops had manually deployed a passenger seat, asked, "Um, okay, where are you going to sit?"

Pops looked around for a second. "Right here, Indian style."

Jack didn't argue. He was growing accustomed to regarding Pops as obviously crazy. He selected the Eyebit to close the passenger door, and as it lowered, Jack couldn't help but notice that the dent and scratch made by the Mustang door were gone.

Seating himself in the driver's side, Jack was confused when the transport wouldn't initiate travel. "Weight exceeds registered passengers," Jack said, repeating what was flashing across his Eyebit screen.

"Oh, okay," Pops said. "Select Manual Entry. Then select Cargo."

Jack, following directions, continued to read the output text. "Estimated weight?" he read aloud from the Eyebit prompt.

Pops thought for a second and replied, "Two hundred fifty plus."

When Jack put in the weight, his Eyebit displayed the outline of the transport and then zoomed in on an outline of the cargo. "***Cargo detected. Unsecured.***" Jack repeated the text. "***Cargo securing straps deploying in 3.2.1.***"

Pops was confused for about half a second before he remembered the cargo straps. "Aaah, shi—"

Swish. The first set of cargo straps shot across the cargo area in a horizontal pattern, so fast Pops didn't have time to move. As the set of straps exploded across the cargo zone, they caught the brim of

Pops's cowboy hat and knocked it clear from his head. The second set deployed at a perpendicular path from the first and formed a crisscross net pattern. The cargo net was aligned in such a way that Pops's head was sticking out through one of the squares. "***Securing cargo... Securing cargo.***" Jack continued to read the text out loud.

Click, click, click, click. The automated ratchet straps cranked down, hunching Pops over the pile of parts while at the same time pushing it into his chest. Pops let out a whine, as Jack continued to read. "***Cargo secured.***"

The transport sparked to life and shot off like a rocket. Taking in Pops's current condition, it was Jack who couldn't help but laugh this time. Pops wasn't amused.

Adding insult to injury, Jack decided a little revenge was in order. He took the hat and wedged it on Pops's head sideways while saying, "Here's your hat back" in a low whisper like you would to a sleeping child.

Pops couldn't help but smile as he thought to himself, *Smart-ass kid.*

CHAPTER TEN

Eyebit Immersion 90%

RESYNCING PREVIOUS SETTINGS...

The transport sliced through the early evening air. As it glided along its virtual rails, it made a low hum that Pops found annoying. *Doesn't have that throaty V8 sound,* he thought as he contorted his body into the most comfortable position he could achieve. He was tempted to talk to Jack but would not allow himself to do so. It would cause Jack to look at him with his Eyebit on, and he couldn't have that.

Jack looked forward with a zombie-like stare as he was immersed in the Eyebit world. There were thirty-nine messages, a movie playing on an endless loop, a soft music overlay, and two waiting calls. Despite all that, his mind was still wandering back to his experience at the reclamation center.

With one swipe of his eyes, every input in his Eyebit was reduced to the bottom left corner of his field of view. The transport continued, streaming toward its destination. Its program didn't allow for the disengagement of the Eyebit while a transport was in motion.

Given his recent enlightenment about manual overrides, he momentarily wondered if there was a way to bend the "no disengagement" rule as well. But something larger had been pressing on his mind. *What did Pops give Bones in exchange for the parts?*

Jack turned to look at Pops, who cut his eyes and looked away to avoid detection. "Tell it you want to sleep," Pops said, as Jack once again faced forward.

With a few swift eye strokes, Jack was able to make his Eyebit fade into the background. Except for the clock icon in the top left corner, the Eyebit screen was as clear as a window.

"There, that's better," Pops said as Jack faced him again.

"How can you tell I'm in sleep mode?" Jack asked, ever curious about Pops's knowledge of the inner workings of something he hated.

"Your eyes aren't bouncing around like a crack-addicted lab monkey. What's on your mind?"

Jack, without hesitation, launched right into questioning. "How did you pay Bones? You physically gave him something. What was it?"

Pops answered with a single word. "Gold."

"Gold?" Jack repeated in disbelief.

"Yep, gold," Pops said very matter-of-factly.

Jack, still confused, asked again, "Gold... Gold-gold? Like the valuable metal?"

Pops squinted. "Yes! Gold, the precious metal. Gold, atomic number 79 on the periodic chart of elements. Gold, the glittery stuff that the James Bond villain Goldfinger obsessed about."

Jack, clearly understanding what Pops meant, asked, "Where did you get it?"

Pops smiled. "A prospector never gives up his spot, boy!"

Jack was having a hard time believing his ears. Had his grandfather physically mined it? *He must have. It's not like he found it just lying on the ground, did he? How was this possible?* Jack's mind was racing with questions.

He drew in breath to speak but didn't. He exhaled and returned to a relaxed position, contemplating. After a moment of reorganizing his thoughts, he inhaled again but failed to form the words. He exhaled and sat back.

"Wondering how and where I come by it?" Pops asked after the entertainment of Jack's breathing had subsided.

"Yeah," Jack said keenly, giving Pops his undivided attention.

"Well, for starters you must know the history. See, this whole area was the site of the first gold rush in America." Pops shifted in the cargo straps, attempting to make himself more comfortable.

He let out a moan before continuing his story. "In the early 1990s the main bank building downtown was constructed on top of an abandoned gold mine. When they drove the spire into the ground, they punched into that mine. The mine was empty, the news outlets reported." Pops shifted his body again.

"However, it had been abandoned at a time in history when there were no metal detectors or modern equipment to seek out hidden gold." Pausing to let Jack absorb what he was telling him, Pops again fought against the cargo straps. They still didn't budge.

"Anyway," Pops continued. "You're probably thinking that I've just gotten into that mine somehow. Well, you're wrong. What I've done is identify the contractor who built the building and, more importantly, where their waste site was... specifically the dirt-removal dumping ground."

The only word to describe Jack's reaction was "flabbergasted." He couldn't believe what he was hearing. Surely people wouldn't simply leave something as valuable as gold lying around, but obviously they had.

"That's amazing!" Jack said as he hung on Pops's every word. "But why are you not rich? Why don't you just go and get all of it?"

Pops had to confess; he had been tempted by that before. By his calculations, there was enough gold not only to purchase the derelict church where his wife was buried but also to pay to have the grounds maintained for at least fifty years.

"Two reasons," Pops said. "One, to manage and move that kind of currency would force a spotlight on me. And two, I'm not a greedy person. I have or can get what I need on my own. Besides, laziness tends to follow wealth, especially today."

Despite seeing the wisdom in Pops's words, Jack couldn't help but wonder about all the ways he would handle wealth. He imagined all the things he could buy. He pictured himself living a lavish lifestyle in the lap of luxury. The transport ride fell silent as Jack daydreamed. As the fantasy wore on, he couldn't help but notice that it was devoid of one thing. Work. Jack's fantasies of wealth were missing any sort of activity that involved him doing anything. He didn't even consider using the money to pay for higher education.

Does Pops think I'm lazy? He wondered. For the first time in his life, Jack was concerned about someone's opinion of him. He found the feeling bizarre. The Eyebit had always paired him with people of similar interests, so making friends had required little effort.

Furthermore, he had never had any kind of job, part-time or otherwise. He knew people who did, but he didn't need to. Sure, he did schoolwork but only because he was made to.

In the Eyebit world, he was popular. He was active. He did stuff. But none of it was real.

As Pops's house came into sight, Jack was coming to understand why Pops hated the Eyebits so much. They didn't encourage people to do anything in the real world. Here was a man who went out into the world and found gold! Real gold.

No matter how hard Jack looked, he would never find gold inside an Eyebit. It was beginning to dawn on him, a small crack of light at first, but soon it would be the blazing sun. Maybe he didn't need an Eyebit either. Maybe, just maybe, he could do something without it.

Chapter Eleven

Eyebit Immersion 89%

Resync complete. Reengage device...

The transport stopped. They had arrived at Pops's house. Still operating under the impression that Jack was sleeping, the Eyebit began the wake-up cycle.

Having never really gone to sleep, Jack spoke aloud before the sunrise sequence was completed. "I'm awake." Upon registering the voice command, the Eyebit redisplayed everything Jack had been doing before he supposedly went to sleep.

Having completed its transportation sequence, the transport raised both doors and retracted the cargo straps. Pops slumped back against the dash and breathed heavily. "Damn," he muttered as he lifted his legs out of the transport.

Standing up, Pops began to shake and shiver as if something was crawling on his skin. "These things make me feel dirty." Dusting his hat off on his leg, Pops faced away from Jack. Avoiding direct eye contact with him, Pops put his cowboy hat on so the rim just covered his eyes. "Wait here. I'll get the dolly."

Jack watched as Pops walked to the house, and he couldn't help but notice that Pops was using his right hand to massage his left arm. Pops went in the front, and unsurprisingly to Jack, he didn't use a key, as they'd left the door unlocked. After only a moment the garage door flung open, and Pops emerged pushing an ancient dolly with a wobbly wheel.

"Don't just stand there, boy. Get to unloading."

Jack jumped at Pops's directive, careful not to look him in the eyes, as his Eyebit would pick up his image. The dolly was quickly loaded, and the two men retreated back toward the garage. As they walked, Jack, without being asked, removed his Eyebit.

As the garage door closed, Jack looked at the transport, realizing that he had not powered it off before removing his Eyebit. Interestingly enough, it had shut down and locked itself when all approved Eyebits had become unreadable.

Jack quickly forgot the transport when he fixed his eyes on Pops's Mustang. The vehicle didn't appear the same as it had before they left for the reclamation center. Not that it had changed in the slightest. Jack was simply viewing it in a different light. It appeared to Jack now more as a refugee, plucked from unimaginable violence and saved from certain destruction.

Jack was certain the car hadn't undergone any changes in their absence, yet somehow it no longer appeared the same ancient piece of rainbow-colored junk it had been. For lack of a better word, he felt pity for the machine. As he stared at the car, he was trying to visualize how the parts they just got would all be incorporated.

Jack's thoughts were interrupted when he felt a fist punch his arm.

"Hey, I said, do you want a beer?" Pops said.

Snapping back to reality, Jack stammered through his response. By the time he got out "I'm not allowed, too young," Pops already had two beers in hand.

"Do you always do what you're told?" Pops asked as he tossed one of the beers in Jack's direction. The next sound to reverberate through the garage was a loud crash, followed by a hiss that was unmistakably from a shaken-up, punctured beer can. Jack hadn't moved as he watched the beer can sail past his head.

"Okay... so your dad didn't play catch with you either, huh?" Pops said as he handed Jack another beer.

Jack took the beer and asked, "Won't you get in trouble if they find out you gave this to me?" He waited for Pops to answer as he watched him drop some old rags on top of the floor where the beer had spilled.

Pops thought about it for a minute. "Yeah... I don't much care." He stamped on the rags to soak up the beer.

Jack wasn't surprised by Pops's lack of regard for the law. He had seen too much today to be surprised anymore. But he still wondered how Pops could not care about the potential punishment involved with deliberately breaking the rules.

Pops said, "Son, when you get to be my age, you've faced, accepted, and made peace with man's ultimate fear. The rest of society's trappings are... well... crap." Pops shrugged as he said "crap," then he set his beer down next to the dolly and began to piece out the parts.

Jack sipped his beer. *Yuck*! He thought and went to join Pops.

Thinking on the subject of age, Pops decided to open up to Jack a little bit. "I do envy you slightly, though," he said as he picked up a piece of cracked plastic. "You're at that perfect age, right smack between ultimate freedom and responsibility."

Jack didn't understand what Pops was referring to. "What do you mean?" he asked, sipping his beer. *Ugh.*

"Well, you wouldn't understand. Only the old understand the power of youth."

Jack sipped his beer and looked downtrodden. "I don't feel powerful," he confessed almost shamefully.

Pops felt sad for his grandson. Before him was a boy who had no inkling of what it meant to become or be a man. "Well, you're at that stage between grade school and university. You're old enough to be able to reason and make decisions while at the same time young enough to not have any responsibilities that force your path in certain directions," he said wisely.

Pops sipped his beer with an annoying sucking noise as he took it between his teeth. "When is your graduation?"

"Two weeks."

"College in the fall?"

"Yes... Maybe," Jack answered half-heartedly.

"Major?"

Jack didn't answer, just shrugged, because he didn't know.

"That's okay, boy. It took me a long time to decide what I wanted to study, and even then, I still felt incomplete."

Pops thought about his words for a moment. In that instant, he realized that he had finally connected with his grandson. They had something in common. Pops decided to run with it. "Hey, how 'bout that, boy? Something we got in common after all!"

At hearing this, Jack perked up. "Really? You didn't know what you wanted to be either?" he asked earnestly.

Pops chuckled. "No, I didn't have a clue. I only knew what I liked." Pops had a momentary flashback to when he was Jack's age. Driving fast, drinking, and women raced through his mind before reality caught back up with him.

"Wait," Pops said as he turned his attention back to Jack and away from his past. "Doesn't that do-swatchit tell you what you will be studying and what you should pursue as a career?"

Jack looked almost embarrassed. "It's giving me error messages. 'Classification failed, choose interest, course unknown' or something like that. So I've been ignoring classification protocols."

Pops was stunned, his heart swelling with so much pride he thought it might burst. "Don't sweat it, boy. Some of the most interesting people in history failed classification."

At hearing this, Jack felt a sense of relief and smiled. Eager to continue feeling better about his condition, Jack jumped in to help Pops move the parts and find out more about how Pops had found his way. "So, what did you do to find out what you wanted to be?"

"Well," Pops said and thought about his response for a moment. "I just did what I liked and stuck to that path and ended up in the here and now. Voilà! I didn't realize it at the time, but I was lucky enough to have an entire summer of pivotal freedom, as I call it."

Jack had never heard of that and was forced to inquire. "What's that?"

Pops smiled to himself, knowing he had succeeded in drawing the boy into something he hoped would be enlightening for him. "So, pivotal freedom is the time just before someone leaves the nest. During this time, they have the sense of security and safety of the home, with none of the responsibilities. Most people have a mode of transportation that allows for adventure. The length of time it lasts is never set in stone. Sometimes it's an hour, maybe an afternoon or a day. For some very lucky people, it's an entire summer."

Pops paused for a moment to craft his next words carefully. "Responsibility degrades freedom." After allowing a moment of silence, he continued. "The end of pivotal freedom is usually marked by the crowding in of society's responsibilities—a parent can no longer support the child, there's an untimely death, or college begins. When pivotal freedom ends, it's over, forever. It can never be reclaimed, regained, or duplicated.

"But I'm sure you've heard all this before," Pops said, as he tossed his empty beer can toward the trash. The beer can hit the wall and fell to the floor. "Ahh, white guy basketball." He got up to put the beer can in the trash.

"I've never heard that before," Jack said as he followed Pops's movements.

"What?" Pops looked confused. "Sure you have. You probably didn't catch the meaning. You know, the story of the man and the horse?"

Jack shook his head. "I don't know that one."

Pops squinted at Jack and flatly asked, "Your dad never told the story of the man and the horse?"

Jack again shook his head. "No."

"Jesus! Okay, well, do you want to hear it?"

"Ummm, sure," Jack said as he reached for his beer and sipped it absent-mindedly.

Yuck.

"Okay, pull up a stool," Pops said as he came to sit back down next to Jack with a

fresh beer.

Jack looked confused. "I don't see any stools."

Pops huffed and shook his head. "It's a figure of speech." After getting comfortable,

Pops began. "Okay... Once upon a time..."

As Pops allowed his tale to unfold, Jack had the fleeting thought he was supposed to be somewhere, but he couldn't remember where. Unbeknownst to Jack, a light was blinking in the transport.

Location tracking engaged... Location tracking engaged...

Chapter Twelve

Tall Tales with Pops

The Man: Chapter 1

"**M**oney's tight right now, boy. We need the basics in supplies! Don't get nuffin' we can't eat, ya hear?" his father said with a slur in his speech.

Charlie didn't like his father. He was cold and cruel and had always struck Charlie as uncaring. The tension between them had been mounting lately, and Charlie wasn't sure how much longer he was going to be able to endure his father's abuses.

"You best be back here by tomorrow, carrying nothing less than you can manage. Get the rest brung out... ya hear?" his father said.

Charlie clenched his jaw, nodded, and turned toward the road. These monthly supply runs were a real treat for him. He got to get away, and he was responsible for himself alone. *Like a real grownup,* he thought as he headed down the dirt road toward town.

Charlie enjoyed the buzz of the city. There was always something happening, something to see, and plenty to do. He located the supplies fairly easily and managed the money well. Well enough, in fact, to sneak himself a little treat.

Women had been on his mind with more frequency, and he knew that the city had any number of whorehouses from which to choose an education. Close to dusk, he decided to stay and not rush back home.

"Back by tomorrow," he repeated to himself.

"Yeah, I hear," Charlie muttered aloud.

He located suitable lodgings and set out to find something to eat. Charlie stepped out onto the street. Darkness had fallen, and the lamplighters were making their rounds. There was a slight nip in the air, as summer was nearly over.

The darkness seemed to bring a strange illumination to the sins of the city. The perpetrators of those sins were emboldened by the power of the night. The women were dressed more revealingly; beggars and thieves were more brazen in their pursuits.

Even the churches bowed to darkness and closed their doors; the saloons and gambling houses seemed the only beacons of company, and even they were dangerous. It was scary. It was exciting. It was rebellious. His mother would never approve. Charlie liked it.

As he wandered the streets, any number of women caught his eye, all very flirty with the young man who they assumed might be easily separated from his money. Charlie was not persuaded... yet. He was hungry, and that urge was paramount.

He wandered Main Street for more than half an hour without finding an ideal establishment. Out of hunger he finally settled for a not-so-respectable-looking place next to a theater.

"I'll never tell my mother, but this food is amazing," Charlie said to himself. He devoured every morsel and ordered more.

As he waited, he took in his surroundings. It was a dimly lit place, not much for décor. His stare fell on the bar and onto a specific bottle of whiskey. Charlie had never drunk whiskey but knew it well. His father had left him with many a whiskey bruise. He hated it.

As he stared at the whiskey, Charlie replayed his father's words. "Money's tight" and "basics in supplies" rang through his mind as he tried to count the money spent on whiskey.

His calculations were broken by the light voice of a young woman who had come to his side. "I spied you looking at me from the bar. Didn't anyone tell you it ain't polite to stare?"

Charlie looked up and was surprised to see a rather attractive young woman perched next to him. Suddenly remembering his manners, Charlie practically jumped out of his seat. It was, after all, the custom to stand when addressing a lady, or so his mother had taught him.

Upon seeing Charlie stand to greet her, the woman said with a sweet Southern accent, "Oh, a gentleman after all."

Charlie smiled and motioned for her to take a seat. "Please," he said.

Not wasting any time, the woman continued. "I couldn't help but notice you seem to be alone. Are you by yourself, sugar?"

Charlie nodded and decided to indulge in the conversation. "Yes, I'm in town tonight buying supplies for my folks in the country."

The conversation was momentarily broken by the server bringing Charlie his second plate of food. Looking up to meet the server's gaze, Charlie noticed that she looked at the woman with an expression that said, "You should be ashamed of yourself."

Charlie sensed the tension between the two women and looked away.

"Well, not everyone in this city is as polite as you are, sugar," the woman said, dismissing the server's disapproving look. "Do you have any friends here?"

Charlie was intrigued by her Southern accent and wondered if she was faking it. He shook his head.

The woman sat back and gasped. "No friends! Well, lord have mercy, somebody should have told you, this city is dangerous for someone with no friends."

Charlie didn't respond, and a moment of silence passed between them. The woman sat forward and covered one of Charlie's hands with her own then spoke in a lower tone of voice. "I can be a friend to you." She smiled slightly.

The following morning...

____

"Wait. Wait. Wait," Jack said, interrupting Pops's story.

"Yes?" Pops sipped his beer.

"What happened during the night?"

"Seriously, boy? You can't infer what happened between these two overnight?" Pops said with an almost shocked expression.

Jack just looked at him blankly.

"Well, to spell it out for you, they had sex. Probably a couple of times."

"Okay, I figured that, but why didn't you simply say that? Why did you have to be all mysterious about it?" Jack shot back at him.

"'Cause, boy, it makes for better storytellin'. Besides, we ain't ever gonna get through this if you can't let your mind fill in the gaps for the things I don't say. Sorry, but this story don't come with pictures. Use your imagination."

"Okay. Fine. Whatever." Jack rolled his eyes at Pops.

"And before you ask, yes, Charlie had to pay for the sex," Pops said sarcastically.

"Multiple times?" Jack responded, matching Pops's sarcasm.

Pops squinted at Jack and said through gritted teeth, "Moving on..."

———————

When Charlie woke the following morning, he found himself alone. As he contemplated the previous night's activities, he decided it was good that she had left before he woke. *Makes it easier,* he thought.

As he stepped out into the brisk morning air, Charlie had anticipated he would see things differently. He expected that with the eyes of a "man," the world would be slightly more revealed to him. It wasn't. It looked the same as it had the day before.

Reluctantly, he stepped out into the street, not wanting to go home but not having a choice either. As he slowly made his way down the road headed out of town, he spied a small Asian man dressed in robes staring at him from across the way.

Charlie tipped his hat and continued on the road. To his surprise, on the corner of the next block was a man who looked just like the one on the previous block. This time the man smiled at him.

Confused but still sure that this couldn't possibly be the same man, Charlie looked back to the corner he'd just passed to verify that a similar-looking man was there. But he found no such man.

Charlie shook it off, didn't tip his hat, and carried on his way. The next block up stood the same man. Charlie was sure this time it was the same person; he, of course, was not surprised to find no one on the previous block corner.

Again, the man smiled and waved at Charlie. Once the two men made eye contact, the Asian man's smile froze on his face, and he stopped waving. As Charlie approached the man, he made a quick gesture and pulled from his pocket a small leather pouch.

Charlie quickly recognized it as his very own change purse. Charlie froze, not knowing what to do. The Asian man stood there, taunting him, swaying the purse back and forth, back and forth, daring Charlie to react.

Charlie thought about his options. *No gun. No sheriff. Nobody seems interested in what I'm looking at.* Sure enough, Charlie didn't know it, but the passersby couldn't see the Asian man. To them, Charlie was a crazy person staring at the street corner.

After a momentary stare-off, the Chinese man stopped smiling, raised his eyebrows, made an O with his mouth, clasped the change purse, and bolted to the right. The last thing Charlie saw was the Asian man disappear into the alley between the Belk building and the Woolworth's.

Charlie had no choice. He had to go after him. He was off like a shot, rounding the corner just in time to see the Chinese man take the next left and disappear again. Hot on his trail, Charlie almost caught him at the third corner.

The Chinese man's robes slipped between his fingers at the entrance to Chinatown. Charlie knew if he didn't catch him now, he would lose him. In his last desperate attempt, he leapt to tackle him, but the man vanished the instant Charlie touched his robes.

Charlie spilled out into the middle of the street clutching a bundle of rags. Standing up, he squeezed and shook out the rags, hoping that his change purse would fall out. When it didn't, Charlie threw a very immature temper tantrum in the street. So much so that he didn't realize he was upsetting the surrounding livestock for sale.

"Hey, hey, hey, you upsetting horse. You stop being child," commanded an elderly Asian lady in broken English.

Charlie felt something poking him in the side and looked down to see a Chinese woman so short she only came up to his chest. When Charlie looked down to meet her eyes, he found that she had her index finger pointed right at his face.

"You act like crazy person, jumping out with robes, scaring things. Where you come from?" She didn't break her stare as she yelled at Charlie.

Charlie calmed himself. "Ma'am, I'm sorry. I didn't mean to scare your horse. Did you happen to see—"

The Chinese woman cut him off before he could finish. "You're sorry? Sorry don't calm horse." The woman pointed back toward the horse, drawing Charlie's gaze. There, not twenty feet from them, a gray and black horse was reeling, desperately trying to break his reins.

Once Charlie laid eyes on the horse, everything else faded out. He couldn't explain it, but he was drawn to the beast. He wasn't afraid, apprehensive, or the slightest bit concerned. He slipped up, grabbed the reins, and pulled the horse down. Humming a tune and stroking his mane, Charlie calmed the animal.

As Charlie petted the horse, he felt a hard lump in the mane. With some slight prying, Charlie discovered his change purse. The Chinese woman had come up to his side. Noticing Charlie's change purse, the woman began to speak to Charlie with a more persuasive tone.

"Oh, you buy horse? I must warn you, he crazy like you. He mostly broke."

Charlie turned his attention away from the horse and toward the woman. "Mostly?" he asked with raised eyebrows.

"Eh, enough."

Of all the temptations the city had offered during this trip, this one was the greatest. With one look Charlie knew he wanted this horse. But why? It was just a horse. He had been around them his whole life and never felt like this before. Was it the color? The personality? Or was it all in his head? The truth was that it was what the horse represented to Charlie—freedom.

The horses he had worked with were never his. They belonged to his father. Charlie pictured himself riding across some great plain, a cowboy outlaw doing what he wanted, when he wanted.

Coming back to his senses, Charlie resigned to live with disappointment. "I can't. My father said—"

The woman cut him off before he could finish. "You... eh... special boy. I give you saddle too. Then your trip home be much faster."

Charlie petted the horse a moment longer in silence. Despite the fact the supplies had been easier to acquire than he thought and he had managed to save money, he was still afraid of his father and attempted to protest. "I-I can't, my father said—"

"You always do what you told?" the woman asked with a scowl. "You have money, you want horse, I sell you horse, you be happy."

Cut off again, Charlie exhaled with a huff. He squeezed his change purse and gave the woman another look. Picking up on Charlie's hesitation, the woman gave him one last pitch.

"You only live once. You know what will happen if you don't take chance. Do you like your life without this chance?"

He didn't, and with that, Charlie was sold. As the two exchanged purse contents for horse reins, Charlie asked the woman one last question. "Why is he 'mostly' broke?"

The woman gave Charlie a sad look. "He not from here. He born at sea and have no home." Charlie wasn't completely satisfied with that answer, but as he drew breath to ask another question, the woman beat him to words. "It okay. Make him faster. You like."

That satisfied him, and he gave the woman a smile, a nod, and a hat tip. Charlie waded into the sea of people and tried to work his way back toward his way out of town, with his newfound freedom in tow.

———————————

With the city firmly behind him, Charlie happened upon a watering hole and stopped to allow his horse a drink. *My horse* echoed through his mind. He hadn't mounted him yet and was contented to lead the horse out of town. Given his experience with horses, Charlie knew that high-spirited animals didn't do so well in busy environments.

Once the horse had had his fill of water, Charlie decided it was time to mount him. "I'm not going to hurt you... okay. We're gonna be friends. Trust me, and I'm gonna trust you... okay?"

It was as if the beast understood him. Charlie watched in amazement as the horse snorted at him, shook his head, and used his teeth to readjust his hat from its propped-up position. "Okay, deal," Charlie said.

From the instant Charlie mounted his horse, he felt different. He had ridden horses for as long as he could remember but never like this. Every time it was always on a planned route. "Only go so far and turn around" was what his father said. Every. Single. Time.

But now, Charlie looked out over the mountains and didn't know where he was going, or how far, or for how long. That was the first drop of freedom. As Charlie sat in the saddle, he contemplated the possibilities of each direction. A smile spread across his face.

His horse snorted and brought Charlie back to his senses. Chuckling to himself, Charlie told the horse, "Okay, what do you think?" Charlie gave his horse a pat on the neck, grabbed the reins, and, with a twitch of his ankle, let out a loud, "Hee-yaah," and they were off like a shot.

Charlie offered no direction and allowed the horse free rein. They crossed several hills before reaching a plain. "Hee-yaah!" Charlie commanded, and the horse sped up. "Hee-yaah!" Charlie yelled again, and the horse went faster still. Now halfway across the plain, Charlie let out one last "Hee-yaah!"

Freedom. Complete and utter independence was laid before him, and Charlie was no longer the same person. He was experiencing what it meant to rebel. He was teaching himself the power of choice. Charlie was pushing the limits of manhood, and in so doing he was becoming one.

Reaching the end of the plain, the horse began to slow of its own accord. Feeling more confident than he had ever felt before, Charlie loosed the reins and threw both his arms out wide as if to embrace the mountain itself. The horse slowed to a trot, and Charlie jumped off. "Whooo!" he exclaimed.

Charlie fell silent just long enough to hear his echo return to him from the mountain range. The two spent the rest of the morning roaming the plain and the surrounding hills. Charlie was deep in thought most of the time. He didn't yet realize it, but his life was never going to be the same. As morning turned to noon, he had decided that he wanted to further his education and not go straight to the fields working beside his father.

He didn't know what he wanted to do with his life, but he did know that it wasn't farming. With the afternoon wearing on, Charlie knew he needed to head home. Tightening the reins and providing direction, Charlie steered the horse toward home. After all, manhood means responsibility, and people were counting on him.

————————————

When he trotted up to the farmhouse, Charlie was greeted with a smile from his mother that faded quickly when she learned that Charlie had bought the horse. "Your father isn't going to be happy."

Charlie didn't respond. He dismounted and hugged his mother.

"Nice horse," a gruff voice said from the doorframe of the house. His father was leaning to one side and drinking what Charlie knew to be hooch. "Put him in the barn and come in. We need to talk 'bout what you got."

There were no open stables in the barn. The family had two horses and an ox. Charlie latched his horse to a pillar and dragged a water trough over to him.

"I'll get you some food when I'm done inside," Charlie told the horse as he closed the barn door and headed for the house.

He knew he was in trouble, and the walk between the barn and house was filled with dread. Sitting at the table, Charlie's father stared at him a long moment before he spoke. He cut his eyes back to the list Charlie had made of total purchases. Charlie had marked all the items that were due for delivery, which was the majority of the list. "When's the rest being brung out?" His father gulped the moonshine.

"Next week."

"*When?*" His father was almost shouting.

"Um, um," Charlie stammered, "um, Wednesday morning, before church."

His father took another swig of shine. "What money did you bring back?"

There wasn't any. Charlie had spent it all.

The silence only angered his father. "What money, boy? I know you didn't spend it all on what's here." He pointed to the list.

"Um, um, I had to sleep somewhere and eat."

"That don't cost that much," his father said after another sip of moonshine. "How much did that horse cost?" He looked Charlie dead in the eye. He may have been drinking, but he was crisp, clear-spoken, and calculating.

"I got a deal," Charlie said, his voice shaking.

"Well? How much?" After another moment of silence, his father shouted, "Answer me!"

Charlie relented. "Fifty-five dollars."

His father smiled, but it wasn't a comforting smile. It was malicious and not designed to make Charlie feel better. "Well, that is a good deal," he said, putting his bottle down, "but it doesn't account for everything."

I'm caught, Charlie thought.

"Let's see..." his father said with a hiss. "This list, food, lodging, that horse. There's several dollars unaccounted for. Produce them."

Charlie couldn't.

"What do the whores cost in town, boy?" his father asked slyly.

More embarrassed that his mother was within earshot than of the fact he had been caught, Charlie attempted to deflect. "I-I-I don't know."

His father let out a *hmph* and picked up his bottle. "Yeah, I don't know either. Ever since I put your mama up, I ain't paid."

Charlie hated his father. The sheer meanness of the man was limitless. Charlie's anger was rising. He had been abused in one form or another most of his life, and he tolerated it well, but he didn't take kindly to malice befalling his mother. Clenching his fists and gritting his teeth, Charlie was about to let loose his anger when his father did the unexpected and completely disarmed him, with a compliment.

"You done good, boy."

Charlie was confused. He gave his father a quizzical look.

"The last thing I said to you was 'Don't get nuffin' we can't eat.' That horse will feed us for a week, maybe more." His father rose from the table.

Charlie's stomach sank, and he felt all the blood run out his face. His father meant to slaughter his horse. He jumped up from the table and approached his father saying, "No, please..."

His father showed no mercy and punched Charlie in the stomach, dropping him to his knees. As Charlie knelt there gasping for air, about to throw up, his father delivered the second blow, this one across the face.

Charlie managed to hold onto consciousness. By the time he saw his father exit the house with his shotgun, his mother was by his side. As the vision of his father shooting his friend rampaged through his mind, anger and the strength associated with it fueled his body. Charlie was only down for a moment. He broke from his mother's embrace and made for the door, reaching it in time to see his father enter the barn.

As Charlie ran, there was no singular thought in his head. He didn't envision his father shooting his friend. He didn't find God or meet the devil. He didn't even recall the basics, like where he was, or his name—nothing.

From the time he bolted from the door till he reached the barn, his mind was blank. Charlie ran like he had never run before. The distance was a good thirty-five yards. If his legs were burning, he wasn't aware of it. If he was breathing heavily, he didn't know it. The fuel provided by rage was all Charlie needed.

When he reached the barn, Charlie didn't slow down. The last thing he saw was his father raising the shotgun toward the horse. With a good ten feet between Charlie and his father, Charlie took aim at his father's lower back, tucked his shoulder, and jumped. He closed his eyes. Just before he collided with his father, he heard the click of the gun's hammer being cocked.

When Charlie jumped, he did so with the entirety of his soul. He hit his father with such force that he broke several of his ribs. Even intoxicated, his father felt the pain. The next sound was the shotgun firing, followed by the splintering of wood. A beam of light from the freshly formed hole in the barn roof illuminated the spot where his father collapsed, clutching the shotgun.

Charlie attempted to wrestle the gun away, but his father's grip was too tight. As the struggle ensued, Charlie realized that his father's ribs were hurt. Three kicks to the already-broken ribs made wrenching the shotgun free less difficult. Enraged, Charlie beat his father. And beat him, and beat him, and beat him. His father offered a struggle for a few minutes but eventually went limp. Charlie resolved to kill him. He would end his life, take him out of this world, and in so doing make it a better place.

By this point, Charlie was kneeling on his father's chest with his hands around his neck. His father was coughing and slapping at Charlie, who did not relent. Charlie was so deep in rage that he didn't feel the teeth bite down on the collar of his shirt till it was too late.

His horse pulled Charlie off his father. The horse dragged Charlie six feet from the broken shell of his father, who, after some time, managed to crawl toward the barn door. Charlie let him go. Charlie was still on his knees, his fists clenched as tears of pure hatred streamed down his cheeks.

He knew his life there was over. Charlie spent the night in the barn, holding the shotgun close to his chest as he tried to sleep. It remained elusive.

The next day he emerged more of a man than he had been when he returned home. Charlie knew he couldn't stay. He packed his belongings, said goodbye to his mother, and promised to write. Charlie didn't speak to his father, but he did leave something to remember him by. As he mounted his horse, Charlie gave one last glance back at the homestead and smiled to himself.

Just behind the house, black smoke could be seen growing more intense. Charlie was sure his father would be in a panic when he discovered what he had done. *Moonshine and fire don't mix that well,* Charlie thought.

Riding away, Charlie didn't know where he was going, what he was going to do there, or what was coming next. That was frightening to most people, but for Charlie it was intoxicating. For him, the unknown was not to be feared but embraced. This made him free.

———————————

"So, he just left? Just like that?" Jack asked.

"Yeah, he sure did," Pops said.

"Wow. I couldn't imagine just up and going like that."

"Well. Every child leaves home at some point. It's part of growing up, which everyone must do," Pops said in an all-knowing tone.

"I guess. So what happened next?" Jack asked with growing interest.

CHAPTER THIRTEEN

Eyebit Immersion 89%

PLEASE REBOOT DEVICE...

The sound of the socket wrench turning stopped as Pops looked at Jack and said, "Hold here." He pointed to a hose with a metal clamp on it. "Okay, where was I?"

"He burned the moonshine shed and left," Jack said.

"Oh right, right. Okay, so when he left the homestead, he befriended an Indian tribe, who took him in." Pops broke into the story again to ask for another tool. "Pass me that Phillips head, boy."

Jack fumbled with the tools on the cart, muttering to himself, "Phillips head... Phillips head..."

Pops peered over his shoulder. "Right there. It's a screwdriver. Remember, Phillips has a cross top, and a flathead is straight." With that hint, Jack was able to locate the screwdriver quickly.

"Okay, so the Indians taught him respect for the land, how to hunt, and the power of the buffalo. He, in turn, showed them the ways of the white man and helped them communicate in English." Pops continued the story, telling how Charlie spent a year living among the tribe. And how he came to be known as "White Man with Horse."

"Leaving the Cherokee was not easy for Charlie, but fact was fact. He was a white man, and when the federal government came to relocate the Cherokee, Charlie was forced out. It was a brutal experience for him but..." Pops stopped talking when his eyes connected with Kyle's.

Jack was still looking at the car when Pops stopped talking. He looked up and followed Pops's gaze. "Oh, hi, Kyle. Is something wrong?" Jack asked, genuinely not realizing he had missed his dinner appointment.

Kyle's icy stare did not break from Pops's as he spoke. "You weren't home like you were told!" Kyle paused for a moment. "We waited." There was another pause before Kyle began again. "We couldn't reach you."

Pops, sensitive to what this line of questioning was going to escalate to, broke in. "Now hold on, son. This isn't Jack's fault. I'm the one who made him take his Eyebit off. I'm the one who kept him here. If you're lookin' to assign blame, assign it to me, not him."

Kyle was not dissuaded. "Damnit, Dad, I let him come here so you could help teach him responsibility, not make it worse."

Pops clenched his jaw and lost the battle to restrain himself. "Yeah, that's the problem with your generation—now. Now. Now. Responsibility is a lesson, you learn it, you experience it, you grow from it, and that ain't fast, ya dipshit!"

Jack, sensing that Pops and Kyle were about to get into another fight, interrupted their conversation. "Kyle, we're late. Let's go. I'll take the other transport home."

Kyle broke his stare from Pops's and turned his attention toward Jack. "Claire is extremely upset."

"I know. We better get going."

Kyle glanced back at Pops and said to Jack, "You're grounded! You won't be taking the transport anywhere!" Kyle had intended to hurt Pops more with Jack's grounding than Jack.

Before he turned to go, Kyle gave his father one last "I dare you" look. It was not returned. Instead, Pops gave Jack a nod and a wink. Which gave Jack a feeling that things were going to be okay. Jack nodded back.

As Pops watched two generations walk out the door, the dull pain returned to his arm, and he began to rub it. The pain intensified to the point of forcing Pops to take a seat. As he sat rubbing his arm, he spoke aloud a single sentence.

"Come on, buddy. I don't know how much more of this I can take."

———————————

By the time the two reached the street, Kyle had already sent the transport home via the autopilot feature. "We need to talk; you're riding with me," Kyle said as the passenger side of his own transport opened.

Sitting in the transport with Kyle, Jack was silent. He was holding his Eyebit and didn't feel the need to immediately put it on. Kyle was controlling the transport, and Jack was content to just listen to the hum of the electricity streaming through the rails.

Kyle began to speak, but not to Jack. "Yeah, I got him. He was with my dad." There was a moment of silence, and then Kyle spoke again. "You can't see him because he isn't wearing his bit." Then Kyle told Jack to put his bit on.

Jack sat there for a moment but didn't comply.

"Hey, I'm talking to you." Kyle stared at the side of Jack's head, but Jack didn't move.

Claire had no patience for Jack's lack of bit participation. She screamed so loud

into Kyle's Eyebit that Jack heard it in the passenger seat. "Put it on!"

Jack reluctantly put on his bit and waited for the lenses to close on his eyes. He was immediately greeted with a full-screen view of a fuming Claire. "If Kyle didn't tell you already, you're grounded!"

Jack didn't say anything. He simply switched the Eyebit off and handed it to Kyle.

Kyle didn't have words. He looked at Jack for a long while, and after some serious reflection, he decided he couldn't be *that* angry with him. This was, after all, his doing. Jack was a quiet, introverted, shy, distant, near nineteen-year-old before Kyle forced the introduction to Pops. This is what he wanted, although not how he wanted it.

"Well, if Claire wasn't mad before, you can bet she is now," Kyle said to Jack, who didn't respond.

The two rode home in silence. The entire ride, Kyle contemplated how to deal with Claire once they arrived. She was going to be cross. Since the advent of Eyebits, people didn't have conversations like those Kyle and Claire had been raised having.

No hellos or goodbyes to signify the beginning or the end of a conversation. In the Eyebit world, once someone was considered a regular contact, the portal to the conversation was always open. It was like being in a large group all the time, and once you were ready to speak, you just said their name aloud. So, when Jack disconnected, Claire essentially got hung up on.

Claire's view of Jack's hang-up was the image of Jack suddenly going black and red lettering typed across her view reading, "***Jack has disconnected***."

When a person disconnected, they saw the world as it was, the physical world, which was gray, calm, dull, and lifeless. The lifelessness was the worst. A mixture of isolation, melancholy, pure darkness, and a chill that made you shake. People who weren't prepared for a sudden disconnection didn't handle it well.

Jack had been spending less and less time connected and seemed to Kyle to be coming out of his shell more. But again, he wasn't fully prepared for this sudden rebellious attitude. Halfway through the trip, Kyle looked over, only to find Jack with his hands and face pressed against the window. It took Kyle a moment to realize Jack had never really ridden in any kind of vehicle without an Eyebit before.

When the transport slid into the driveway, the two sat in the car for a moment. Kyle was contemplating either supporting Claire or defending Jack. Either way, one of them was going to be angry.

Being reasonable for a moment, Kyle understood this was partly his fault and decided not to go on the defensive against Claire. "Listen," Kyle said, handing the Eyebit back to Jack. "Claire is going to be angry. If you apologize and put this on, she might be willing to reduce your grounding." Jack took the Eyebit and waited for Kyle to open the door without saying a word.

Jack jumped out of the car and walked briskly toward the house. Of course, he had to wait for Kyle to catch up because the front door wouldn't open without an Eyebit. Kyle was in no hurry. Once inside, the two found Claire in the kitchen, standing with one hand on her hip and the other on the counter, tapping her index fingernail.

Tap. Tap. Tap. Tap. Jack found the sound annoying. Once Claire saw Jack and Kyle in front of her, she began to speak to Kyle.

"It's about time!"

Kyle knew that it would be best to just let Claire finish, and then he would try to speak.

Claire turned her attention to Jack. "I just don't know what's going on with you. A few weeks ago, you were fine. Then you started going to your grandfather's, and now you're different."

Jack was silent, not because he didn't have anything to say, but because he was clenching his jaw in mounting anger. Claire continued her barrage of comments regarding her dissatisfaction with Jack's actions. "You used to be such a well-behaved boy, but who is this person? I don't know him. Why don't you wear your Eyebit as much? Don't you want to be normal? Not much good happens to people who don't fit in."

Attempting to force an opportunity, Kyle tried to squeak out a defense. "Claire, I think Pops has been good for Jack. Before he just sat there like a lump." Kyle's argument was cut short by a look from Claire that he knew too well.

Returning to Jack, Claire said in a tone that implied a threat, "Put your Eyebit on, please."

Jack didn't respond, just clenched his jaw.

Claire said, "Look, you're already grounded for two weeks. Do you want to make it three?"

No response.

"I don't think you understand what 'grounded' means. It means you can only go to school and come home. No games, no friends, no music, no Pops!"

That got Jack's attention. Methodically, Jack opened the arms of his Eyebit and gently set it on his face. A quick moment later, he was connected. He was immediately assaulted by a view of Claire's talking head.

Jack stared at her for just a moment before turning the volume on her down. Then, one by one, he started closing all the running programs. Streaming movie, closed. Streaming audio, closed. Friends and family communication link, closed. School link, closed. Transport control, closed. Eyebit connection controls, closed. It took Jack at least two minutes to close all the programs his Eyebit was running.

Had he been calmer, he might have been surprised at how much stuff was auto-streamed, all the time, but he wasn't. Finally nothing else was on his Eyebit except Claire, muted. Jack amused himself for just a moment with the fact that her lips were moving with no noise. With a swipe of his eyes, he clicked the volume button, and Claire was unmuted.

The pure silence he had been in for the last few minutes shattered. Claire was screaming at him. That was the last straw. Jack squared his shoulders and looked Claire in the eye, beyond the Eyebit. He stared her physical eyes down, and with an eye swipe, he closed her conversation window.

Claire's view of Jack went black, and red lettering streamed across her screen. ***"Jack has terminated the conversation."*** Silence immediately fell upon the room. As the black screen faded, Claire found Jack's gaze locked on hers.

Kyle, not believing what was happening but knowing what he was going to have to deal with later, rolled his eyes and muttered to himself, "Ohhh shit."

Jack had had enough. Once he had Claire's and Kyle's attention, he held them in deafening silence before turning toward the door. He ordered the front door open and stepped outside. Jack breathed deeply three times before he reached up and turned his Eyebit off. Removing the bit from his face, he set it on the ground next to the front door.

Jack stepped out onto the sidewalk. His rage had mounted to the point he thought he might explode. The energy had to go somewhere; he didn't know what to do or how to handle it. All he knew was that he couldn't be still. He had to act. A brisk walk turned into a jog, which quickly turned into a sprint. Jack ran till his legs ached for relief, and then he ran some more.

"Ahhh!" he screamed into the night, as he ran faster than, he was sure, any human had ever run before.

Chapter Fourteen

Eyebit Immersion 88%

Connection Failure

Exhausted, Jack stopped running. The pain in his legs was a hot burning fire like he had never felt. He fell to his knees, put his hands over his eyes, and breathed as if he had been held under the tide too long. Once he had caught his breath, once the pain had turned into a medium burn, once his body had cooled itself, Jack felt better. He couldn't explain it, but a kind of peace washed over him. The anger was gone.

He took stock of where he was. He didn't know. He was sure his sleeping quarters were close, but he didn't recognize how to get there from where he was. Then it dawned on him: he had never been outside without his Eyebit before.

Exploring the fact that he was essentially "naked" out in the world—at night—Jack tried to remember an experience that might have been similar enough to help him through his situation. Once when he was younger, his Eyebit had been knocked off while he was playing on the school playground. He didn't know what to do then either.

Being a child, he reacted like a child would and began to cry. One by one the other children encircled him; they didn't know what to do either. They just watched, as silence fell over the playground, as his cries became the only sound.

Eventually—and it seemed like an eternity in the mind of a child—a "big person" came and put Jack's Eyebit back on. Then everything was better. The children resumed their play, and Jack was awash in the warm fuzzies provided by constant connection.

"Well, I'm on my own tonight," Jack muttered aloud and stood up. By backtracking his actions, he was confident he could retrace his steps and find his way. "I'm not crying this time," he said to himself as he took the first step toward home.

As he walked, Jack couldn't help but notice the silence. Without his Eyebit, without the constant stream of data, movies, music, talking heads, transport alerts, blah, blah, blah, the world was quiet. It took a few minutes for what that meant to sink in.

Silence. Silence enshrouded him. Not even the hum you find when a body of people was present. Most people had been driven indoors by the lure of their Eyebits. ***"Safety is indoors"*** was the sunset message provided by the Eyebits. Not even a passing transport was to be heard. The transport system shut down after a certain time anyway.

Jack took in the night as he walked. It was pleasant, warm and breezy. The trees were in bloom. Spring was in the air. Jack sneezed. *What the hell?* He thought and sneezed again. He stopped, feeling another sneeze coming on. His face contorted, and he let out a sneeze so powerful snot flew from his nose and landed square on his lips.

He clasped a hand over his mouth and froze. He didn't know what to do. There were no tissues available. He thought about wiping it on his sleeve, but the idea of snot on his suit repulsed him. Besides, he didn't know how snot would react with his bit suit of clothes. "Grass," Jack said aloud then dragged his hand across the yard of an abandoned house.

Continuing his walk home, Jack was lost in thought when a slight rustle, more than a breeze, split the silence of the night. Jack stopped dead in his tracks and desperately looked for the source of the noise. He heard it again, this time louder. Jack's heart rate went up, his breathing deepened, and his pupils dilated.

He heard the rustle again, closer, and he nearly jumped and took off in a run. More paralyzed by fear than empowered by bravery, Jack stood his ground. He isolated the rustling to a bush and eyed it until something furry jumped out. Jack couldn't quite make out its shape in the darkness, but once it barked at him, he knew.

Jack exhaled deeply and spoke to the dog in an uninviting tone. "Damn dog, you scared the shit out of me!" The dog barked at him again. "Where's your Petbit?" At the word Petbit, the dog growled at Jack and turned toward the abandoned house.

Hmph, Jack thought. *Domesticated animals are usually friendlier than that.* Returning his thoughts to his journey home, he turned and continued the task of retracing his steps.

He found his home easily enough, and as he approached the front door, his Eyebit was right where he had left it. He put it on, pushing the button on the arm, and with a flash he was connected.

He didn't see much at first. Remembering he had turned everything off before he left, he let the bit run its start-ups. ***"Checking vitals... Checking vitals... Checking vitals..."*** flashed across the screen. ***"Allergy alert... Allergy alert... Anti-Allergy Protocols*** *initiated.*" Almost instantly Jack's nose cleared up, and he could breathe freely. Not realizing he had been mouth breathing since his run, Jack closed his mouth and resumed breathing through his nose.

When Jack decided he was ready to enter the house and face his parents, he pulled up the house controls and turned toward the door. To his surprise, there was a digi-note that simply read "Three weeks." Jack knew for the next three weeks it was school, home, and room. His Eyebit would be restricted, and he was about to be super bored.

Jack stood at the door and thought about the next three weeks. He wasn't looking forward to it but knew it was happening whether he liked it or not. He breathed deep, squared his shoulders, jutted out his chin, and opened the door.

"I'm not gonna cry about it," he told himself and crossed the threshold like a man.

The house was shut down for the night. He thought about eating something but wasn't hungry. With nowhere else to go, Jack went to his room. He sat down on his bed and took stock of what programs were available. School link; Friends—talking only, no program joining; Transport, restricted to approval; Wardrobe program. Even his room decorations were limited to posters.

I wonder? Jack thought for a second. "Theon, I'm looking for something," Jack said aloud, speaking to his Eyebit. In a moment the screen went dark and an elderly man with white hair, wearing Roman robes and carrying a scroll and quill appeared. The old man opened the scroll and positioned the quill to write.

"Hello, Jack. What may I help you find?" the man asked.

Jack smiled. "Car, automobile, Ford Mustang."

Theon's quill twitched, he examined the words, scratched his head, and turned away from Jack. Behind him were ancient bookshelves that held countless scrolls. Theon dug through the stacks until he found the one he was looking for.

"*Ah-ha!*" Theon exclaimed. Without turning around, Theon tossed a scroll over his shoulder, and it opened as it flew toward Jack. Listed on the scroll were titles and links to the various articles named.

Ford, Henry: Defining America

Ford introduces the Mustang

How fast is too fast: Ford and Shelby

Ford repays federal bailout

Mustang goes coupe

Ford, defines the middle class

Ford, Model T, for the common man

Actor killed while racing a custom Mustang

Ford, Mustang 2007 Owner's Manual

Ford vs. Chevrolet and the winner is...

Ford assumes control of all automobile manufacturing

Learning to drive, a how-to guide to your Mustang, muscle car, Buick, pickup truck...

Ford, Mustang 1983 Owner's Manual

Ford, on trial for monopoly marketing

Why the Mustang is king of the road

America's love affair with cars Ford, Chevy, Dodge

Preston Tucker takes on the big three: Ford, GM...

Ford, Mustang 1994 new body style

Ford, Mustang 2015 redefining the pony

Ford vs. The Federal Government

Local woman killed when she lost control... Mustang

Gas prices too high, Ford discontinues manufacture of low-yield vehicles, Mustang...

Ford Motor giant, no more. Federal Government rules monopoly

Federal Government assumes control of Ford Motor Company, manufacturing ceased...

Ford, Mustang 1982 Owner's Manual

Ford, Mustang 1978 Owner's Manual

Ford, Mustang 2014 Owner's Manual

Buying tires for your... Mustang

Flash of genius and the betrayal of the Ford Motor Company

Person-Driven Cars Outlawed! Federal Transportation Group (Formally Ford...

Ford No More... Cars replaced with Auto-driven Transports, bits corps to develop...

Environmental concerns force Ford Motor Co to develop electric cars

Ford, Mustang, a colorful history

Ford, wins the Daytona 500

Mustang, Special editions, Shelby, Roush, Boss, California Special, Cobra...

Ford, Mustang 1999 Owner's Manual

Jack scrolled through the titles. There were mounds and mounds of things related to Mustang. One title jumped off the screen at him. "*Learning to drive, a how-to guide to your Mustang, muscle car, Buick, pickup truck...*" Jack reached up and gently touched the link with his index fingertip.

The screen on his Eyebit went black. In the center was a tire spinning and spinning. Jack was slightly annoyed at having to wait for the program to load. As he waited, he reminded himself that the older programs took a little longer for Theon to find.

After about five minutes the tire disappeared and a tall, lanky man appeared wearing a cowboy hat, which reminded Jack of Pops's hat, but bigger and more decorated. The man also had on what looked like a blacked-out Eyebit. It didn't immediately occur to Jack that he wasn't wearing an Eyebit. It was a pair of sunglasses. "Howdy," the man said. "I'm Richard Petty, and I'm gonna teach you how to drive."

The significance of who Richard Petty was was lost on Jack. "Hi, Richard, I'm Jack." The two carried on a conversation as if Richard were physically present.

"Hello, Jack. What kind of car do you want to drive today?"

"Mustang," Jack said excitedly.

"Mustang, huh? Well, I'm a Dodge man myself, but okay."

Jack sat still for a moment, and then he heard an engine roaring through his room. He didn't appreciate the sound of the throaty, powerful V8 engine, but Richard did.

"Man, that does sound good!" Richard said.

Instantly the Eyebit program put Jack behind the wheel of a Mustang coupe that looked very similar to Pops's Mustang.

"You wanna drive a stick or an automatic?" Richard asked.

Jack thought for a moment. He didn't know. "Ummm, what's the difference?" Jack asked as he gripped the steering wheel.

"Well, simply, one requires more attention but gives you more control. The other takes less attention but steals control."

Jack was still confused, so he decided to put it to Richard. "Which did you drive?"

Richard answered immediately, as if he had been asked that question before. "Well, I'm a racecar driver. It's all about control for me, so stick."

"Okay," Jack said. "I wanna learn both." He looked over at Richard, who had sat in the passenger seat.

Richard gave Jack a nod and a slight one-sided grin that caused his mustache to twitch. "Okay then, let's get started," Richard said and turned to face the windshield.

Jack faced forward as well. Beyond the windshield was an open road. They were in the desert. The only thing other than the road and the sand was a sign that read Route 66.

Jack roared down the highway.

"Yeeeh haaaw!" Richard yelled over the sound of the engine and the wind blowing through the windows. "How fast we going now?" Richard asked as he tried to shift to see the odometer himself.

Jack's eyes were as wide as saucers, and he was breathing through his mouth again. He tore his eyes away from the road for a split second, just long enough to get a quick read on the odometer. "Ninety-five!" he shouted back at Richard.

"Faster!" Richard yelled.

Faster! Faster, faster, Jack thought as he gripped the wheel harder.

"Push the gas pedal all the way down!" Richard screamed at Jack while grinning from ear to ear.

Jack pushed the pedal to the floor. The engine responded with a roar and a tug. Jack felt himself sink even farther into the seat.

"Whooo!" Richard yelled.

Jack wasn't paying attention to the time. They could have been at this for hours for all he knew when Richard instructed him to ease off the gas and bring the car to a stop. Jack stopped in the middle of the street, right in the center of the dotted line.

He sat for a minute catching his breath as Richard looked around in the car. The two were listening to the engine idle when Richard began to speak in such a calm tone that Jack had to remind himself that he was interacting with a computer simulation and not a real person.

"Son, all you needed was wings on this thing and you'd have been flying!"

Jack thought for a moment, not understanding what Richard meant. "But I don't want to fly."

Richard was silent then chuckled. "Okay, then." Richard paused before saying, "Anybody ever tell you to read between the lines?"

Jack nodded. "Yes. Lately, they have."

"Okay," Richard said. "That was an automatic, and I think you have that down pretty good."

Jack nodded.

"You're ready to move onto a stick shift, but you should take a break first."

"No, I want to keep going."

Richard refused to allow the program to run further. "Jack, you've been driving for ten hours. That's Knoxville to Disney World. You must take a break." Jack breathed in to put up another protest, but Richard spoke before he could get a word out. "See ya tomorrow." Richard tipped his hat to Jack and faded away.

Jack's Eyebit screen gave a countdown. ***Program available in 8 hours...7:59:59...7:59:58...***

With a swipe of his eyes, Jack minimized the countdown clock. He laid back on his bed and began to process what he had learned. His heart was still beating hard. He hadn't taken notice before now. Putting his hand on his chest, he was impressed with how forceful it felt. Unable to drive for several hours and still grounded, Jack decided to research some of the other things Pops had mentioned.

"Theon, I'm looking for something."

Instantly the old man walked out of the blackness as the library appeared behind him. "Yes, Jack?"

"Please provide information on the following things: Bones, starship, gold, cyberbully, and knock 'em stiff," Jack said.

Theon's quill twitched, and he turned to the stacks. The scrolls with the least amount of information appeared first.

Knock 'em stiff: noun, slang, nickname for homemade alcohol. First coined during the Civil War. Popularity surged during Prohibition. The name is symbolic of the hangover associated with drinking it: "It'll knock you dead."

Gold: noun, a chemical element with the symbol Au and atomic number 79. In its purest form, it is a bright, slightly reddish yellow, dense, soft, malleable, and ductile metal. Chemically, gold is a transition metal and a group 11 element.

Cyberbully: noun. Nickname for someone who uses social media and other technologies to assault another person.

Bones: noun. Any piece of hard, whitish tissue making up the skeleton in humans and other vertebrates.

Starship: noun. Starcraft or interstellar spacecraft. A theoretical spacecraft designed for travelling between stars, as opposed to a vehicle designed for orbital spaceflight or interplanetary travel. The term is mostly found in science fiction because such a craft has never been constructed.

Jack read the definitions of the words he'd requested and was unimpressed. Pops was such an odd character; these terms must have other meanings. *Read between the lines, Jack,* he told himself and tried to figure out how to do that.

"Theon?" Jack called.

"Yes, Jack?" This time when Jack called for Theon, a pile of scrolls appeared in the bottom left corner of his screen. The scrolls began to shake, and Theon's head popped out of the pile.

"Cross reference the following five words and display the connections: Bones, starship, gold, cyberbully, knock 'em stiff."

Theon's head plunked back down into the scrolls, and the entire pile began to shake. Much quicker than the driving program had, a single scroll appeared.

Star Trek*: TOS (The Original Series) Cast and Crew... Bones played by...*

Starship Enterprise Logs, all series...

Enterprise – 1701, -A, B, C, D, E, F, G, H, I...

Star Trek, *canceled... producers cite lack of interest*

9 Southern states refuse to air Star Trek, *interracial relations cited...*

*"*Star Trek *is the future, and science is the new religion," philosophy of...*

*The last philosopher... "*Star Trek *is the future..." buys the Catholic Church*

Bones vs. the Doctor: which is the best medical officer?

Gold shirts, red shirts, blue shirts: understanding the Star Trek *uniform*

*The last philosopher demolishes Notre Dame... "*Star Trek *is the future..."*

DeForest Kelley and the role of Bones... "Damn it, man..."

"Why Star Trek*?" The last philosopher's first interview*

Reaching the Star Trek *the last philosopher envisions*

"Warp 9.5 to the future": The last philosopher's keynote speech

Video file: Star Trek *series: all related television shows, viewable here*

The last listing caught Jack's attention. *This... Star... Trek seems like it was a big deal,* Jack thought. He decided to see what it was about. Unsure if his grounding would permit him to view the file, he reached up and touched the video file link.

A strange symbol Jack had never seen before appeared on the screen before him. It looked like a solid *A* sitting on top of a circle. Again, a long wait preceded the booting of the file associated with *Star Trek.* Annoyed, Jack thought, *Jeez, how old is Pops?*

After five minutes the symbol faded away. The screen was solid black, dotted with... stars, or so Jack assumed. The next thing to present itself to Jack was a voice.

"Space, the final frontier..."

CHAPTER FIFTEEN

Eyebit Immersion 87%

RECOMMEND 12 HOURS OF UNINTERRUPTED CONNECTION...

Jack didn't know how long he had been in his room watching *Star Trek*. He knew it was over a day but couldn't stop watching. Even though he didn't prefer this old form of entertainment, he was fascinated, nonetheless.

The way people his age were entertained was to experience it through Eyebits in the first person. So, if *Star Trek* had been an Eyebit program, he would be able to experience *Star Trek* life as Spock, not just by watching Spock. The conclusion was predetermined, but he could alter the story slightly and directly interact with the characters. Jack's entertainment world was very much like the holodeck first introduced in *Star Trek: The Next Generation*.

Not interacting with the program was both relaxing and stressful for Jack. On the one hand, he didn't have to do anything, just let the story play out. On the other hand, he didn't know what he was getting into. He was used to programs that were selected by the Eyebit based on personality type, and Jack always liked his programs.

So far, he liked *Star Trek*. The plot was good, the characters were complex, there was danger along with a sense of safety, almost every character survived, and the ship always carried on. Somewhere around season three of the series *The Next Generation*, Jack decided to take a break from the show.

He emerged from his room and headed for the kitchen. Both Kyle and Claire were there. Claire was facing the stove, using her Eyebit to cook. *Must be breakfast,* Jack thought. Jack didn't acknowledge their presence but merely opened the refrigerator.

"How's it going, Jack?" Kyle asked, breaking the awkward silence. They hadn't spoken since he'd grounded him last week.

"How do you think it's going, Kyle? I'm just going to school and sitting in my room," Jack snapped.

Kyle huffed and tried to remain calm. "Well, remember why you got grounded in the first place, and hopefully you'll learn something."

Jack had been walking away while Kyle was speaking. He stopped dead in his tracks and turned around to face him. "And what, exactly, was that, Kyle?" Jack asked with disdain in his voice.

Kyle gritted his teeth so hard his temple visibly flexed. "Well, if you don't know, maybe you need another week to figure it out."

Jack didn't say a word at first. He merely unloaded the foodstuff from his arms onto the table next to him. At this point, Claire was facing Jack as well. Jack very calmly looked over at Claire, reached up, and switched off his Eyebit. Then, turning his attention back to Kyle, Jack issued his response. "Make it so, Number One!" He then gathered his food into his arms and retreated to his room.

Jack had been grounded before, but this occurrence was different. Time didn't seem to move as slowly. His classes at school even seemed different lately, as he found himself pinging instructors with questions. Mostly about where and why things were the way they were.

His history instructor was particularly frustrated. "Why is George Washington considered the first president if he was a general during the Revolutionary War? Wouldn't the person who was president during the war be the first president?" was just one of the daily questions with which he peppered his instructors.

<hr>

Kyle had been standing outside Jack's door long enough to doubt his decision. Jack had been grounded for two and a half weeks, and they had barely seen him. Usually by this point in a grounding, Jack was desperate to get his Eyebit turned back on.

Sometimes Kyle even got him to do some cleaning. *Not that cleaning-bits let this place get dirty much,* Kyle thought. This time was different. Jack seemed almost like he was enjoying being disconnected. Claire was pushing to have his grounding lifted. She didn't think it was right to leave Jack isolated for so long.

Kyle had refused to even consider the idea until Jack's school called. They were worried about his recent behavior. Jack had always been such a good and complacent student, but lately, he was "acting out." He had been speaking out loud in class, asking questions nobody was concerned with, and challenging his instructors.

"It would be a shame to blemish his permanent record this close to graduation," the school principal had said to Kyle, which he rightly interpreted as a threat.

Bullshit! Was Kyle's first thought, then he calmed himself before he challenged him. "I see. Did you tell Jack that?" he asked through gritted teeth.

"We did," the principal said flatly. "He asked us if he could see his record. Which is what led us to call you."

Kyle couldn't help but smile when he heard that. He was proud. "So, what you're telling me is that my son questioned the imaginary threat you hold over these kids? And you don't know what to do?"

Silence. He didn't know how to respond. Then: "Your son?" the principal stated dryly. "Yes... *Jack* is questioning authority." His snarky tone underscored Kyle's use of the term "son."

Continuing in a voice with a slightly empowered undertone, he spelled out for Kyle the cost of rebellion. "While the permanent record may be fictitious, the compliance and conformity credits required for graduation are not. Failure to meet those requirements could hinder *Jack's* graduation."

It hadn't occurred to Kyle till then *why* he'd taken Jack to Pops in the first place. Despite the Eyebits Corporation's best efforts, the subconscious was still an assertive presence. His son was just like everyone else: same thoughts, same ideas, same clothes, same, same, same.

Kyle wasn't raised that way, and his subconscious had been eating away at him. If there was one person in the entirety of the world who could teach his son independence, it was Pops. Kyle decided to compromise on Jack's grounding.

Jack had just shifted into fifth gear when Kyle emerged into the spectrum of his view. Until this point, Kyle's Eyebit had told him that Jack was utilizing the Theon Library program but not what that program was accessing. Once Kyle appeared, the driving program paused, and Jack gave Kyle his undivided attention.

"I wondered what you were doing in here. Now I know." Kyle looked around for a moment; the car and Jack were in a mountain landscape with snake-like roads and no other cars.

His eyes eventually fell on the paused passenger. Raising his hand and furrowing his brow in confusion, he asked, "Is that... Richard Petty?" as he moved in closer for a more precise view.

"Yes," Jack said. "He was a racecar driver. When I asked him what a racecar was, he didn't stop talking for the entire car ride."

Kyle raised an eyebrow. "Yeah, he was a racecar driver," Kyle said with a touch of sarcasm.

Jack, not picking up on it, launched into some of his experiences over the last few weeks. "Did you know that there used to be more than one type of transport?"

Kyle thought for a second. "You mean a car. More than one type of car."

Jack shook his head. "Yes!" he said enthusiastically. "I've driven a pickup truck, convertible, SUV, Jeep, and something Richard called a James Bond car."

Kyle couldn't help but grin as he listened to Jack and thought back on his own teenage driving experiences. "Yeah, I did. You know, I used to drive an old Chevy pickup myself when I was your age."

Jack couldn't believe his ears. "Really? Where did you get it?"

"Pops bought it for me. It was my first car. He taught me to drive it too." The two fell silent for a moment as Kyle thought back. Then he said, "So, are you driving a stick or an automatic?"

Jack turned up a corner of his mouth and gave Kyle a sarcastic expression. "Stick, of course."

"So, other than submerging yourself in the twentieth century, what else have you been doing in here?" Kyle asked as he sat down on the bed beside Jack.

Jack didn't have an answer; he had done nothing but practice driving and watch old TV shows. "I, ummm, I was... it's just that..."

Kyle, sensing that Jack was uneasy and near embarrassment, broke in with a story to try to relate to him.

"*Star Trek*, huh? You know I used to watch all those with Pops. I thought they were pretty good shows. *Voyager* was always my favorite."

The stress danced away from Jack's face as his eyes widened. "I like *Voyager* too!"

"You don't say," Kyle said. "Who's your favorite character?"

Jack thought about it for a moment. He wasn't sure. Until recently he had always played as the characters, not simply watched them. "Paris, I guess. The pilot."

Kyle was a little surprised to hear that answer. Usually, it was the main characters that won favor. "Why Paris?"

"I don't know. I guess because he reminds me of Pops a little bit, alive in the future but obsessed with aspects of another place and time in history."

Kyle was stunned, not by the insightfulness of Jack's observation, but by the fact that he'd arrived at it on his own. Keeping the conversation going, Kyle offered his own favorite character up for discussion. "I always liked the Doctor."

Having not given the old *Star Trek* TV shows much thought since he was young, Kyle thought for a moment about why he liked the Doctor's character more than the others. "It was his attitude that always got me. I found the Doctor to be the most dynamic. He was controlled by everyone on that ship, and despite that, he was determined to grow beyond it." Feeling that he was finally connecting with his son, Kyle tried to expand the conversation. "You know, Pops always liked Seven of Nine."

Jack rolled right along with him. "Why?"

"You know, I'm not sure. Probably something to do with the Borg. Pops hated the Borg." Silence fell as the two men considered the Borg persona and wondered why Pops hated them the way he did. "You know what?" Kyle said, slapping Jack's knee. "Let's stop sitting here wondering about it. Let's go ask him." Kyle stood up and headed for the door.

Jack, remaining seated, just followed him with his eyes.

"Oh!" Kyle exclaimed as he snapped his fingers. "You're un-grounded."

And with a few swipes of his eyes, Jack's Eyebit lit up, and he was awash in the programs that had been restricted for him. One by one the different programs Jack had been running before he was grounded reappeared in his field of view.

With the emergence of the programs, Theon and Richard got smaller and smaller until they were nothing more than two blinking dots in the upper right-hand corner. ***143 new messages. Music streaming active, bedroom decorations re-applied, view screen interactions reengaged.*** Jack was nearly overwhelmed. It took him a few moments to acclimate to the reconnection.

Once he got his bearings, he realized that Theon and Richard had been minimized. Switching off the music and view screen interactions, he was able to keep the Theon and Richard programs active. After all, he still had more driving to do.

"You coming?" Kyle called. He had managed to walk to the outside of Jack's bedroom during the time it took Jack to reorganize his programs.

"Yes!" Jack answered as he jumped off the bed and headed for the door.

Chapter Sixteen

Eyebit Immersion 86%

DO NOT DISCONNECT DEVICE.

The transport whisked through the afternoon air, speeding toward its destination, brought to life by the constant stream of electricity being injected through the magnetic rails that lined the streets. Jack, riding on the passenger side, moved his hands left and right, driving an imaginary steering wheel. Every time the transport shifted or jumped, Jack shifted imaginary gears. The only thing missing from this scene was engine noise.

Kyle watched this performance from the corner of his eye, fearful that being detected would end the show. As he observed Jack making the best of his environment naturally, not artificially, he couldn't help but reflect how far he had come. The last time he took Jack to visit Pops, he was nothing but a pile of blinking, twitching, drooling human flesh.

The transport came to rest in front of Pops's ranch-style house. Jack was still flipping turn signals and pretending to park as Kyle got out of the transport.

"Come on, Speed Racer. Let's go," Kyle said with a slight smile that got bigger when he saw Jack reach down and pull the imaginary parking brake.

As the two walked to the front door, they both disengaged their Eyebits in an identical fashion that would convey to any observer that these two were obviously father and son. They both took notice of the recently pruned bush animals that were expertly trimmed to appear as the animals would in the wild.

Approaching the front door, Jack walked beside Kyle, not behind him. They reached the door at the same moment, and both looked down at the latest Robox delivery that had been left on the doorstep. They both bent down for the package but were interrupted by an audacious sound coming from the garage.

Vaaarooommm. Vaaarooommm. Glub, glub, glub... Bang!

This was immediately followed by a voice the two men knew well. "Shit!" Pops exclaimed.

Kyle, chuckling to himself, turned the front doorknob and found it unlocked. *Of course.* The two entered and headed for the garage. "Dad!" Kyle called out to alert Pops of their presence. "Dad, we're coming in." Kyle's call was met with silence. He inhaled to call out again.

Jack stopped him. "He heard you."

Kyle gave him a confused look, and Jack said, "He always hears you. He just doesn't answer because he knows that annoys you."

Kyle huffed and shook his head. "Okay."

As they neared the garage, a few familiar noises became more pronounced—a turning socket wrench, a radio... No, it was an old movie.

When they were standing outside the garage entrance, the dialogue of the movie was clear: "The first rule of fight club is..."

Kyle immediately recognized the movie and announced their presence to Pops by entering the garage quoting it. "And what's the second rule of fight club, Dad?"

"The second rule of fight club is... you don't talk about... *this car*!" Pops poked his head out from around the propped-up hood to find Kyle and Jack staring with slack-jawed amazement. "Shut your mouths, boys. You is letting the flies in."

Displayed before them was a completely put-together car. A Mustang, to be exact. The pile of junk that Jack had seen in the spare parts a few weeks ago was now fully incorporated. In their presence was a dead and forgotten car, reborn.

"Y'all look like you seen a ghost. My ticker didn't give out already, did it?" Pops asked as he tried to call Kyle's and Jack's attention toward him.

"Dad! This is... Wow, it's really coming along! Was that the noise we heard, this thing's engine?" Kyle asked as he reached out to touch the hardtop above the driver's door.

"Yeah, it's this design. It's giving me fits," Pops said as he took a step back from the engine. "Hey!" he exclaimed as he snapped his fingers. "I'm glad you're here. I need somebody to rev her up while I look at the engine."

As Pops opened the driver-side door for Kyle to get in, you would have thought it was Christmas. Kyle could scarcely recall being so excited. "You want... me... to..." Kyle stammered. Pops only raised both eyebrows at him and nodded. Thus prompted, Kyle eased his butt into the seat. He was surprised at how well an old bucket seat held up to the test of time.

He thought hard, trying to recall the next steps in prepping an old car for driving. Seat adjustment was next on the list, but he didn't have to do that—he had, after all, inherited Pops's height. He gripped the steering wheel and lost himself for a moment.

"Okay, start her up!" Pops called from under the hood.

Kyle snapped back from a distant memory of driving to pick up Claire in the last car he'd owned. He reached down and turned the key. Nothing. He turned the key back and then tried again. Nothing.

Pops waited a moment, grinning, wondering if Kyle would figure it out. He didn't. "It's a stick. Push the clutch in, then turn the key… I know it's been a while."

Kyle rolled his eyes and brought his left foot into the car, pushed the clutch, and turned the key. *Vrrrooommm!*

Like a horse that had just been spurred, the Mustang roared to life. Kyle gripped the wheel with both hands and smiled a big, open-mouthed smile.

"Okay, gas it!" Pops yelled from the front. Kyle gripped the wheel tighter and gently pushed and quickly released the gas pedal. The Mustang responded a second later with a roar and a slight rock that moved the car a bit from left to right. Kyle was a little startled by the movement but remembered that old muscle cars did that.

"Again!" Pops yelled.

Kyle eagerly hit the gas, and as the car rocked, he grinned even bigger. "Oh yeah," Kyle said to himself as he felt his entire body crackle with power.

"Again!" Pops yelled. "Longer this time." Kyle was happy to oblige.

Pops had called Jack to his side under the hood while Kyle was gassing the engine. "Look there," Pops said as he pointed to the tube jetting off the engine. "You see that hole?"

Jack did see what Pops was referring to but was confused. The engine he was looking at didn't look like the same ones he had been studying with Richard Petty.

"Okay, that's good. Cut it!" Pops yelled to Kyle. As the beast powered down, Pops kept his eyes fixed on the engine.

The engine didn't immediately stop but admitted several glubs, pops, hisses, and one bang before it finally found a resting state.

Pops hummed as he cupped his chin with his left hand. "What's making it want to keep running like that?" he wondered aloud. Pops looked over at Jack and exclaimed, "I know! We need a beer!"

Jack furrowed his brow. "Beer?"

"Yeah!" Pops said with a devilish grin. "You want one?"

Jack shrugged. "Sure."

Pops nodded. "Okay." He called out to Kyle, "Son, we're having a beer. You want one?"

Kyle, who had finally emerged from the car, looked at Jack, who stared at him with a wide-eyed expression conveying a desire for approval. Kyle was so juiced from having been exposed to the awesome power of the outlawed car that he approached the offer with a caviler attitude. "Yeah, I'll have one."

Pops fished three home-brew bottles from the ice box and kicked over two crates to create makeshift seats. The three men sat down and shared a table as adults for the first time. Three generations of men, spanning over one-hundred years of life, had put their differences aside and found common bonds. They didn't say much at first because words weren't needed to accent the pleasure they were finding in each other's company.

Just before the silence got awkward, Kyle let out the question he'd used as an excuse to get Jack over to Pops's in the first place. "So, Dad, Jack was wondering why you liked the Seven of Nine character?"

It wasn't the conversation starter Kyle thought it would be. In fact, Pops just stared at him for a moment before asking, "What?"

After taking another healthy swig of home brew, Kyle elaborated. "You know, Seven of Nine from *Star Trek: Voyager*, the Borg drone turned human."

Pops continued to stare, not believing his ears.

Kyle said, "See, we were talking about our favorite characters. Mine is the Doctor, Jack likes Paris, and I remembered you always liked Seven of Nine. And we were wondering why?"

Pops was flabbergasted and unwilling to directly answer the question without further understanding of what prompted it. "So that's an interesting form of punishment. You grounded him and made him watch *Star Trek*?"

Much to Pops's surprise, Kyle laughed. Pops couldn't recall the last time he had seen Kyle laugh. To his pleasure, Pops was treated to a flash of his long-dead wife dancing across his son's face.

Kyle swigged his beer again then answered with a zeal that surprised Pops. "No, Dad, he found the old TV shows on his own and watched them all, every last one."

Pops could sense Kyle's pride. He looked at Jack. "Wow, boy, I'm impressed." Pops had to find out how much of the *Star Trek* universe Jack had absorbed. "What are some of your favorite episodes?"

Jack pondered it a moment, sipped his beer, and answered. "I liked the one where Picard gets a new heart from Q. I also liked the one where Worf was constantly moved from reality to reality." Jack thought a moment longer and sipped his beer again before raising his head. When he did look up, he realized that he had Pops's and Kyle's undivided attention.

He wasn't used to this. "In *Voyager*, I liked the one where the time travel guy kept changing the present, and the one where Q had a son."

Jack quickly put his head back down, as if he were about to be scolded for having an opinion.

Pops, sensing that Jack needed some reassurance, spoke with a twinge of both pride and sarcasm in his voice. "Well, good for you, boy. There may be hope for you yet."

Jack smiled to himself; he wasn't used to positive reinforcement. The men sat finishing their beers and idly chatting about *Star Trek*. During the course of the conversation, Pops had to be reminded of the original question, not because he was forgetting it, but because he was avoiding it by constantly changing the subject. The truth was, he was enjoying the moment enough to dread its end.

Finally pinned into a corner, he relented. "Okay, fine! Seven of Nine represents hope to me." He gulped down the last of the home brew then continued. "She was raised as a Borg and barely knew any other life. Despite all that, despite being hopelessly addicted to the system, she was still able to break free and find herself."

Jack and Kyle looked at Pops, waiting, knowing he had more to say. "The Borg are the *Star Trek* universe's biggest threat or fear. Loss of self, loss of individuality, and loss of freedom are all paralyzing to an enlightened society." Forgetting his beer was empty, Pops put the bottle to his lips, only to be greeted by nothing. "Eeeh, anyway," he said, setting the empty bottle down beside him.

"Hmm, interesting," Kyle said as he turned his bottle straight up and drank down the last of his beer. Setting it on the ground, he stood up and wiped nonexistent dirt off the ass end of his pants. "Well, we gotta get going. Come on, Jack."

Jack didn't even have a chance to move before Pops jumped up to protest. "You boys leaving already? You just got here."

Facing away from Pops, Kyle grinned then turned with a cocked eyebrow. "Yeah, Dad, it's the weekend, and I have stuff to take care of."

"Sure, sure," Pops said. "Well, you boys are always welcome here. So it's no problem if Jack wants to stay."

Jack had already moved back to the hood of the car and peeked his head around it to look at Kyle, hoping for permission.

Kyle thought for a moment then said, "Why not? Okay, Jack, I'll send the transport back for you."

Pops grinned broad enough for Kyle to take notice. "Thanks, boy," he said with sincerity in his voice.

"Okay, Dad. You kids enjoy your playdate!" Kyle called back as he left the garage.

Pops called out, "Good talk, son." Turning his attention back to the car, Pops addressed the situation at hand. "Okay, Jacky, let's try to patch that hole. Hoses are hard to come by nowadays."

CHAPTER SEVENTEEN

Tall Tales with Pops

THE MAN: CHAPTER 2

"This is called duct tape. Pretty heavy-duty stuff, so it should do the trick," Pops said as he displayed the roll to Jack. "Now, I need you to lift the hose so I can get this around it."

"Okay," Jack said as he lifted the hose gingerly so as not to cause any more damage.

"Good. Now don't move," Pops said as he circled the roll over and over the hose, covering the hole. Once the hose's color had changed from black to mostly silver, he stopped, tore the tape, and squeezed the hose as if the last little bit of force possessed magic. "Okay, moving on." Pops straightened up and looked at Jack. "What's on your mind, boy? You're awfully quiet."

As usual, Jack went direct to the point. "I was wondering what happened next."

"With...?" Pops asked, trying to draw out the rest of Jack's thought.

"Charlie and the horse."

"Oh, well, okay, you're still interested in hearing that, are you?" Pops asked, a little surprised.

"Yes. I tried to find the rest of the story while I was grounded but couldn't locate it anywhere," Jack said, his tone questioning.

"Yeah, boy, didn't I tell you that? That story has been told orally through our family for generations."

Jack didn't respond.

"Okay, well, where was I before your dad burst in last time?" Pops asked.

Jack perked up. "He had been living with the Indians but was being forced out."

Pops thought for a second. "Oh, right, right... Okay. So..."

Under the order of President Jackson, all Indians were being relocated to reservations, and Charlie wasn't allowed to go. The Indians were losing not only their homes, but also their birth and burial places, along with all their other holy places. What happens to your religion when what you worship—the mountain, river, and sky—is taken from you? Your religion dies.

Charlie and the tribe had to part company, but before doing so, the chief had asked Charlie to be the "steward of the land." Despite having no legal claim to the land, Charlie agreed to pay homage and honor the Indians that had cared for him. He was humbled by the request and vowed to protect the land.

"Care for the land, and the land will care for you" was the last thing the chief said before the army soldier shoved him with the butt of his rifle.

"Move along," the soldier commanded.

Charlie stood by helplessly as he watched his friends being marched two by two off the land. Most were barefoot, some were crying, and all were destitute. A tiny spark came to life inside Charlie, which ignited the same flame of rage he hadn't felt since he'd last seen his father. He let out a howl, and before he knew what was happening, he had connected his fist with the jaw of a Union infantryman.

The infantryman was on his knees as Charlie tried to wrestle his gun away. Before he could relieve him of his firearm, he felt a hand grab his shoulder. In the throes of uncontrollable rage, Charlie thrust his elbow into the face of the hand's owner, knocking him back five feet.

The third attack came from directly in front of him. That infantryman lost teeth when Charlie swung an uppercut that reverberated through the soldier's body. As Charlie began to bear down on the third man, he was blindsided. The captain's gun butt struck Charlie in the side of the head.

The power associated with rage left him. Just before he blacked out, he heard the captain say, "He's a white man. Leave his horse." Then all Charlie saw was darkness, void, nothing.

In a flash, images crowded Charlie's unconscious mind. He was in an Indian ceremony where the chief spoke clear English.

"We give you the power of our people with the understanding you will care for the land." The chief thrust a stick into the fire and drew his hand down Charlie's cheek, streaking paint the entire length of his face. "You are its custodian."

Then in the background, at the far corner of the ceremony, stood Charlie's father, who said "Ya hear?" When Charlie turned his attention back to the chief, he was gone, and Charlie was alone. Even the fire had died out and was merely glowing embers. Charlie felt something wet on his face and brought his hand up to wipe it away, then again and again. Awake!

Charlie's eyes flicked open to find a horse snout rubbing his chin, lips, nose, and forehead. He sprang to his feet and surveyed his surroundings. Everyone was gone. The remnants of a campfire smoldered nearby. Charlie was suddenly awash in pain from the spot where the captain had struck his head. Dabbing at it, Charlie found his hand stained red with blood.

Not only had the federal government relocated all the Indians in the area, but they had also gone out of their way to destroy the agricultural legacy that was left behind. Charlie lingered on the land for as long as he could—weeks, maybe months. But hunger finally drove him to a more populated area.

"What was he eating?" Jack asked, breaking into Pops's story.

"What?" Pops asked.

"There wasn't anything there, no grocery stores or anything, right? So what did he eat till he had to go to the city? Like, how did he make it as long as he did?"

"Well." Pops thought for a minute. "I suppose he hunted and fished. He planted. Don't forget the Indians taught him a lot of stuff."

"So why did he go into the city then? You said he got hungry."

Pops, realizing the glaring plot hole in the story, thought for a minute. "You know what? He got lonely and wanted to learn more stuff. He thought it would be a good idea to go to college. So, he did. Happy?" Pops said proudly.

"Yeah, okay. That makes sense. It's not like he had power or anything. I'd get lonely too. I don't think I could live without power and stuff."

"You know, I always roll my eyes when I hear people say that. You could if you had to. If the chips were down and you had no other choice, you'd find a way." Pops's tone was superior.

"I suppose so." Jack turned his attention back to the car.

"Anyway," Pops said as he launched back into the story.

While in the city, Charlie was able to further his understanding in the ways of the world. After his encounter with the soldiers, Charlie figured out that brute force would not be enough to summon his will into reality. Sure, it had worked on his father, but he was weak and just one man. The Indians were forced away by an entire army.

Charlie spent years learning, improving, and growing. He didn't sleep much during that time, as he had to earn money while attending classes. He studied law, agriculture, and finance. Even though he enjoyed agriculture the most, he showed real promise in finance. So much so that he caught the attention of his instructors. To most people, the math associated with high dollar amounts was incredibly intimidating, but Charlie was able to disregard that by simply saying, "Eh, it's not *my* money."

A few days before the graduation ceremony, everything changed. After leaving a meeting with one of his finance instructors, Charlie was returning to the horse tie-up, and then he saw her. Even from a distance, Charlie was able to make out her shape.

She was shorter than him but still tall for a woman. As he traced his eyes down her neck to the swell of her bosom, to the collapse of her waist, to the obvious flare of her hips, and down through her legs to her feet, Charlie was impressed. She wore pants, which was not the custom for a lady of the day, and that alone interested him even more. As he drew nearer, her fine features became clear. She had a complexion with a reddish tint; long raven-black hair; and deep, soulful chestnut-brown eyes. She was an Indian.

That was it. Charlie was finished. He had met a lot of women while at university, but this one was different.

"You're petting my horse," Charlie said with a smile. He had startled her a bit, and she took a step back from Charlie, closer to the horse.

The horse let out a snort, and the woman snapped her head to the left, looking toward the horse. The movement was such a jerk that it caused her hair to flip. Love at first sight? Maybe. Reaching to pet the horse in response to his snort, she answered Charlie.

"He would say that you belong to him."

Charlie let out a little laugh. "Yes, I suppose he would." Charlie was not accustomed to being without words while talking to women, but this time he was coming up short. Losing his cool and feeling desperate to captivate her, he spurred the conversation on with an open-ended question.

"There's a whole row of horses to pet here. Why did you choose mine?" Charlie asked, sounding more accusatory than charming.

Without returning his stare, she answered him with a sass that only deepened Charlie's infatuation. "You should know why! It's the same reason you chose his company in the first place. This one is special."

It was a good thing Charlie had already completed all the requirements to graduate from university, because he did nothing over the last few days of his education. He spent every available moment with Laura. Even though he addressed her by her English given name in public, he privately called her by a shortened version of her Indian given name.

Charlie called her "Wilds," shortened from "Wild Like Beast." To Charlie, she was every bit a free-spirited animal who bore little respect for her captors. Like him, she'd been taught by the Indians that everything was about partnerships with their surroundings. Ownership was a white man's concept.

Laura didn't immediately open up to Charlie, but once she learned of his past and his time with the tribe before displacement, she found herself equally drawn to him. She had been courted before but had never really felt a connection with any of the suitors, mostly because she wasn't being courted by anyone who had any understanding of her heritage. To her, Charlie was a rare find.

Wilds had been made to attend a white man's school since the settlers came in. The government said it was to "help them assimilate." In truth, it was a covert way to get rid of the "Indian problem." She had been a captive in the white man's schools since she was a girl. White man's language, culture, beliefs, and laws were all forced on her. She was made a Christian, even though she didn't believe in Christ. She was made to speak only English, but she secretly practiced her birth tongue. She was made to learn to sew and wear cumbersome dresses. But it didn't take her long to sew the dresses together into pants. Had she been a man, she would have been beaten into submission. Wilds had only survived by outwardly conforming enough to avoid detection. To Charlie, she was perfect, and he was in love.

As graduation came and went, Charlie revealed his plans to her. He had managed to file for a piece of land with the claim's office. Charlie was set to take "white man's ownership" of the same land the Indians had put in his charge. As part of his plan, Charlie asked Wilds to accompany him.

"I figure that it would do me well to have a partner in this endeavor—"

She cut him off. "Yes!"

Charlie smiled. "You don't know what I was going to ask."

Wilds gave him a look to convey that she did. "You want me to go with you, right?"

Charlie stammered; she had completely disarmed him. "Well, I... It's just... Well, the last few days have really..." Charlie was flustered, and his condition only worsened when he looked at her.

Wilds, meeting Charlie's gaze with two raised eyebrows, waited patiently.

With a huff, Charlie completely exhaled and drew in a deep breath. "Yes," he said plainly. "I want you to go with me."

There was no room for silence. Wilds responded immediately. "That's what I thought. So back to the original statement, before you got embarrassed. Yes!"

The only preparation they needed to undertake was outfitting a wagon for homesteading. The land Charlie intended to occupy was a few days' travel from any major city. His possessions were few, and Wilds's were less. She had been a prisoner in the white man's world for too long and was looking forward to shedding the trappings of her oppressors.

The pair enthusiastically set out at first light. Even Charlie's horse seemed excited. Charlie gave a slight snap of the reins, and the horse leaped into stride, yanking the wagon so hard that both Charlie and Wilds nearly ended up on their backs. They were off, together.

The journey was relatively uneventful. Upon his arrival at the claim, Charlie's breath was taken away. It was more beautiful than he remembered. The area where the wagon came to rest was on a flat plain squared off by a string of trees, perfect for cabin building. Farther ahead ran a stream that was approximately twelve feet across and two feet deep at the deepest point.

Best as Charlie could tell, it was probably fed by the majestic snow-topped mountain in the distance. *Wow, what a view,* Charlie thought as he stepped out of the wagon, took off his hat, and breathed as deep as he could. He didn't understand it, but the air here seemed clearer.

Over the next weeks, months, and years, the couple prospered. They lived a minimalist lifestyle and survived off the land. They grew their own food and traded when they could. Children were a blessing they had yet to receive during this phase of their partnership. Fortunately, children didn't concern them at this point, which was another oddity about this unlikely pairing. Time marched on, and they lived their lives peaceably.

One day, as Charlie was hammering the wooden shingles to the roof of his newly constructed barn, he spied a horse rider in the distance. The rider was approaching the homestead as if he had business or, moreover, as if he thought he had the right to be there.

Wilds and Charlie were immediately on the defensive. Strangers weren't always welcome. The last one was the census man, and that didn't go well at first.

To stop the stranger from getting too close to the main house, Charlie and Wilds walked a good ways up from it and greeted the rider. Charlie wasn't wearing his hat; he was holding it. He hoped it would appear to the stranger as a sign of respect, but it also concealed his Colt revolver. The rider slowed and stopped but did not dismount.

"Howdy, stranger," Charlie said, trying to sound sincere. "You lost?"

The stranger eyed Charlie for a moment then announced himself. "No, sir, I have business here."

Charlie wasn't interested and was already losing patience. "State your business, and be on your way then."

The stranger said, "By order of the federal government…"

Those words started a blaze in Charlie, and he took a step forward. By this point, Wilds had ahold of his arm and slowed his advance with a clasped hand on his bicep.

The stranger continued, "It is decreed that a postal route be established to further the communication efforts of the United States Government."

Charlie stopped and considered what the stranger had just said. "Postal route?"

The stranger said, "Yes, sir, I'm your post rider. Are you Charles?"

Charlie couldn't believe what he was hearing. "Yes, I'm Charles."

"I got mail for you." The post rider reached into his shoulder bag, which Charlie hadn't noticed till then. The post rider extracted a bundle of paper all addressed to Charlie. There must have been fifteen pieces of mail there. As the post rider handed Charlie the bundle, he asked, "Got anything going out?"

Charlie didn't verbalize an answer; he couldn't find the words. He merely shook his head.

"Okay," the post rider said as he turned his horse to face the direction from which he had come.

"Wait!" Charlie yelped. "Where did this—and you—come from?"

The post rider looked back, confused. "The post office, in town. See you next week."

Charlie was still confused. "What town?"

The post rider, still riding away from the couple, called back. "Boom town... A few miles thataway." He spurred his horse on and headed away.

Still wanting more information, Charlie called out, "Why is there a boom town?"

Without slowing, the post rider yelled back a single word that answered all of Charlie's questions. "Gold!"

Charlie and Wilds stood silently for a while, watching the post rider fade into the distance. Once he was out of sight, the couple retreated to the main house, abandoning the shingling for the remainder of the day.

They poured over the correspondence for the afternoon and early evening. There were several messages from one of Charlie's former instructors, mostly asking for advice and assistance with finances. There was a newspaper from the town press, a sheriff's announcement, a wanted poster, and a copy of the town charter.

Wilds had no mail; it was all for Charlie. Nonetheless, she delighted in reading his mail as if it were hers. She was particularly fascinated with the newspaper. She even took down Charlie's dictation in response to his ex-instructor's pleas for help.

Over the next few months, especially during the winter, the idea of civilized living snaked its way in. Charlie and Wilds were receiving correspondence regularly. Charlie was finding that his counsel could earn him money. He had even managed to set up a bank account. By winter's end, a longing was on both their minds, if not on their lips. Spring normally meant planting, but this spring Charlie was interested in growing another type of green.

CHAPTER EIGHTEEN

Eyebit Immersion 85%

RE-CONNECT TO AVOID CONSEQUENCES.

"Wow, I couldn't imagine," Jack said as he handed Pops his empty beer bottle.

"What do you mean?"

"Well, they have nothing. No power, no running water, no toilets, no Eyebits."

Pops scoffed at Jack's observations. "Yeah, true. But at least they are free. Living only on your wits, gettin' by, or die tryin'! That's adventure, boy!" Pops stopped himself, as he didn't want this to turn into a lecture. "You want another?" he asked, holding up the empty bottle.

Jack shook his head as Pops retreated to the fridge. Jack continued to talk to his back. "Well, they aren't free like we're free."

Pops popped the top on his home brew. "That so?"

Jack looked at him, confused. "Well, yes. We have modern conveniences plus the freedoms the country was founded on."

Pops's eyes nearly bugged out of his head. "Oh, help me, Jesus. You think you're free?"

Jack was taken aback by Pops's reaction. "Am I not?" he asked almost fearfully.

Stopping himself again, Pops began with a disarming exhale. "Well, what you must understand is that the idea of freedom is more than just a word used to describe having choice. It's a perspective. A free man can be ensnared by situations just as easily as someone born into captivity." Pausing a moment to let that sink in, Pops sipped his beer. "So, if you work your whole life to pay for your power, running water, toilets, or Eyebits, are you free?"

Jack was beginning to understand. "But not everything is bad," he countered. "Toilets carry dirty water away and replace it with clean water."

"That's true. Some things are good and worth the sacrifice of some freedoms. Choosing to spend some time making earnings to pay for those things is an act of choice, which is freedom. What you have to be careful about is becoming a slave to it. Do you need a gold-plated shitter for one hundred times the cost of a porcelain one?"

Jack thought about it for a moment. "No, I guess not."

"Right," Pops said, "'cause you'd spend the next thirty years paying for it."

Reflecting for a minute, Jack was coming to understand where he was in life, riding on the edge of his pivotal freedom. "I don't pay for that stuff." He looked at Pops almost defiantly.

"That's true. But you ain't one hundred percent free either. You're a slave to that fuckin' thing you wear."

Jack was getting irritated. "How's that?"

Pops was hesitant to answer and secretly employed a little reverse psychology. "Eh, you don't wanna hear this. You won't like it." He paused a moment. "Better tell you later. Hand me that bolt."

Jack complied but insisted, "Tell me now."

Pops looked away and smiled. "Better not. You're not gonna like it, and when you see what I see, you're gonna get even madder. Trust me, ignorance is bliss. Now that washer, please."

Jack grabbed the washer for the bolt, and as Pops reached for it, he clamped his hand around it. "Tell me now!"

Pops looked up and met his eyes. "Okay, but don't say I didn't warn ya."

Jack released his grip and gave the washer to Pops.

"Okay, what's your favorite food?" Pops asked as he slipped the washer down the screw shaft.

Jack thought for a quick second. "Um, steamed broccoli, baked eggplant, and rice."

Pops's shoulders dropped as he craned his neck to look Jack in the eye. With an overly sarcastic tone, he said, "Sounds yummy. You get that from the cafeteria, do you?"

Jack again answered quickly, as if he were pre-programmed. "Yes, every day."

Pops felt a twinge of pity for his grandson and in that instant knew that he was setting him on the right path, even though it was going to be painful. "Okay, so tomorrow before you select your favorite food, take a step back, disengage your Eyebit, and then come back and tell me what your favorite food is."

The next day, Jack went through the motions. He got up, showered, selected his suit's clothes display, caught the transport, and arrived at school. The day was progressing normally. Outside of some graduation preparations, there wasn't much of note, till he got to lunch. Following Pops's advice, he collected his tray and filed into line.

Displayed before him was the food buffet. From Jack's view, it was sparsely stocked with bins of various fruits, vegetables, and whole grains with big gaps between the different bins. He had never questioned the purpose of the gaps before. Jack breathed deep, reached up, and disengaged his Eyebit. The cyber world flashed away, and he stood before the food buffet in astonishment.

All the empty spaces between the bins were filled in with... foodstuff he didn't recognize. There were strange dairy-covered triangles, crust-covered chicken parts, and salt-covered golden sticks of potato, to name a few. Jack was so enamored by what was before him that he had forgotten he was holding up the line.

He was brought back to his senses with a shove from the ant mill behind him. Quickly he grabbed everything he had never eaten before and shoved it onto his tray. Thinking even quicker, he reengaged his Eyebit. Knowing that he wouldn't be able to pay for his selections without being connected, Jack approached the checkout person.

From Jack's point of view, he stood before this person holding a tray of nothing. He knew there was something there because of the weight of it. The checkout person looked at Jack's tray and then up at him. "Hungry?" she asked with a cocked eyebrow.

"Starved," Jack answered.

Jack located a table where no one else was sitting, disengaged his Eyebit, and proceeded to spread out the food. He sat down before it and reengaged his Eyebit. Once connected, he found the food had disappeared. He clenched his jaw.

"That's fucked up," he swore under his breath. "Theon!" he called out.

"Hello, Jack. How may I help you?" Theon answered as he stood in Jack's visual field.

"Identify the foods on the table," Jack commanded.

Theon turned his gaze to the table and said, "Hmm." Because of Jack's Eyebit settings, the foodstuff wasn't initially visible to Theon either. Jack sat patiently as Theon screened through several light filters till he found one that displayed the food. "Ahh, there we go."

Jack looked over to his right at the first plate of food. A white line blinked around the shape of the food, and Theon defined it. "This is pizza," he said.

Jack had heard the term before, recently. "What's pizza?"

"Pizza is an Italian food item composed of bread, tomato sauce, cheese, and assorted toppings usually made of meats or vegetables. This particular piece has pepperoni, green peppers, and onions," Theon answered.

It only took Jack a few moments to remember where he had heard the term pizza before. It was *Star Trek: Voyager*, in an episode where Tom Paris attempted to convince Neelix to make him a pizza.

Jack shifted his field of view to the next item on the table. The same white line that had flashed around the pizza flashed around the next item in line.

"Fried chicken," Theon said. Then French fries, then a hamburger, then a hotdog. Jack was a little overwhelmed, but regardless he was resolved to try them all, if even just a taste.

During his feast, Jack disengaged his Eyebit. It was just him and the food without any distractions. Being disconnected caused him to miss his next class. Unconcerned, he spent the remainder of the time wandering the halls without his Eyebit on.

He had never attended school without the aid of his Eyebit, and he discovered that without it he couldn't even find the location of his next classroom. The first twenty minutes of his modern tech-less exploring experience were spent just trying to get his bearings.

The walls of the hallways were bare. Passersby were of little help; they didn't know how to communicate with someone who wasn't connected. At first, he almost panicked, but then he remembered that all he had to do was reengage and the Eyebit would take care of everything for him. With the knowledge of this safety net, Jack continued his exploration of a place he had been most of his life but had never *really* seen.

Despite the highly technically connected world, some things remained. Old laws supported old technology's continued existence. As Jack traversed the halls, he eventually came across an illuminated sign, with red lettering, hanging above a door.

He stood and stared at it for a long moment. It wasn't new. It had always been there. He had seen it before but paid it no mind. Before now, it was just one of the few things that shined through the Eyebit screen every time someone looked at it. It boldly announced its presence and forced its meaning on the world, regardless of the status, place, or language of that world. Exit.

The sign had taken on new meaning. Jack was seeing it as no longer annoying or intrusive to the harmony of his Eyebit world, but more as salvation. Drinking in this new enlightenment, Jack considered all the possibilities this one worded sign implied. Exit.

Beyond these walls, the outside, no longer in the building, away. All these thoughts crowded their way into his mind simultaneously. As he tried to imagine what world lay beyond those double doors, another *E*-word swept away all the other thoughts in his mind. That word was *escape*!

That single word spurred him on. Escape was exactly what he needed. His cares and concerns about the potential threats beyond the security of those walls were gone in a flash. As he lurched forward, he heard Pops's voice in his head. *But at least they are free. Living only on your wits, gettin' by, or die tryin'! That's adventure, boy!*

Wham! Jack slammed into the door with such thrust it swung open and smacked against the wall. He crossed the threshold and found himself in the central courtyard. Taking in the basics, Jack surveyed the concrete walkways; they were in a square pattern. Awnings covered them. Just beyond the concrete lay a grassy area randomly spotted with picnic tables.

When Jack approached the tables, he discovered they were in a haphazard state of disrepair. To his surprise, they were made of wood. Upon close examination he was able to make out messages... No, not quite. They were names. They had been carved into the wood a long time ago. "Joe sat here. Class of '20."

The wood was heavily weathered, and most of the scratches had faded away. As he continued his survey of the grounds, Jack's attention was pulled to the far corner of the lot. As he neared it, he discovered a small garden. At the entrance to the garden was a well-weathered plaque that stated the purpose of the space.

CHAPTER NINETEEN

Eyebit Immersion 84%

LOCATION SERVICES TRACING...
TRACING...

Jack stood staring at the plaque. He traced his fingers along the surface and took in the feeling of the raised type. He wondered how long it had been there and whether he would have ever noticed had he not taken his Eyebit off.

IN HONOR OF:

Richard Carl Wolfe: *The Last Philosopher*

He shook us free and showed us the future.

Memorial Garden

Jack entered the garden via a gravel pathway that had been laid years ago. The garden had been maintained but not walked on. As he traversed the pathway, Jack spied a floral-drone watering and pruning away. The garden was covered with a variety of greenery.

Shrubs, trees, wildflowers, and vines, just to name a few. Near the end of the path grew a small patch of tulips. Every color Jack had ever seen was before him in a rainbow patch of flowers that gently swayed in the breeze. Jack reached out to touch one of the flowers but was interrupted by the unmistakable sounds of doors opening, people, and business.

Realizing that the time had come for his next class, Jack quickly exited the garden and made for the concrete awnings and the groups of people being led between classes. As he approached, it took him a moment to realize he wasn't connected to his Eyebit. His big clue came when he started to notice all the people were dressed the same. Without being connected, he couldn't see whatever everyone had chosen to display as their clothes suit.

All Jack saw was everyone wearing white—pants, shirt, shoes, and of course an Eyebit. As he approached the edge of the concrete, he paused a moment and looked over his shoulder at the bright colors he was leaving behind. Turning back to the crowds of conformity, he reluctantly put his Eyebit back on and stepped into the ant mill.

Jack's Eyebit wasn't fully engaged before he stepped into the crowd. Someone knocked his shoulder hard enough to spin him one hundred eighty degrees, which landed him face-first against the crowd. Jack was tossed this way and that as the force of the mindless march washed over him. He was being pushed and shoved hard enough to keep his Eyebit from fully connecting with his eyes, retina, and brain.

The lenses were down, and he was getting flashes of connection, but every time someone hit him too hard, the connection was lost. Jack's first thought in this panic was to push back against the crowd, but if he had learned anything over the last few months, it was that sometimes to win, all you had to do was hold your ground.

Jack squared his shoulders, tucked his chin down, bent his knees slightly, and clasped his hands at his chest. Moving his shoulders with the blows allowed his head the ability to stay level long enough for a secure connection to be established. Jack raised his head and smiled. It had worked.

However, Jack's victory was short-lived. As the crowd began to wane, a straggler was rushing by and not paying attention to where she was sprinting. *Wham!* She hit Jack with such force they knocked foreheads, and both fell to the ground. They both sprawled out on the concrete, and their Eyebits turned solid red and initiated ***Injury Protocol***.

As they directed the two not to move, the Eyebits simultaneously ran diagnostics of their injuries. Each Eyebit traced its owner's brain and mapped the neural circuitry to where the nerves were signaling pain. Once the diagnostic was complete and they had determined that no injuries were present, the Eyebits stood down their medical alerts and instructed the two that they could move.

Jack was first on his feet and came to help up the girl who had hit him. Once he got a look at her, Jack was knocked down again, metaphorically.

Looking beyond the Eyebit, the girl made eye contact with Jack. "I'm so sorry," she said. "I didn't see you there."

Jack couldn't respond. He was speechless. Besides, he wasn't given much of a chance. The Eyebits had reasserted their dominance, and she was off.

Jack suddenly understood what Pops had been telling him about how Charlie felt when he saw Wilds. There are times in our lives when the walls we build around ourselves are brought crumbling to the ground. Some of those times it's subtle, but most of the time it is violent.

Change rarely calls on us at a moment of our choosing. Often, we find ourselves blindsided by what is seemingly a normal day. As we are left holding the remains of a lifestyle that ended only moments ago, we wonder, *How will I carry on?* Whether the destructive force is the death of a loved one, a new job, or a move to a new home, the results are the same: our former selves are over.

The saving grace of change is that it's not always unwanted. Sometimes, if we are lucky, it's a girl. The details of the introduction aren't important. She's there, and we find ourselves willing to do anything to catch just a moment of her attention, even if it means tearing down our walls ourselves, by the handful. Jack *got it* now.

Jack might as well have skipped his last class. He spent the entire time reading the profile of the mysterious girl who knocked him on his ass. He didn't even realize the class had ended until the Eyebit alerted him.

The rest of the day and night were spent deeper in the Eyebit-connected world than he had been in months. Jack was frustratedly sure that the Eyebit could help him get an introduction, but he kept coming up short again and again.

After what seemed like hours of trying, he took a break and practiced driving with Richard Petty. Once he got bored with that, he spent the rest of the night watching old TV shows. He had recently discovered *The Dukes of Hazzard*, *Supernatural*, *Knight Rider*, and cartoons. He particularly liked cartoons, especially the superhero-themed ones.

Despite all the visual stimulation, he still drifted off to sleep. As he waited in the place Peter Pan called Neverland, that silent spot between asleep and awake, two images greeted him: Pops with his car and this girl.

CHAPTER TWENTY

Eyebit Immersion 82%

RELINQUISH MANUAL SETTINGS.

"I like chicken wings and pizza," Jack said to announce his presence at the door of Pops's garage. Pops was standing at the hood of the car, cupping his chin. He ticked his eyebrow up as if Jack had always been there.

"Yeah, now that sounds like a teenager." Pops approached Jack, rubbing his arm. "What did your parents say when they found out you've been eating everything you weren't supposed to?"

Jack thought back on the conversation they had had that morning before he came over. "It was strange. Claire was disappointed that I didn't make it to graduation, and Kyle was surprised that I had made it this far." His tone was confused.

Pops nodded at Jack. "Yeah, supposedly once you graduate or turn eighteen those stupid things open up the rest of the world your parents had been hiding you from."

Pops contemplated the implications of the accepted social norm of blocking aspects of the world from children until a magic age. Then suddenly, boom, the veil is off. Hope you can deal.

"What a fucked-up world," he said.

Jack, as usual, didn't fully understand. "What else am I missing?" he asked excitedly, knowing Pops would tell him the truth.

Pops thought about his answer for a moment. "Well, there was once a time in this country when the answer to that question was simply missed opportunity." Pops flashed back to his youth and faded away for a moment.

"Pops? Hey, Pops?"

The sound of Jack's voice broke in and Pops snapped back to the present. "What? I'm sorry. I didn't catch that."

Jack flatly repeated his question. "But what do I do to get more opportunity?"

Pops gave it some thought. "Yes, I suppose that when everything is controlled for you, it's difficult to find new and exciting opportunities. So for you, I guess one should say missed exposure."

Silence fell over the room, and Pops let that thought bubble for a moment. He saw no reaction in Jack. Figuring he wasn't catching his meaning, Pops decided to put his thought into action.

He snapped his fingers and exclaimed, "I know! We'll go to the mall! You have the transport, right?"

"Yes, but why the mall?"

Pops squinted at Jack and dropped his shoulders. "See, exactly, missed exposure!" Pops said sadly.

Jack couldn't believe what he was hearing. "You want to expose me to the mall?" he asked sarcastically.

"No!" Pops exclaimed. "I want to take you on an adventure."

Jack, still sarcastic, said, "At the mall? Why?"

As he excitedly scuttled around the garage, Pops was convincing himself at the same time he was convincing Jack. "Time to face fear," he said.

"Fear? You are afraid of the mall?"

Pops stopped dead in his tracks and looked Jack square in the eye. "God, yes! Aren't you?"

Jack looked at Pops as if he were a crazy person. "No."

A smile spread across Pops's face, and Jack could tell he liked that answer. "Yes! Right attitude, boy! Good! Now we need supplies. Get me a beer. You want one?" he asked as he set back to hustling around the garage.

"No, Pops, I am okay. It's 9:30 in the morning."

Pops kept moving. "Right! Good call. Whiskey it is."

Bang... Crash...

Jack stood still in the garage and watched Pops flail about.

"You seen my hat, son?"

Jack didn't move. "It's on top of the car."

Pops's head shot up from the passenger side. "Ah... there you are." He quickly came around the car and stopped face-to-face with Jack. "You ready? Let's go."

As the transport shot along its preprogrammed, predetermined, pre-laid roadway, Pops fidgeted in his seat. Attempting to distract himself from his current predicament, he conversed with Jack.

"So, when you took your Eyebit off at school, did you just stay in the cafeteria, or did you do any exploring?" He sounded genuinely curious.

Jack, of course, had an answer. He desperately wanted to tell him about the girl but was completely unsure of how to ask him what to do. He instead asked about the garden, specifically the name on the plaque.

"Yes, I explored the halls and found a garden that stood in memorial to a..." Jack paused a moment as he attempted to recall the name. "Richard... Carl... Wolfe. I think that was the name."

Pops nodded. "Yes, that was his name. The last philosopher. Do you know why he is called that?" he asked, looking forward.

"I don't even know who he was," Jack said, careful not to look at Pops while wearing his Eyebit.

Pops rolled his eyes. "Yeah, right. I mean, seriously... what do they teach you kids in school?" Pops huffed. "I am a little surprised, though, especially with all your delving into old pop culture stuff, that you haven't at least stumbled across something related to him."

Jack was silent and waited for Pops to continue.

"In a nutshell, a philosopher is someone who questions things. Throughout the ages, their job description included the duties of doctor, leader, soothsayer, inventor, and spiritual advisor. As history marched forward, the duties became more defined to include only questioning." Pops paused momentarily for Jack to confirm his understanding up to this point. Jack nodded.

"Okay, well, up until Richard came along, humanity was bound by the confines of religion. Just after the turn of the millennium, the number of people who attended religious services was on the decline, in fact, so much so that the institution of Judeo-Christian belief began closing a lot of churches, mostly due to a lack of funding."

Jack broke into the conversation with a question that took Pops by surprise. "Is that what those half-demolished buildings with gravestones are?"

Pops gave a prideful but sad smile as he nodded, thinking of his wife's grave. "So, the last philosopher was an atheist, which means that he didn't believe there was a god. Seizing on the decline of the religious infrastructure, he began to buy churches, one by one. Once he acquired enough, he had control of the denomination, and once he had control, he closed it down, liquefied the assets, and donated or invested them in the education system."

Pops stopped his history lesson to reassert his surprise that Jack hadn't seen anything about Dr. Wolfe. "And you don't know about this guy? Even with your *Star Trek* searches?"

Jack shook his head.

"Jesus!" Pops exclaimed. "I knew it was bad, but people *really* don't care about anything nowadays, do they?"

Jack didn't respond.

"Okay, well, one of his most famous quotes is 'Science is the new religion, and *Star Trek* is the future.' The last philosopher understood the crippling power of religion, and one of his most powerful gestures was to personally flip the switch on the dynamite charges of a church that was being demolished."

Pops recalled an ancient memory and shared it with Jack. "You know, I was there when he destroyed the Notre Dame cathedral after he bought the Catholic Church." Pops turned to face the side of Jack's head. "I suppose to you, Rome is just the headquarters of European education?"

Jack nodded.

"Yeah, well, when I was your age, it was the center of the entire Catholic world and led one billion people." Pops purposely let the conversation go stale at that point to get Jack engaged. It worked.

After a minute of listening to the electric hum of the transport, Jack decided on a question. "So, how did he get his start? How was he able to buy religion?"

That was the question Pops was looking for. "Well, he started as a life extension researcher, had a breakthrough, and extended the life of everyone on the planet. That led to a best-selling book. This, in turn, led to even more popularity, and it wasn't long before he was leading the scientific community. At this point, he gained access to nearly infinite investment funds. Once he was able to direct that, he showed the world what it would be like without the confines of religion. That act freed humanity from thousands of years of bondage. It empowered the individual and set the world free." Pops bit his lower lip and waited patiently for the next question.

"So what happened? Religion is gone, but we don't travel to the stars like in *Star Trek*... I don't even think we aspire to... I know I don't."

Pops grinned. "The short answer is that, well, nobody cares." Pops reflected for a minute. "Turns out that religion was more than just a system to maintain order and reinforce fear. Religion provided a moral compass, as it were. It gave people motivation, purpose, and a reason to strive for something. Regardless of what religious doctrine you held, it served to provide a sense of... worth. Without those fundamental truths that support the evolution of human nature, we got lazy, really lazy." Pops could tell Jack was connecting the dots and paused for his comments.

"So it's like Charlie's Indian tribe. When they were forced away from the land where they worshipped the mountains and the sky, the religion died."

Pops nodded. "Yeah, exactly."

Jack's interest was piqued, and he was enjoying the conversation. "So, the last philosopher bought Christianity. Were there other religions?"

Pops huffed. "Oh yes, many. Hinduism, Buddhism, Islam, Judaism, Mormonism, Scientology, and many others."

Jack immediately asked the obvious question. "What happened to all those? Did the last philosopher buy those too?"

Pops didn't have to think about the answer at all and immediately responded. "Yes and no. He bought all the American-based ones—Scientology and Mormonism. Some just quit caring, like the Jews. If there was one religion that suffered throughout history more than the others, it was Judaism. 'God's chosen people' eventually got tired of getting shit on and said, 'Screw this.' The Muslims met the worst fate. They were wiped out."

Jack interrupted. "Wiped out? What happened?"

Pops deviated from where he'd planned to go next to answer Jack's question. "Well, China happened. The Muslims had the most violent of the extremist religious advocates. Essentially, they said, 'Believe in what I believe in, or I will kill you.' A terrorist attack on the capital led to China's response of wiping them all out, all of them, even the peaceful ones. Sadly, having struggled with the extremist Muslims for decades and being unable to resolve the issues themselves, the Western countries of the world did nothing to stop China." Pops paused to let Jack absorb that history.

"As for the Hindus, they began to question the divinity of the cow, and the Buddhists simply vanished. It was believed they fled higher in the mountains of Tibet, but no one ever found any evidence of it," Pop said with pity in his voice.

The premise of religion perplexed Jack. At its core it all boiled down to one thing—faith. The trust in something unmeasurable, much less tangible, was beyond him. Imagining what it would have been like to have lived in a time where religion ruled, Jack began to feel sorry for those people who suffered under the ignorance of faith.

Pops broke into Jack's thoughts. "Don't go thinking you're better off, boy. You ain't. You just traded one god for another. This one you happen to wear on your face." Pops smirked.

Something about Pops's tone irritated Jack. "I don't worship my Eyebit!"

"Ha! Okay, Mister I-didn't-know-what-pizza-was," Pops retorted. "Seriously, think about it. You can't get through an entire day without it. It's nearly impossible to function in society without its presence. Even now! This very instant it's controlling your thoughts, as we speed mindlessly toward its temple." Pops crossed his arms and continued to face forward. "If that ain't worship, I don't know what is!" he said grumpily.

Tension was mounting, and that was the last thing Pops wanted to add to. "Are we there yet?" he joked after a couple of minutes of less-than-comfortable quiet. Jack didn't get it.

Pops took a swig of whiskey and coughed. Jack had not questioned the mindlessness of the Eyebit before. Until recently, it just was and had always been. Before, Pops was just stubborn and unwilling to change. Before, the Eyebit brought order, comfort, and convenience to his life. Before, Jack thought he was... free.

"So, I get how religion went away, but how did we get here with the Eyebits?" Jack asked.

"What do you mean? How did the masses come to accept it and give up their freedoms? Is that what you want to know?"

"Yes. That."

"Well, it depends on how far back you wanna go. Books gave way to newspapers, which led to magazines, comic books, movies, and television. Throw in the telephone somewhere back there, and here we are. Blame could technically lie with any of those." Pops paused a moment before continuing.

"Personally, though, I think it went downhill with the advent of smartphones and social media. Those specific inventions came without a feeling of any kind of threat. Which, in turn, groomed people to readily accept the next logical step, wearable technology. It started small—smart watches, rings, ankle bracelets, then bam! Here's your Eyebit. By then it was too late."

Jack thought about what Pops had said. It didn't surprise him that every form of media Pops listed he could find in the Eyebit world, easily. All of it was right there with just a few eye swipes.

———————

The mall approached in the distance, and Jack noticed Pops's body stiffen with discomfort. Pops eyed the structure with a slight tilt of his head. "It's bigger than I remember."

The transport stopped at the main entrance, the doors popped open, and the two men climbed out. Jack slid his eyes over to the park function, the transport doors closed, and it shot away.

Pops stood away from the main entrance, making fists with his hands and clenching his toes. The dull ache in his left arm returned, and he released the tension in his hands as he rubbed his shoulder. The two walked slowly toward the door, and this time Jack was the confident one and Pops was in tow.

Chapter Twenty-One

Eyebit Immersion 80%

Alerting Tech Support

Jack and Pops walked through the open doors. It didn't go well. Pops immediately ducked off to the right in fear. He kept his hat on, shielding his eyes from any Eyebits that might detect him. He rocked his body and crossed his arms nervously as he stared at the floor. Anxiety was about to overtake him.

It was obvious to Jack that something was wrong. He came to Pops's side and, without looking at him, simply asked, "What's wrong with you?"

On the cusp of a panic attack, Pops was overcome with fear and stuttered a response. "I... don't... know that I can do this."

Jack, still not understanding why they were there in the first place, attempted to bring him to the point. "Right, okay. Well, do what, exactly? I still don't know why we are here."

Pops was distracted. Jack observed his gaze and followed it. Pops's eyes shifted from person to person. To Jack, they were just people going about their business. "What's the problem?" Jack demanded, growing afraid there might be something physically wrong with Pops.

"What do you see, boy?" Pops asked as he rubbed his hands together nervously.

Jack looked around. "Stores, walls, people?" He wasn't sure what Pops was asking.

"Okay, right. I don't see the people you see. I see zombies! I see the Borg! All dressed the same! All wanting to hold me down and force one of those fucking things on my face! Ever searching to rob me of myself and make me one of them," Pops confessed nervously.

Jack couldn't help but let out a little laugh. Pops shot him a look. Understanding that Pops was serious, Jack let the smile fade away from his face. Thinking quickly, Jack took charge of the situation. "Okay, the Borg, huh? All right, what we do know about the Borg?"

Pops didn't respond.

"They won't bother you unless they perceive you as a threat... right?" Jack let that idea sink in as Pops began to come around. "So you'll have to be non-threatening. Don't do anything to get their attention, and they won't bother you. Now I'm going for a walk. Are you going to let me go alone?" Jack asked confidently. Pops emerged from his shell, and the two descended deeper into the hive.

They walked around for a bit, more window-shopping than anything. Of course, Jack saw more of the advertising than Pops did. To Pops, it was mostly bare walls, but now and then they passed a clothing store with a window display. Every so often a passerby would brush too closely to Pops, and he would jump defensively.

"You know, when I was your age, every other store was a clothing store. I only count five now," Pops said, attempting to distract himself.

Jack thought for a moment of Kyle's desire for regular clothes. "I never understood that," he said. "One set of clothes all day seems like such a wasted commitment."

"Yeah, yeah," Pops said. "Don't believe everything the Eyebit advertisers would have you believe. Clothes are an expression of personality. Someone's clothes say a lot about that person. What do you convey to people if your outfit changes throughout the day?" Realizing that he'd left a hole in his logic, Pops elaborated. "At least pick a theme. Western, punk, rocker, businessman... something." Pops waved his hand at a shopper walking by whose clothes were changing every few moments.

"See this hat, son?" Pops said as he tilted his head toward Jack. He was still careful not to make eye contact.

"Yeah, Pops, how could I not?" Jack said, referring to the enormity of it.

"Smart-ass! Anyway, I've had this hat since your father was your age," Pops said proudly.

"Smells like it," Jack said, laughing a little.

"Oooh, funny guy." Pops cracked a smile.

It didn't take long before the two happened upon a long line leading to the largest store in the mall. The Eyebit store was the size of a department store. It was located at the far west wing of the complex. The line to get into Bithaven extended almost to the center of the mall.

"What are all these Z-faces in line for?" Pops asked.

Jack knew, but if Pops didn't know, telling him wasn't going to go well. Jack thought for a moment and decided to make Pops pull the information out of him. "The transition prep," he said casually.

That wasn't enough for Pops.

"Transition to new hardware," Jack said.

"Oh yeah? Did they finally figure out how to make that thing wipe your ass for you?"

Disarmed, Jack let out a small laugh. "Ha! No, it's a soft piece that actually goes in your eye."

Pops stopped walking, reached out, and grabbed Jack's arm, careful not to face him as he spoke. "It's what that goes where?"

Jack sighed. "It's a soft bit that you put directly on your eye."

Pops was turning pale. "So, it's an Eyebit that touches your eyeball? Like a contact lens?" He sounded fearful. "How do you turn it off?"

It was too late for Jack to soften the blow. "You don't. They even encourage you to sleep in it."

Pops's mouth fell open, and his arm started to hurt. "That's just fucking stupid!" Looking back toward the line, Pops asked the next dreaded question. "When? When does this lemming march to the sea happen?"

Jack didn't have the answer Pops was looking for. "That's unknown. The company wants it to be a surprise, but they have said it will be before the new year. Claire doesn't even know, and she works there."

Pops stared at the line, and his thoughts drifted. As he pictured the future world filled with willing slaves, the lyrics to the song "The Sound of Silence" began to play in his head. As he thought of the people in the song worshipping a false god, Pops saw in his mind's eye the population of the world on its knees before a giant statue with white glowing eyes. He didn't realize it, but Pops had started to hum aloud.

Jack strained to hear. "What did you say?" he asked.

Pops snapped back to the present. "Oh, nothing. I was just reminded of a quote from Henry Adams." Pops drew a deep breath and shared the quote with Jack. "'Man has mounted science and is now run away with. I firmly believe that before many centuries more, science will be the master of men. The engines he will have invented will be beyond his strength to control. Someday science may have the existence of mankind in its power, and the human race commit suicide by blowing up the world. Not only shall we be able to cruise in space, but I'll be hanged if I see any reason why some future generation shouldn't walk off like a beetle with the world on its back, or give it another rotary motion so that every zone should receive in turn its due portion of heat and light.'"

Pops's words had little effect on Jack, mostly because he didn't fully understand their meaning. Pops had expected that. "See, boy, Adams wrote that during the American Civil War. He was referring to the technology arising out of the conflict. He was speculating that one day the technologies we create will rule us or destroy us." Pops paused for a moment to reflect on his interpretation of the quote. "Or that's how I take it, at least."

The two stood staring at the line for another moment before Jack spoke. "You know, before a few weeks ago I would have thought you were crazy, but then I had pizza, something that was right in front of me my entire life. Now, I'm worried you might be right... and that scares me!" Turning his attention back toward the line, Jack pointed and asked, "But how do you fight that?"

Pops gave a half smile. "Don't conform, ever! Never! Conform! Make the world deal with you. You've got to force it to think, to reason. You have the power, son, the same as me, the same as them. You just have to use it!" Feeling spunky, Pops said, "Here, I'll show you."

The two backed away from the line to the Eyebit store and headed for the food court. They filed in line at a fast-food place and patiently waited their turn. They didn't speak, but Jack's mind was racing. *Oh shit, oh shit, oh shit* was all he could think.

CHAPTER TWENTY-TWO

Eyebit Immersion 75%

EMERGENCY COMMUNICATION INCOMING...

"Welcome to McDonald's. Please engage your Eyebit, and place your order," the associate behind the counter stated to the brim of Pops's cowboy hat. Knowing Pops didn't have an Eyebit, Jack started to move into position to mediate for him. Pops jutted his arm out and stopped him.

"Ain't got no bit... It's being repaired. One small black coffee," Pops said as he kept his head down, hiding underneath his cowboy hat.

The associate was silent for a moment, trying to come to grips with what to do. "Ummm, sir, a small black coffee is ten dollars. If you do not have an Eyebit, how will you pay for your coffee?"

"With this!" Pops said as he slapped his hand down on the counter. When he withdrew it, there lay a ten-dollar bill.

The associate looked down but didn't touch it. "What's that?"

"Well, I'll give you a hint. It has a picture of Alexander Hamilton on it," Pops answered.

"Sir, I don't understand what Alexander Hamilton has to do with ten dollars, but if you want coffee, you need to get your Eyebit and come back."

Pops had him right where he wanted him. "I see. Get your manager for me, sonny."

Jack could only watch in worried fascination.

The associate swiped his eyes, and the manager appeared from the back of the store.

"What seems to be the trouble here?" the manager asked the associate, who answered with confusion in a hushed tone.

"This customer doesn't have an Eyebit and is trying to pay for his coffee with that." The associate gestured to the paper on the counter.

The manager mistakenly decided to push the issue. "Sir, this is a paperless location."

Pops was not dissuaded. "So you're refusing payment?" he asked, defiant.

"Sir, from where I'm standing, you have yet to present payment," the manager said.

Pops slapped his hand on the counter and reclaimed the ten-dollar bill, holding it directly in front of the manager. "It's right here, Z-face. Federally insured, mint printed, United States currency. It's a crime for you to refuse it."

Clearly, the manager had a fight on his hands. "I'm sorry, sir. What did you order?"

Pops, still holding the money, answered through clenched teeth. "Small. Black. Coffee."

The manager decided that a small coffee wasn't worth holding the line up and simply comped the coffee for Pops. "Okay, sir, no problem. I apologize for your wait. Here's your coffee."

Pops slapped the money back on the counter. As he and Jack walked away, they heard the manager talking with the associate. "Those older people sometimes get confused. If you encounter something like that again, just give it to them and show it as a senior citizen comp."

Looking back over his shoulder, Pops watched the manager examine the ten-dollar bill, shrug his shoulders, and put the money in his pocket.

"And that is bucking the system. Understand?" Pops said to Jack.

Jack didn't understand. "If the goal was to get free coffee, why didn't you just let me pay for it?"

"Sheesh, kid, the goal wasn't the coffee. The goal was to break social norms, the goal was to force these morons into the world, the goal was troublemaking." Leaving Jack in silence, Pops sipped his coffee. "Ahh, don't you ever go changing," he said as he looked at the cup affectionately.

Jack thought for a moment and then came up with the question Pops was hoping for. "So what does breaking social norms get you? Why do it?" Jack asked, cutting to the bitter core of Pops's entire personality.

"You mean besides free coffee?" Pops said with a smirk.

Jack furrowed his eyebrows. "I thought you said the coffee didn't matter?"

Pops bowed and shook his head. "Boy, if you don't start to read between the lines, these conversations are going to go in circles forever. It was a joke." Pops inhaled deeply. "Now look, simply put, when you break out of the mold that society puts you in, you can change the society. In essence, you make a difference. You can change the world. Ever hear of John P. Nobody?" Pops asked with all the seriousness he could muster.

Jack shook his head.

"Really?" Pops exclaimed. "The greatest, most respected, best all-around file clerk in history? Never in trouble a day in his life? Mr. Reliable? Ms. No-misadventures? Mrs. Normal? Do any of those names ring a bell?"

Of course, Jack hadn't heard of any of them.

"Exactly, 'cause they didn't do shit. Well, except exactly what society told them to."

Pops had made his point. With that description, Jack was able to visualize how Pops viewed the world, specifically the people in it. "Okay, so how do you do it? And I don't mean try to pay cash everywhere. How do I learn how to break the mold?"

Pops's smile was so broad that all his teeth were on full display. "And that, my boy, is the right question. Breaking social norms is a form of rebellion, and rebellion is... well... it's doing what you're not supposed to do." Pops continued to speak as the two slowly walked the corridors of the mall and surveyed its vendors of conformity.

Pops was faced with a conundrum; how does one teach rebellion? How does someone ignite the flame of passion and turn it into social change? Something that had always come naturally to him was now a foreign concept to his own flesh and blood. Thinking back on his own life, Pops tried to remember the events that had led him to now.

Ultimately it boiled down to one simple principle: he didn't like being told what to do. Not overly profound, but not something a born conformist could just accept. Fortunately for Pops, Jack was already breaking the mold. He just didn't realize it.

"Well, did you not realize you're doing it already?"

"I am?"

"Yes, sir!" Pops said confidently. "I hear that you're causing trouble for your teachers, and what did you think eating pizza and chicken wings ahead of schedule was?"

"I was just doing what I wanted to do."

"Here, here! Spoken like a true revolutionary! Careful. That kind of thinking and those kinds of actions lead to independence," Pops said sarcastically as the two happened again upon the end of the line leading into the Eyebits store.

Pops stood staring in silence for a moment as an idea formulated in his head. Looking farther down the corridor, Pops spied an exit halfway up the line off to the left. Leaning over toward Jack, Pops all but whispered, "Are you able to have the transport pick us up at any exit?"

"Yes, why?"

Pops rubbed his hands together. "An act of rebellion. Like Jeess-sussss, I am going to lay hands on the sick and dying and give them new life!" Pops's voice had changed to mimic that of a Southern Baptist preacher. Jack, of course, didn't get the reference. Pops had his hands raised to the sky as if he could grab something from the heavens and bring it to the earth. "Better call the transport, son. We're gonna be leaving very soon."

Jack swiped his eyes and had the transport routed to their exit. "Thirty seconds."

With his grandson standing by his side, Pops surveyed the line. The sick and dying didn't move. They just stood like sentinels lost in their sweet oblivion, waiting. Being Eyebit-less, Pops was able to stand next to the last person in line without being detected. With the stealth of a jungle cat, he reached up and disengaged the Eyebit of the last person in line.

Flash! The person's knees buckled, and they began to stumble. Pops didn't stop. Flash! The next person in line didn't fall over but instead let out a yelp, which made Pops chuckle. Next. Flash! The third person Pops disengaged instantly threw up on the person standing in front of them. Next. The fourth person began to weep and wail.

Pops still didn't stop. With each new release he put one foot in front of the other in a kind of march, slightly swaying his hips and jiggling his shoulders. He was dancing, if only to the music in his head. Pops didn't realize it, but Jack was able to hear him humming.

As they neared the end of the line at the exit intersection, Pops wasn't trying to hide it anymore. Caught up in the moment, he was singing and dancing as he "healed the sick and dying."

Jack should have been mortified, but he wasn't. Jack should have stopped Pops, but he didn't. Jack should have tried to help those people put their Eyebits back on, but he couldn't. As he and the dancing, singing, madman hustled toward the waiting transport, Jack took one last look back at the pile of sniveling, wailing, confused, "healed" people.

"Don't feel bad for them. They're the lucky ones," Pops said as they burst through the exit doors. "Whooo, that was fun. Thank you for bringing me here and helping me face that fear."

Jack was dumbfounded. "Umm, sure." Composing himself for a moment and recalling the times Pops had called him a smart-ass, Jack jested, "So much for not appearing threatening to the Borg, huh?"

Pops laughed. "Yeah, right, no kidding. Whoops." Taking a moment to bask in the sunlight, Pops spied a drone making its way toward the mall. "See, we didn't threaten them that much. This one isn't attacking." Pops scoffed as a young man about Jack's age neared them. "Gah, that thing is just sooo tacky," Pops exclaimed.

Jack had picked up on Pops's multiple comments about the way the Eyebit looked and decided to ask him about it. "What thing? The Eyebit? All that guy has on is that and his display suit."

Pops looked at Jack, confused. "Right, but how do you get past the Eyebit on his face when you talk to him?"

Jack thought about it for a second. "Well, I don't see it."

Pops was still confused. "You don't see it? Do you mean that you've gotten used to it and ignore it? Or do you mean you physically don't see it?"

Jack had to remind himself that Pops had never worn an Eyebit, so he couldn't have known.

Pops grabbed the young man who was about to pass them and turned his shoulders so that he was facing Jack. Pops pointed to the stranger's Eyebit and asked Jack directly, "Do you see this thing on his face or not?"

"Hello, Jack, I see that you are interested in…" The stranger's and Jack's Eyebits connected and selected commonalities.

"Shut up, Z-face. Nobody's talking to you," Pops said quickly. "Jack, do you see his Eyebit? Or is it invisible to you?"

Jack looked beyond the profile display of Karl and their shared interests. All he saw was a face, nothing else. "I don't see anything. It's invisible."

Pops squinted and brought his hand to his chin. "Interesting." Breaking away from his thoughts, Pops grabbed Karl's shoulder and steered him away from Jack. "The hive's calling. Be gone with you."

The transport had been waiting this entire time, and the two climbed inside. The doors closed, and they were off with a flash and a streak.

As the two sped away from the mall, Pops was exhilarated. He had faced down a fear, dove into the mouth of the devil, and emerged unscathed. He likened his feeling to that of an old-time bank robber on the getaway.

His exuberance was further reinforced as he looked back at the shrinking mall and the swarm of para-medical-drones called there, no doubt, in response to the mass disengagement... Or better yet, to an act of techno-terrorism. The feelings swelled, and he could no longer contain his excitement.

"*Whooo!* That's living, boy! That's what it's all about."

Pops thought of how to best convey his zest for the experience of life to Jack, but how does one describe the color red to the blind? To Jack, what just happened was a grumpy old man at the mall. If Pops was going to ignite a fire, he would have to find a common interest and encourage it.

Silence had momentarily fallen over the transport when Pops was struck with an idea. "You got a girlfriend?" he asked bluntly, with zero tact.

Jack was taken aback. "Um, well... ummm, no."

"No? Don't want one or can't get one?" Pops put on a faux-surprised tone and said, "Doesn't the Eyebit select someone for you?"

"It will, but I haven't been all that interested in its choices," Jack said, a twinge of disappointment in his voice.

"That doesn't surprise me. You've been wearing your Eyebit less and less, and your natural hormone levels are returning to normal." Pops paused for a moment then said, "So let me ask it a different way. You got your eye on anybody?"

Jack felt his stomach drop. He couldn't answer, but Pops, in his wisdom, knew that silence was just as good an answer as words.

"I see," Pops said. "Let me guess. You have nothing in common with her, but she is the most beautiful thing you've ever seen."

Jack was flabbergasted and looked in Pops's general direction with wide-eyed amazement. "How did you know that?"

Pops shook his head. "Well, if the Eyebit searches for commonalities in people and isn't able to find any to get you an introduction, then ergo, you have nothing in common." That was the *in* Pops was looking for. "How's that choice working out for you?" he asked, leading Jack down the path of self-awakening.

"What choice?"

"The choice that drives the entire human race, to do something or to not do something. Are you going to go after this girl or are you not? Are you going to follow your heart or are you going to conform?"

Jack knew what he wanted. "I want to go after her."

Pops smiled. "All right. Let's work on that then."

CHAPTER TWENTY-THREE

Eyebit Immersion 70%

ARE YOU OKAY? PLEASE CONNECT.

"But not right this red-hot second. There are some things I need to take care of first," Pops said as he started to look around his garage.

"Um, okay. Can't you just tell me?" Jack asked.

"No. No, I can't. Not everything you want in life is at your fingertips. Not anything worth having, anyway! Despite what that stupid thing on your face tells you, getting the girl you want is something you have to work at. And frankly, right now, boy, you ain't ready." Pops paused a moment before asking a semi-hurtful question. "Let's say you were suddenly faced with an opportunity to talk to her, *without* your Eyebit. What would you do?"

Jack didn't have an answer.

"Uh-huh, that's what I thought. You're gonna need some personality skills if you want to pull this off, 'cause that Eyebit ain't gonna help your ass."

"Okay, fine. Well, what do I do while I'm waiting?"

"Jesus, son, I don't know. Here, research this," Pops said as he took a plaque off the wall and handed it to Jack.

"What's RRF stand for?"

Pops rolled his eyes. "That's why I said research it. It'll do you good anyway. I can't believe they didn't teach you this in school."

———————————

The transport sliced through the early evening air, speeding toward its destination.

"Theon, I'm looking for something," Jack announced aloud, summoning the search-engine program.

"Hello, Jack. What can I help you discover today?" the computer simulation asked.

"Display everything you have on RRF," Jack commanded.

Theon turned to the wall of scrolls that had appeared behind him and began tossing out scrolls onto the floor.

RRF: Recruitment Video

RRF: How to dismantle religion

RRF: Jesus Christ, conman: water to water, not wine

RRF: The Muslim Extinction

RRF: Wolfe Corp treats FGM (Female Genital Mutilation) for free

RRF: Buddhists Disappear

RRF: Midnight interview with the devil (Dr. Wolfe)

RRF: Dinosaurs, giants, and unicorns missed the ark... oops

RRF: The last Jew

RRF: Get to know the "saint" of atheism, Madelene Murray O'Hare

RRF: From a Baptist church into a porn and liquor store

RRF: Understanding and combating religious propaganda

RRF: Church Demolitions: 100 churches simultaneously destroyed

RRF: Dr. Wolfe attempts to buy Notre Dame

RRF: Dr. Wolfe attempts to buy Westminster Abby

RRF: Mormons and debunking Joseph Smith

RRF: Wolfe Corp loses battle to relocate all cemeteries

RRF: Understanding that L. Ron Hubbard was a science-fiction writer

RRF: What happens when you believe in religion: the Waco, Texas disaster

RRF: Why God hates you

RRF: Mormons have no right to call Scientologists crazy

RRF: Using the Bible against Christians: a tutorial

RRF: Good Guy Satan

RRF: Wolfe Corp attempts to vaccinate against religion

RRF: Wolfe Corp demolishes the Wailing Wall

RRF: Assassination attempt on Dr. Wolfe

RRF: Wolfe Corp develops revolutionary interface, wearable technology

RRF: Why God is a shitty parent

RRF: Dr. Wolfe uses AI to render an image of Muhammad

RRF: The taking of the Vatican

As Jack skimmed the titles, he was convinced they were enough to convey what the Religion Resistance Forces had been. He now had a better idea of what all the old buildings that were surrounded by cemeteries once stood for. Feeling the twinge of impatience, he skipped to the last video and activated its play function.

Jack's Eyebit faded to black. When the picture returned, a much older Dr. Wolfe addressed the audience of virtual viewers.

"Good day, friends. Everything that follows is a record of the victory of science and reason over religion and fear," Dr. Wolfe said as his image faded away.

When the image returned, Dr. Wolfe was facing the camera, standing behind a podium with the letters RRF projected on the wall behind him. The image of him there was not as aged as when the video started, but he was surely fifteen years older than the previous videos Jack had watched. It didn't take long for Jack to realize that Dr. Wolfe was delivering a motivational speech to a large group of people, a very large group of people.

"Good morning. In a few hours we will be engaged in the largest gathering of nonbelievers in the history of the world. Make no mistake about our mission. We are here to demand the immediate and unconditional surrender of the country known as Vatican City. Our cause is unique in many ways. Never before has a group of culturally diverse people this large put aside all their differences and wholeheartedly embraced something truly better. The time of religion is over! We've been oppressed and silent for too long! No longer are we going to cower in the shadows.

"As members of the Religion Resistance Force, you are tasked with being above those you oppose. Let me be clear. They have weapons... You do not. They employ ignorance... We do not. Their judgment and logic are clouded and flawed. Ours is resolute. They are weak! *We! Are! Strong!*"

The Eyebit screen faded to black, but Wolfe's voice still narrated the images on the screen. A topographical map of Vatican City was divided by colors into four sections, north, south, east, and west.

"The circle will encompass the entire city as we move inward. The lines will become more condensed and reinforced. As we descend on Saint Peter's Square, the remaining Swiss Guard will be the most intense. It is important to remember that they view their jobs as a calling. They will defend the square violently, if necessary," the voiceover of Dr. Wolfe stated as the video zoomed in on the center of the map. When the map faded away, an older Dr. Wolfe stood before a simple black background. "We went in prepared for the worst. What we found was nothing like what we expected."

The next scene was a shaking news camera narrated by a field reporter capturing the action as it unfolded. "We're here reporting live on the northern front alongside Captain Rivers." The camera cut to a thin man with black hair. "So far, the RRF has met with little resistance. It is expected to intensify toward the center, but we are already starting to combine with the eastern and western fronts."

The next scene was of two captains conversing as the reporter attempted to relay the information to the audience.

"They seem apprehensive," the reporter said as he grasped his earpiece. "Okay, okay, we're continuing forward. We have met no resistance, and there was worry of an ambush." The reporter's eyes darted back and forth as he pressed the earpiece farther into his ear. "Okay, the four corner scouts are reporting back... This can't be right, can it?" the reporter asked as he broke eye contact with the cameraman. "Okay, we are being informed that the city is abandoned."

The camera zoomed out, and Jack watched in anticipation as the two captains raised their arms and signaled the army to march forward. The camera jostled as the reporter and cameraman walked at a light sprint, keeping pace with the army. The reporter spoke into the microphone, constantly relaying the events as they unfolded to the audience.

"We're converging on Saint Peter's Square. So far, we haven't seen a single member of the church," the reporter gasped, short of breath.

Jack watched in wide-eyed amazement as the armies marched across the square and burst through the doors of the church. The captains of the four fronts personally broke down the doors to the throne room. The reporter rushed in after them, the camera leveled and focused on the center of the room.

Seated on an ornate throne in the middle of the room was an old man wearing a disgusted and bitter look on his face. The four captains and the reporter approached him with a good deal of caution. The man didn't make eye contact with them, nor did he respond to their questions.

Without verbal confirmation, one of the captains held a device to the old man's eye. The captain examined the results and stated to the camera, "It's him." At almost the same moment, another member of the RRF reported to a captain, "It's all clear, sir."

The camera turned to the crowded army standing outside the doors. There was a stir among them, and they divided down the middle to allow Dr. Wolfe passage. For this, the pope looked up. Dr. Wolfe walked into the room as if he owned it, not as if he'd purchased it, and as if he'd been victorious in battle.

He graciously approached the pope and spoke as if he were conducting a business trade. "I am here to negotiate terms of surrender."

The Pope didn't stand but looked him in the eye. "You've already taken it all! This house is empty." He spoke in a raspy voice as if he had been crying.

The screen faded out as the transport pulled into the driveway of Jack's home. Jack sat in the dark of the unengaged transport for a moment, absorbing the history he had just witnessed. The world he lived in now was so calm, peaceful, and serene. Orderly... Dull.

Was what he watched real? Armies, surrender, and excitement. That couldn't have been real life. As Jack sat pondering what it would have meant to be young during that time, he suddenly understood his grandfather just a little bit better. *No wonder Pops hates living now,* Jack thought to himself as he walked in the front door.

When Jack entered the house, he found Kyle sitting on the couch, lost in the trance of the Eyebit world. "Kyle," Jack said aloud, but Kyle didn't answer. Realizing that he wasn't connected, Jack put on his Eyebit.

Almost immediately after the flash, Kyle responded. "Oh, Jack. Hi, son. I didn't see you standing there."

"I said you're... Never mind," Jack said as he cut right to the conversation. "You're old. What was the world like with religion in it?" Jack asked, unaware of how rude he was being.

Kyle furrowed his brow and shot Jack a look of disgust. "I'm not that old, jackass." After a moment of silence, Kyle continued. "Son, it's not polite to say someone is old," Kyle said as only a disapproving parent could. "Anyway, I don't know. There was no religion in the world by the time I was old enough to remember. You should ask Pops. I'm sure he remembers." Kyle paused. "Seems like he was a member of a group that campaigned for ending it."

Jack pondered a moment. "What group? One like the RRF, the Religion Resistance Force?"

Kyle's eyes sparked with recognition. "Yeah! That's it, the RRF! Wow, I haven't heard that in a long time. Not since I was a kid." Kyle breathed deeply as he reminisced on his own childhood. "Dad always invited his buddies to our house, and they would talk for hours and hours."

Jack couldn't believe what he was hearing. "You're telling me that Pops was in the RRF? He was there when the pope surrendered? He knew Dr. Wolfe?"

Kyle gave him a confused look. "Well, son, I don't know all that. I just remember him being involved somehow," Kyle answered, bewildered.

Jack was befuddled. "How have I not heard about this before?"

Kyle gave Jack his best disapproving dad look. "Well, son, did you *really* care?"

That comment hit home with Jack, because the truth was, he hadn't. "I have to go ask Pops about this. Why didn't he tell me?" Jack said as he turned to head back toward the transport.

"Um, not tonight you don't," Kyle called back to Jack.

"Why not?" Jack asked without turning to face his father.

"'Cause it's late, and I said."

Jack was resolved. "I'm going!" he said in defiance.

Kyle, irritated, said, "I've locked it down. No. You're. Not."

Jack knew that there was nothing he could do to activate the transport once it was locked down. Only a person with ownership authority could activate it, and Jack didn't have it. Jack didn't say anything to his father as he passed him on the way to his bedroom.

Alone in his room, filled with teenage angst and with no other outlet, Jack decided to drive. Calling for Richard, Jack suddenly found himself sitting behind the wheel of an antique sports car. The engine was humming, and Jack gripped the wheel so tight he could feel the vibrations the engine was putting off.

"Where we going?" Richard asked.

"Somewhere new."

As Jack ripped through the Italian countryside in what Richard called a Ferrari, he was consumed with the thought of what it must have been like before the world became what it was. Realizing that the driving program probably predated the Reason Revolution, Jack asked, "Richard, can we get to Vatican City from here?"

Richard's response excited Jack as he shifted to a high gear. "That-away," Richard said as he pointed to the right side of a fork in the road.

Pops stood over his workbench fiddling with a derelict but functioning recording device. Once satisfied with his results, he plunged it into a backpack that already held a set of solid black clothes and an old-fashioned QWERTY keyboard.

Donning his cowboy hat, Pops slung on his backpack, pushed his bicycle out of the garage, and closed it behind him. As he peddled into the night, he was gleeful with anticipation for what he had planned. Halfway through his trip, he was struck with a thought that brought an even bigger smile to his face. *I haven't had this much fun in years.*

Chapter Twenty-Four

Eyebit Immersion 65%

Let us help you. We love you.

Just when Jack had tired of doing donuts in Saint Peter's Square, he heard a strange tapping on his bedroom window. He sat on his bed for a moment to see if the noise repeated itself. It did. He muted his audio feed. The noise came again. This time he jumped up and switched off his Eyebit.

He approached the window with a great deal of caution. His heart raced as he reached out and pinched the curtain with his first two fingers. He pulled it open as he simultaneously jumped back and let out a small yelp. Before the curtain fell back in place, Jack caught a glimpse of Pops's cowboy hat and a broad smile.

"Pops?" Jack exclaimed. He pressed as close to the window as he could. "What are you doing here?"

Pops brought his index finger to his lips. "Shh, shh, shh. Be quiet," he said, trying to calm Jack down.

"What are you doing here?" Jack asked again in a hushed tone.

"Let me in." Pops looked around nervously.

Jack looked confused. "The front door is locked. Kyle will know if I open it."

Pops shook his head. "No, open the window."

Jack furrowed his eyebrows. "I can't without my Eyebit, and Kyle will know."

Pops rolled his eyes. "No, boy, just do it manually." Pops raised his arm and pressed his index finger against the windowpane, pointing to a metal latch. Jack reached up and turned the lever. Once done, Pops pressed his hands against the window, and to Jack's surprise, it raised with little effort.

Pops thrust a hand through the opening. "Help me," he commanded Jack, who found himself struggling to pull Pops in the window. "Jesus, son, put your back into it." Pops let out a slight moan as his torso dragged across the window frame.

Pops hit the floor with a dead thud. Any harder and he would have shaken the room. "Jesus, boy, if you're gonna go against the world and get that girl, we're gonna have to teach you how to do that stealthily. I was in and out of your grandma's room without making a sound."

Jack helped Pops to his feet, still whispering as he asked again, "What are you doing here?"

Pops was looking around. "This your room?" He sounded confused. "Kinda boring." Jack was not dissuaded and only stared at Pops. "Right, right, right, okay," Pops said as he took his backpack off. "I need your help."

Jack was surprised to hear that. "You need *my* help?"

"Yes, and stop repeating every question you hear. It's annoying," Pops said as he threw his backpack on Jack's bed. One by one he pulled out the contents. Pops handed the black clothes to Jack as he discreetly slipped the recording device into his pocket. "Here. You'll need these."

Once the contents were displayed on the bed, Pops unfolded a thick sheet of paper. "Okay, this is a map." Jack took a moment to touch the paper. He was surprised to feel how slick and smooth it was.

Pops let him do that for a moment before the smart-ass took over. "Okay, Lenny... that's enough," Pops said, referencing *Of Mice and Men*, which Jack didn't get. It came as no surprise when he had to physically remove Jack's hand from the map.

"So, here's the deal. There's a part I need. The car won't run without it. I finally tracked one to this location," Pops said as he pointed at the map. "Problem is, this guy won't trade with me. Dill-hole won't even acknowledge me because I don't wear an Eyebit."

Jack piped up. "So you want me to talk to him for you?"

Pops snorted. "Hell no! Screw that guy! We're gonna steal it. I need you to drive me."

The two men stood in the dark, in front of the transport.

"Now what? I told you Kyle locked it down for the night," Jack said.

Pops huffed. "Oh, ye of little... Well, I guess in your case that would be... no faith." Pops held up a computer keyboard and patted it. "All right, boy, we got thirty seconds from the time you open the door till it alerts your dad someone is messing with his ride."

Jack watched as Pops crouched beside the door.

"Ok, boy.... Now!"

Jack didn't react. He only stood there, waiting, with no intention of opening the door. Pops, expecting the door to open, lunged at it. He slammed into the side of the transport with such force it rocked from side to side. "Eeeh... Good one!" Pops said with a slight chuckle. "Okay, seriously this time."

Jack swiped his eye, and the door popped open. Pops jumped into the driver's seat with his hand at the ready. Jack observed that the tip end of the keyboard cord had a "Pops-made" adapter fitted at the end of it.

Pops fiddled with the dash for a moment before he found the corresponding slot and plugged it in. The transport sprang to life. Across the inside of the windshield scrolled the words, ***Welcome, Technician. You are now in diagnostic mode.***

"Hot damn!" Pops exclaimed as he clapped his hands together. "Okay, boy! You're up. Engage your Eyebit, and don't freaking look at me," Pops commanded and scooted over to the passenger side.

Jack engaged his Eyebit and slipped in on the driver's side. "Okay, now what?"

"Now this stupid contraption thinks it's being serviced," Pops said with a smile and a nod. "Which means all the alerts are suspended."

Jack was still unsure what the implications of this were.

Pops picked up on his lack of understanding. "Which means there are no official records being made." A long pause indicated to Pops that Jack still wasn't making the leap. "Which means... we can go anywhere, and nobody will know."

Once it dawned on him, Jack was still concerned. "What if Kyle looks out the window?"

Pops smiled. "Yeah... Well, you've got a choice here. Find out what I've got in store, or go back inside and follow the rules. Feel that twist in your stomach when you think about getting caught? Feel that quickened thud in your chest? Are your fingers tingly?"

Jack thought for a moment; he felt all those things and more. "Yeah, I do." He swallowed.

"Feels good, doesn't it? Like an electricity running through you?"

"Yes. It. Does," Jack answered, hinging each word on a breath.

"You're not dead after all! Let's go."

CHAPTER TWENTY-FIVE

Eyebit Immersion 62%

PLEASE LET US MAKE YOU FEEL BETTER.

As the two rode to what Pops called a "junkyard," he assured Jack of how easy it was nowadays to simply take what you wanted. "Back in my day, they used to have what was called junkyard dogs, vicious animals trained to chase a man down and tear him to shreds."

Jack had never seen a violent dog. In Jack's world, they were all calm and controlled, mostly by the Petbits. Sure, his dog barked, but he never snapped at him or hurt him.

"See this?" Pops said as he lifted his pant leg, revealing a calf muscle with scarred puncture wounds in it. "I got this breakin' up a dog fight."

Drifting back into an ancient memory, Pops paused a moment and cast his eyes downward. "Lucy... She was a good dog, just trying to protect a little boy." Pops blocked the memory out and returned himself to the present. "Anyway, vicious animals, junkyard dogs were. They would usually only respond to one command, and of course, you never knew what it was." Pops spent the rest of the ride recounting the exploits of junkyard dogs. He embellished the details, especially of the ones he'd run from.

The transport glided to a stop, and Pops pulled out the map and began to explain the layout to Jack as he disengaged his Eyebit. "Okay, the part we need is here," Pops said as he pointed to an *X* in the center of the map. "It's located inside the engine housing of the car. Now, to get to it, we're gonna have to follow this path." Pops traced a roundabout way with his finger.

Jack was silent for a moment as he studied the map. "And you know all this, how?"

Pops cocked a smile. "Don't worry about the how, boy. Worry about the now."

Jack rolled his eyes. "Okay, whatever."

"That's the spirit! Let's go!" Pops said as he jubilantly hopped out of the transport.

The two men stood examining the fence. "You know, there was once a time when fences were over six feet tall and covered in something called barbed wire," Pops said as he threw a leg over the three-foot fence topped with no additional security measures. Jack copied the behavior.

Pops spotted his opportunity. "Whoa, whoa, whoa, hold on a sec, son." Pops put his hands on Jack's shoulders. "Turn around. I think you caught your drawers on the fence." Keeping one hand on Jack's shoulder, Pops squeezed it just hard enough to keep Jack from feeling Pops clip the tiny MP3 player on his belt. At the same time, he pressed the play button, which started a twenty-five-minute countdown.

As the two men traversed the graveyard of cars, Pops felt compelled to share his feelings on the matter. "You know, these places always saddened me... So much death and dis-*car*-dment." Pops let out a sigh as if he were releasing some great weight that was dragging down his soul. "Every one of these cars has a story to tell. Some happy, some sad... So many great adventures left to rust and decay. See that one?" Pops pointed to an old Jeep with oversized tires and a winch on the front. "That one spent a lot of time off-road, in nature. There's still mud spray on it."

The two men walked on. "That one is a family station wagon." Pops drew nearer to the vehicle and reached inside to feel the seats. "Yep, those indentions are from a child seat."

Moving on, Pops spied a convertible. He didn't speak, just let the movie of his mind play. He remembered an earlier time when his wife was alive and Kyle was a small child. They were driving up the California coast, with the top down. "A million years ago," Pops muttered to himself.

"What?" Jack asked, breaking into Pops's memory.

"Huh? What?"

"I said, what's that long one?" Jack pointed to a limousine.

"Oh, right," Pops said as he pulled his gaze away from the convertible. "That's a limo. It's what people with money used to be driven around in. They had bars and TVs in them. It was a luxury thing." Pops scoffed. "That was, of course, before the world of transports. Imagine it: going somewhere in a car and having to be involved in what was going on around you."

Jack raised his eyebrows and shook his head. He had, after all, been learning how to drive and found Pops's comments somewhat relatable. Succumbing to the impatience only a young man understood,

Jack disregarded Pops's comments about how things used to be and endeavored to press on.

"Which way is the car we're looking for?" he asked.

Pops easily pulled himself away from the limo and directed them onward. As part of his plan for the evening, Pops purposefully misled Jack around the junkyard in different ways. Being careful not to double back for fear Jack would recognize a landmark, he was able to extend their trek around the lot for twenty minutes.

"There she is," Pops said as he pointed to a Mustang that, to Jack, looked an awful lot like the one in the garage. But this one was missing a lot of stuff—both doors, a roof, and all four wheels. "Okay, keep a lookout, just in case," Pops said as he lifted the hood, which promptly fell off. "Shit! That was loud." Pops scoffed and hurried his movements. "Ahh, yes! Pay dirt! Here, hold this." He handed an unrecognizable car part to Jack.

"Great. Let's go!" Jack said in earnest.

"Wait!" Pops commanded. "We need to grab some other things."

"What? Why?"

Pops didn't look at Jack, just kept digging and handing Jack parts. "'Cause, I came round trying to make a deal for that part. If it is the *only* thing that disappears, then they will have a good place to start looking for where it went."

After just a moment of silence, Pops's head slowly peered up from the engine bay. He addressed Jack without looking at him. "Did you hear that?"

"Hear what?"

"Shhh!" Pops jerked his arm up, putting his index finger to his lips.

A moment later, they both heard it. A low, throaty, nonhuman growl.

"Oooh, you're a big girl, ain't ya," Pops said, still not looking at Jack. His eyes were fixed on the source of the noise, which Jack couldn't see.

"What is it?" Jack whispered.

"It's a dog! A really big dog," Pops whispered.

Jack's eyes widened. "I thought you said they weren't used for this anymore."

Pops didn't look at Jack. "Okay, don't move! Here's the deal. She can't chase us both. You're faster and have a better chance of making it. Take this." He handed the last car part to Jack without taking his eyes off the dog. "We got what we came for. Now we have to get out."

The growls were growing louder, and Pops wasn't speaking above a whisper. "The transport is in a straight line, that way," Pops said as he pointed directly behind Jack. "Now, I'm gonna start moving and try to distract her while you make a break for it. Wait for my signal."

─────────────

Jack had never run so hard in his life. He knew Pops had given him the signal, but his distraction plan hadn't worked. The dog was right on his heels. The barking got louder and louder; the faster Jack ran, the closer the dog got. His mind went blank—no thoughts, no planning, no concerns for tomorrow, no fear of getting into trouble with whoever might care. He just ran.

Adrenaline flowed, his eyes dilated, his nostrils flared, and he ran for his very survival. He knew the dog was snapping at his heels when he spotted the fence and the transport just beyond. He knew the dog wouldn't pass the fence, or at least he hoped so. With no time to think, Jack threw every bit of energy into his legs and sailed over the fence.

Jack hit the ground and skidded to a stop on his chest. Not knowing if he was still being pursued, he began to scramble to his feet but then felt hands on his shoulders. Helping him to his feet, Pops began to check Jack for wounds. In so doing he managed to stop and unclip the tiny MP3 player that had been barking.

Jack looked at Pops in complete surprise. "How did you—" Jack was interrupted by his own efforts to catch his breath.

"Get here before you?" Pops completed his sentence as Jack nodded, doubling over.

"You didn't run in the line I told you to. You led that dog on one hell of a chase! And damn, son! The way you jumped that fence, you looked like Superman flying through the air." Pops beamed.

"Who?" Jack asked between gasps.

Pops rolled his eyes. "Never mind. The point is when most people jump, they try to keep their legs under them, but not you! That was some good jumpin', boy!"

Looking back at the fence, Jack had the clarity to notice the dog that had been chasing him wasn't there at the edge of the fence where he expected it to be. "Where's the dog?" he asked as he panted, trying to catch his breath.

"Oh, ummm, she done run off. Yeah. Yes, yes, they usually retreat back into the yard once they chased off whoever," Pops said, hoping he sounded convincing.

With adrenaline still in his veins, Jack's hands and legs were shaking.

"Come on, son, you gotta burn that shit off or it's gonna keep you up all night." Pops looked around and thought for a moment. "How would you like to build some muscle mass in your upper body?" he asked excitedly.

"Umm, okay, like where? A gym or something?" Jack looked around.

"Hmph, yeah, the gym is everywhere. Just take in your surroundings. Back in my day, I worked out with rocks! I didn't have no barbells or Eyebit fitness programs."

Jack gave Pops a deadpan stare. "Okay, whatever! What do I do first?"

Pops smiled. "Okay, grab that metal pole, and stand in front of that tire. Now raise that pole above your head and swing it down into the tire, hard. As you do it, tighten your stomach muscles." As Jack slammed the pole into the tire, he felt his muscles tighten, and his hands and legs weren't shaking anymore.

"Yeah, good. Just like you're chopping firewood." Pops showed Jack workout exercises for the better part of an hour. Nearing the end, Pops could tell Jack's energies were spent. "Come on, son. I need you to take me home," Pops said as the two turned toward the transport.

"How you feeling?" Pops asked as he slapped a hand on Jack's shoulder.

"Tired" was all Jack said.

"Yeah? Good. Now, tomorrow you're gonna be sore in places you didn't know you had, but trust me, it'll be a good sore."

Jack was still breathing deeply as Pops tapped away on the keyboard. Pops let out a sigh as he raised his leg and kicked the dash. "Piece o' junk!" he exclaimed as the car came to life. "Okay, away we go! Yeehaw!" Pops let out a shout as the transport slinked along its predetermined path.

The silence the two men shared was brief before Jack asked, "So what happens next?"

Pops was unable to resist the to urge to be a smart-ass. "Well, we arrive at my house, and I go inside."

Jack shook his head and faked a laugh. "No, what happens next with Charlie?"

Pops feigned surprise. "Oh, you're still interested in that, are ya? Well, all right, where did we leave off?" Pops scratched his head.

"Charlie was being tempted to move to the city to make money," Jack answered quickly.

"Oh right, right. Okay, so they did move to the city..."

Chapter Twenty-Six

Tall Tales with Pops

The Man: Chapter 3

Charlie and Wilds had been living in the city for many months now. The homestead had been put on hold while Charlie pursued his career, as it was coming to be called in America. He didn't sell the land. Even though the law said it was his to sell, Charlie still believed he was a guest on it.

Maybe that was the root of his desire for the city. He had given his horse on temporary loan to a horse and buggy company. There was a strict understanding, in writing, that the horse still belonged to Charlie, and he could claim him anytime. With his other life temporarily paused, Charlie worked to provide their every heart's wish for himself and Wilds.

They had left the homestead at the onset of fall when the leaves were changing. There were no leaves in the city. Wilds never felt right about the move, but out of respect for Charlie, she indulged him in his explorations.

Charlie had been engaged in services with a new financial institution under the leadership of one J. P. Morgan. Morgan was a banker, a powerful one at that, who demanded the absolute best of his employees. Charlie was compensated extremely well for the work he performed. The more he worked, the more he made. The math was simple.

Winter in the city was not like winter in the country. Despite the snow and the cold, the life of the city trudged on. The heat generated by the city itself seemed to soften the impact the snow had. The market didn't stop, so Charlie didn't stop.

At first, it was very difficult for his body to adjust to the ability to work past sunset. In the country, farming meant when the sun rose, you rose; when it set, you set. Gaslight and the newfangled electric light, funded by Mr. Morgan, meant that someone could work well into the night hours.

It was often well after dark before Charlie returned home to Wilds. She was usually already in bed. She had told him once to rouse her. Sometimes he did. Sometimes he didn't.

Wilds wasn't made for the city; she hated it. She had taken to spending most of her days in the park. She despised the park, the white man's attempt to control nature. Something they created to make themselves feel better about murdering the gods of her people. Planned, scaled, selected plant life, approved animals, and visitation hours.

Unfortunately, if she wanted to be remotely close to any semblance of country, this was all she had. So, she endured. She sat and basked in the falsehoods of manufactured nature. She did her best to ignore the wayward sidelong glances of people who still feared and hated the

Indian. When the hours expired at the park, Wilds wandered home to an empty apartment and waited for Charlie to return. Sometimes she would cook for herself, sometimes she would have food prepared and bring it home, and sometimes, she just didn't eat. This was her life now.

As winter had given way to the spring, Charlie had taken to walking to work in the mornings. He had always enjoyed being outdoors. Despite the city air being different, he still breathed deeply and enjoyed his mornings. His body had mostly adjusted to artificial light, but not completely. He still strained to read after the sun went down.

Longer days meant that he could work later into the evening. Charlie didn't walk home after dark much, as the city was still dangerous and he had money in his pockets, which made him a target. Spring was upon the city, after all, and with that added warmth, the poverty-stricken and desperate spilled into the streets. Charlie found the beggars the most annoying. *They just sit there. Find employment, for Christ's sake,* Charlie thought as he looked down his nose at them every day.

Charlie took the same path to work daily. Despite the variety of beggars, Charlie never gave charity. Most of the time they got enough charity from others to allow them to move to another section of town. Charlie figured that a beggar's strategy was to present a new face every so often to help passersby be more open to paying them to go away. It seemed to work. Charlie had taken notice that about every other week or so, he would see a familiar face. However, lately, there was one who didn't move.

He was sitting at the same alleyway corner every day. This person seemed to watch for Charlie specifically. When he saw him coming, he would rise to his feet, extend his hand in Charlie's direction, and say a single word: "Please." This always unnerved Charlie. The beggars usually didn't speak to a person of his stature.

Charlie never made eye contact with this pathetic waste of a man. Something else that disturbed him was that this beggar never asked anyone else for charity, just Charlie. Unsure if he was being paranoid, Charlie could swear the beggar watched him walk away. This went on for several weeks until one day the beggar said so much more than "please."

On a seemingly normal day, Charlie was making his way toward the bank when he encountered the beggar, and he began his dance of avoidance. He managed to pass the man and put him to his back. *Home free,* Charlie thought.

It was then he heard an all-too-familiar voice. "You'd do well to be reminded of your roots, boy! Ya hear?"

Charlie instantly stopped walking. His pupils dilated, he clenched his jaw, and felt his heart race. He slowly turned on his heel and looked his father in the eye.

To his surprise, it *was* his father, but he was thin, gray, and old. Charlie could scarcely recognize him, especially with the long beard. Now standing a mere two feet away from him, Charlie stared at his father, waiting for him to speak.

"You hear from your mother?" the old man asked in a raspy voice.

"Yes, she told me she left shortly after I did."

The old man cracked a smile and cackled a little. "Yeah, she did that. Did she also tell you that I was sleepin' it off on that day when the census man came round and she informed him I was dead?"

Charlie flashed a sarcastic smile. "Yes, she did. I got a good laugh out of that one."

The old man twitched an eye at Charlie. "Yeah, I bet you did. So what'd she do? Go back to whoring?"

The rage swelled up in Charlie, and he snapped. A swift right hook connected square with his father's jaw and dropped him instantly to the ground. The punch didn't knock him out, and the old man wrapped his arms and hands around his head to protect himself.

Charlie stooped over and calmly whispered in his father's ear, "If I ever see you again, you're a dead man. Ya hear?" Time had not softened Charlie's hatred of his father.

Charlie proceeded to the office and put in a full day's work. On his way home, he looked out the window of the carriage at the corner where he had met his father earlier. The corner was empty. When Charlie arrived at the apartment, he found Wilds fast asleep. She seemed to be sleeping a lot lately.

He chose not to wake her. His sleep was restless, and he rose before the sun. He was careful not to disturb Wilds as he slipped out of the apartment. When Charlie passed his father's corner, he found it vacant. As spring passed into summer, Charlie tried his best, but he could not put the encounter out of his mind.

Life was getting back to normal when another chance encounter brought his paused life back to the forefront of his thoughts. It was a particularly hot morning in the city, and when it was muggy like that, the filth that lingered on the streets smelled exceptionally horrendous. Charlie decided to treat himself to a carriage ride to work.

The ride started smooth enough, but when he was almost to the office, the cart began to jerk and shake violently. Charlie did his best to steady himself but eventually toppled over onto the floorboards. He heard the crack of the bullwhip and the driver shouting. Charlie stuck his head out of the window. "What the hell?" he shouted.

"So sorry, sir. This stupid horse was never broken properly." He cracked the bullwhip again but dropped his hand too low, and the tip struck the horse across the back. Charlie immediately recognized his horse.

He kicked the carriage door open and climbed out. The driver was about to flick the whip again when Charlie reached up and caught his arm in midair. "Stop," Charlie said as he forcibly removed the whip from the driver's hand.

Charlie slowly walked to stand in front of his friend. He didn't like what he saw. His horse had a lower weight than when he'd last seen him. He also had a wild, crazy look in his eye that he had never seen before. Charlie could tell his friend recognized him. He could also tell he wasn't pleased to see him.

When Charlie brought his hand up to pet him, the horse nosed his hand away. Charlie was confused and attempted to pet him again. This time the horse shook his head violently and then pushed Charlie's entire body away. Charlie was stunned and deeply saddened by what had just happened. He hadn't many friends in this world, and now it looked like he had one less.

Charlie made it halfway back to the driver's carriage, let the whip fall to the ground, and said to the driver in a low, flat, depressed tone, "I'll walk from here."

The driver looked at Charlie, confused. "Sir, the bank is there." He pointed to Charlie's place of employment. Charlie looked wearily back at the bank and sighed. He didn't go in.

Charlie wandered the city for the entire day. He and Wilds had been there for months now, and he'd never really explored it much. How could he? He worked constantly. As Charlie wandered the streets, he reflected on his life up until that point. Reliving his past, he could easily count the things that brought a smile to his face—his horse and Wilds. Charlie had gotten so lost in the fast-moving world that he barely thought about much else.

With the advent of the wire, he could communicate cross-country and broker same-day deals. With Western Union and Wells Fargo supplying the papers nearly round the clock, the money was there for the taking. Charlie came to realize he had gotten caught up and left his true self behind. What was worse was that he had sacrificed his only friends in the process.

Toward the end of the day, Charlie decided to return home and speak with Wilds about something he had put off way too long. When he arrived, he was surprised to find that she was not there. Figuring she was out shopping, he waited for her to return. Seconds became minutes, and minutes faded away into hours. At sunset, he was becoming concerned and was near panic.

Wilds was always there when he came home. Had he been in his normal frame of mind, he would have realized that his normal time to return was still two hours away. Only then did he understand. Only after sitting in silence, only after that solitude, did he fathom what she must go through every day.

Searching through her things in an attempt to ascertain where she might have gone, he landed on page after page of pictures of the woods, landscapes, and countryside. It was then he heard a knock at the door. Charlie's eyes were met with Wilds's, and she quickly looked at the ground. His gaze then took in the two constables who held Wilds by the arms.

"This squaw claims to live here and know you. Is that correct, sir?" one constable said with contempt in his voice.

"Yes, sir, it is, and I would appreciate it if you let her go." Charlie made the request calmly, battling down his rage.

The officers blinked and looked genuinely surprised that Wilds had been telling the truth. "Well, it looks like we've got a squaw chaser after all! Ain't never seen one of them. You know these things have fleas, right?" one of the constables said as he undid the restraints.

"She had constructed a teepee in the park. When we asked her to vacate, she became violent and began speaking Indian words," the other said.

Charlie looked at the officers skeptically. "Took both of you, did it?"

One of the policemen gave Wilds a shove and sent her sailing into Charlie's arms. "Next time we'll take her to the pen. Maybe she can build a teepee there."

Charlie didn't break eye contact with the constable who'd shoved Wilds. He held it till the door was completely closed. Charlie helped her to the bed and gave her a once-over.

Her wrists were cut and bleeding from the ropes used to tie her. After she washed and they ate, Charlie decided then was as good a time as any.

"You know, if we were married, you might not have those problems."

She only stared at him. Charlie moved to her side and presented an engagement ring. "Laura, will you do me the honor of being my wife?"

There was a long pause before she reached out and covered the ring box. She looked Charlie in the eye with anger. "No," she said plainly.

Charlie was confused. "I don't understand." He rose from the floor.

Wilds stood and faced him. "That's not my name, and you know it's not my name. You've never called me that until just now." She diverted her eyes and began to collect the dishes from the table.

Facing away from a slack-jawed Charlie, she continued to speak. "I'm not staying." Her voice was clear and unfaltering. She meant what she said.

Charlie could offer little argument. He knew that tone. Her mind was made.

CHAPTER TWENTY-SEVEN

Eyebit Immersion 60%

LIFE IS EASY WITH US AND HARD WITHOUT US.

Pops stopped the story as the transport arrived at his home. "Well, thanks for the lift," he said as they pulled up outside. "Also, thanks for the help. There's no way I could have outrun that junkyard dog."

Jack gave Pops a half smile and nodded.

"So, here you go. I'm gonna set this contraption to go to two addresses before it deletes the history," Pops said as he typed away on the antique keyboard.

Jack raised his eyebrows. "Two addresses?"

Pops didn't meet Jack's look, just typed at an impressive speed. "Yes, the second address needs to be your address, but the one before can be anywhere you want."

"But where else would I go?" Jack asked as he watched Pops gather his things and unplug the keyboard.

"Anywhere. Use your imagination." Pops climbed out of the transport.

Jack thought a moment but was unable to come up with anywhere. "What if I just go home? Will that mess anything up?"

Pops let his shoulders drop and stooped over to look inside the transport and face Jack. "Really? You can't think of anywhere? Nowhere that you might like to know where something... or somebody might be?"

Jack broke eye contact for a second then looked back at Pops. "No, not really."

Pops exhaled deeply. "Well, give it some thought. I'm sure you'll come up with something," he said as he situated his things. "Say, what color did you say that girl's hair was?"

Pops didn't have to look at Jack's face to know how it lit up at the thought of her. "Guess you already know where she lives?" Pops gave him a moment to let the seed of that idea blossom. "Look *at* her house, not *in* it! That's creepy. You're just gonna cruise by. Never know when you might need that information." As Pops walked away, he smiled, very pleased with himself.

Jack fought with the Eyebit for a moment. More and more it was becoming harder to use. Before, everything was automatic and he didn't have to think; now asking for something was a chore. Pops's words echoed in Jack's head: "That thing is supposed to help you. If you can't find a way to make it work for you, then you don't need it." Jack repeated aloud, "Make it work for you."

Instead of trying to access the girl's address directly, Jack commanded the Eyebit to display the names and addresses of everyone he went to school with. Once he found her name, he then set the Eyebit to search for compatible people on the same street as the girl. *That will at least get me close enough*, he reasoned. ***Would you like me to alert Smith, Andrew that you are en route to his location?*** " the Eyebit displayed.

Jack selected No as the transport sped away. "Display map," Jack said. "Indicate my address and my current location in relation to the destination." To his surprise, his home address wasn't that far from hers. Just a few miles. *This whole time, she was right there,* Jack thought as he let his mind slip into a fantasy about being able to reach this girl on foot if he had to.

Jack was nervous while climbing out of the transport. His heart raced as he casually walked past her house, trying not to stare, but at the same time desperately hoping for just a glimpse. His mind and heart were locked in a struggle to both look and look away. His breath caught when she emerged from the front door.

The thrill of glimpsing her—*There she is!*—was short-lived when a boy he didn't recognize followed her out. Jack's heart sank as he watched them embrace, and a strange feeling churned in his gut. As he made his way back to the transport, he contemplated that age-old question: what does that guy have that I don't?

"He's got what everybody in the world has! That stupid thing telling them what they should have, not necessarily what they want," Pops said as he handed Jack a block of sandpaper. "You're gonna have to find a way to get her attention while fighting that thing, and that's just to get her to talk to you. Once you've done that, then you're gonna have to make her want to be with you without that thing. After that... well... you'll figure it out."

Jack was hanging on Pops's every word, hoping for a glimmer of insight as to what he should do. "That's it?" Jack asked, a twinge of irritation in his voice.

"Yep, that's it." Pops stood back from the car. "Come here, boy, look at this."

Jack stood by his grandfather, looking at the car they had spent the last several months putting together.

"Wow, that's good shit right there, boy."

Jack only saw an antique car. "Yeah, it's a car." He was curious as to what Pops saw that he didn't.

"It's not just a car, boy. It's the embodiment of everything we've done together. It's a symbol of our triumph, and it represents ultimate freedom! It's a big FU to the established order! It's not just a car!" Pops thought for a moment. "Plus, look at how much it's changed. Remember what it looked like when you first came here? Look at it now! We're getting ready to paint it, and then it's done!"

Before them sat a fully reconstructed, hard-top Mustang that had been assembled from a rainbow of parts.

"You gotta look at what it will be. Don't be consumed by what it is. We've got what's called a vision! Find its inner potential," Pops said as he put his hand on Jack's shoulder.

As the two set to work sanding the body of the Mustang, Jack was struck with a thought. "What's her name?" he called to Pops on the opposite side of the car.

"Eh? I don't know. She's your girlfriend," Pops sassed back at Jack.

After a moment's pause, Jack said, "No, the car! Not the girl."

Pops was surprised by Jack's question. "Why do you assume it's a her?"

Jack's response was dry and thought out. "Well, in most everything I've been watching lately, the vessel, be it a ship, plane, rocket, or car, is usually given a girl's name. If not, they are called by words that imply femininity, like baby or girl or she."

Pops was genuinely impressed with Jack's insightfulness. "I never really thought about it like that," he said as he sanded. "Truth is I've been struggling with a name since I found her." Pops paused to rest his elbows on the hard top above the driver's side, facing Jack, who mirrored his position. "A name is the most important thing to an object. It must encompass the past, present, and future. It must convey a meaning and sense of purpose, while at the same time being a definition of the name-bearer. Essentially, the object's name is its source of power."

Jack hadn't considered all that. He had only thought of the matter in simple terms.

Reading into Jack's blank stare, Pops endeavored to explain further. "Okay, so have you watched the *Deep Space Nine* series as part of your recent *Star Trek* immersion?"

Jack's face lit up with recognition.

"Okay, so the ship in that series is named *Defiant*. Now, that name perfectly fits the criteria of what the ship stands for. It's of the Federation, but it is built for war, which is contrary to what the Federation preaches. It has a cloaking device, which is also against the rules. Nothing about the name *Defiant* conveys obedience."

As Jack processed what Pops was saying, he could only think of other *Star Trek* ship names. "So, *Voyager* fits because the journey from the Delta quadrant to the Alpha quadrant was essentially a voyage," Jack said as he came to understand the symbolism in naming things.

Pops nodded. "Right! Exactly! Now you're getting it."

Turning names over in his head, Jack arrived at another question. "So, what does it mean when it's named after a person? Like the *Farragut*?"

Pops was again surprised by Jack's insightfulness. "Good question, boy! Usually when a ship bears the name of a person, it's done in honor of that person. So the *Farragut* was named in honor of David Farragut, who was in the Civil War."

Jack now had a clear understanding. "So like the General Lee, which was a person and later the name of a car."

Pops chuckled. "Yeah, sure, but it was also a couple of boats. Names can be used on multiple vessels more than once. Just ask Forrest Gump, who named twelve shrimping boats *Jenny*. But to answer your question, the best I've been able to come up with is either Freedom's Revenge or Last Raft for Cuba." Pops waited for Jack to laugh, but he didn't.

Pops tried to keep the conversation rolling. "I guess I could go with Dolly or, hell, with the pain this paint job is gonna be, maybe I should just skip it and call her Coat of Many Colors." Silence filled the garage.

"Is that a joke?" Jack asked.

"Guess not," Pops said as he turned his attention to sanding.

"Why would you take a raft to Cuba?"

"You wouldn't. Nobody would. But that's kinda the point. Never mind. I guess. Keep sanding."

As the two worked, Jack continued to ponder names. "Has there ever been a name that was a person or a ship that you considered perfect for its bearer?"

Nothing sprung to Pops's mind. "Not that I know of. Not in real life anyway."

Jack was becoming fascinated by the meaning of names. "Well, what research have you done?" He pushed, hoping Pops would somehow reveal some missing piece of information he didn't realize he was holding onto the whole time.

"Some." Pops wasn't ready to reveal that he had been borderline obsessing about the right name since he first laid eyes on her.

Jack couldn't let it go. "You should name her something epic. Something like, 'Awesome Giver'."

Pops just stared at Jack. "What the hell did you just say?" he asked sarcastically.

"You know... Awesome means filled with awe, and the car gives it."

It took every bit of Pops's resources not to laugh at Jack's attempt at name-giving. "No," he said quickly as he turned away so that Jack didn't see him grin. "Look, if this name thing means that much to you, I'll let you do the honors." Pops thought on it a moment. "Just so long as it's something cool and I like it. Deal?" Pops extended his hand to invite the time-honored custom among men to signify a bonded word.

Though Jack had heard about handshakes and had recently witnessed Pops and Kyle exchange one, he was unfamiliar with the custom. Once Pops explained all the nuances of it, along with how and when to properly apply one, the men shook hands. They sanded late into the night in silence.

CHAPTER TWENTY-EIGHT

Eyebit Immersion 57%

REENGAGE NOW TO FEEL BETTER.

It had been several days since Jack was dutifully charged with finding the perfect name for the antique machine that Pops was sure would be the ultimate FU to the system. He had scoured everything he could find—old TV shows, old movies. He had even managed to break into an abandoned library. He had considered himself lucky when it had contained books, real books. But unfortunately, all of it amounted to nothing.

Why is this so difficult? Jack thought as he finally turned to technology.

"Theon, I'm looking for something," Jack said.

His Eyebit went dark, and Theon appeared before him. "Yes, Jack, what may I help you find?" the computer program asked.

"I'm looking for a name, but not just any name. Cross reference the following ideas:

Ship, freedom, adventure."

"Where would like to book your cruise too?" Theon asked.

"Nowhere. Okay, try this. Freedom, car, driving, speed."

"Driverless cars are the way of America. Is this what you are looking for?" Theon asked.

"No, no, no. Try this. Name, girl, car, freedom."

"Baby names with the meaning freedom. Is this what you are looking for?" Theon asked.

"Yes, better. What's in that?" Jack asked, prompting Theon to display the information.

1. Amnesty

2. Anaya

3. Avasa

4. Busela

5. Elefteria

6. Feronia

7. Isra

8. Malaya

9. Najya

10. Saoirse

Jack scrolled through the list, saying each name aloud. "Nah, none of those fit," he mumbled to himself as he pondered what to search for next. This exchange went on for what must have been hours. Nothing fit, not just right, anyway. "Okay, new search… Start over," Jack said as he let out a huff.

But Jack's attention was pulled away as Kyle interrupted him. He let himself into Jack's room and sat down on the bed next to him. "Son, you've been here for hours. What are you working on?"

Jack launched into a lengthy explanation and recap of everything that had taken place since Pops had given him the opportunity to name the car.

"Wow, that's a hell of a chore," Kyle said. "What have you come up with so far?"

Jack didn't have an answer. He just shook his head and shrugged his shoulders.

"I see," Kyle said. "Well, you know, your grandfather tends to get hung up on things. Sometimes it's best to pick something and run with it. Pops has been known to make a mountain out of a molehill, as my mom used to say."

That didn't make Jack feel any better.

"You know how you came to be named Jack?" Kyle asked.

Jack shook his head. But then he suddenly realized that he might know. "Was it Pops's father's name?"

"That's right. I always liked it, and here you are. Jack."

Being correct combined with the sense of approval from his father made Jack smile.

"Relax, take a break. It'll come to you," Kyle said as he slapped Jack on the knee and stood.

As he neared the door, he offered another piece of advice. "Take the word car out of your search, and add rebellion, south, pride, C.H., and Boyd." Kyle pulled the door closed as Jack took to the search.

It didn't take long. "Perfect!" Jack thought to himself as he sprang up and headed for the door. Kyle was in the living room when Jack went hurriedly past.

"Figured it out, I see," Kyle called after him.

Jack stopped in his tracks and craned his head back around the corner. "May I borrow—"

Kyle cut him off. "Come on. I'll go with you."

―――――――――――

"Oh good, boys, you're here," Pops said as he looked over and saw Jack and Kyle standing at the garage door.

Jack stood transfixed in slack-jawed amazement. What had once been a "coat of many colors," as Pops had called it, was now a deep-blue masterpiece. The paint seemed to sparkle, as Jack looked closer. Even the wheels seemed to shine.

"You call that chrome," Pops said, as if he were reading Jack's mind.

When Jack ran his hand along the hood, it was smooth to the touch. He had never seen anything so old look so amazingly good.

"Awesome is the word you're looking for. You know, filled with awe," Pops said as he stood beside Jack with his hand on the hood.

Jack continued to circle the car, inspecting every part. He ran his hand over a section he had been sanding just a few days before. He found it to be perfectly smooth, like it was brand new.

"Wow, Belle! Nice," Jack whispered.

"What's that?" Pops asked loudly to call attention to the fact Jack was mumbling.

"Jack's come up with a name I think you'll like," Kyle said, breaking his gaze from the car.

"Okay, let's hear it," Pops said.

"La Belle Rebelle," Jack said, and he puffed out his chest.

Pops was genuinely impressed. "The Civil War Confederate spy," he said as he looked over at Kyle with knowing insight. "That's actually... It's really... really good, I'm not gonna lie."

Kyle winked at him and tilted his head back toward Jack, conveying silently that Jack deserved the credit, even though Kyle sparked the idea. Pops obliged.

"Not bad, boy! Not too bad at all! La Belle Rebelle it is." He chuckled. "Damn, son! That's a great name! I even like calling her Belle for short. Hot damn! Come on, you've earned yourselves a beer!"

The three men sat in silence just staring at Belle, each reminiscing over the last few months, thinking about the individual parts they put together, the struggles and the triumphs, everything that led them to what the car had become. As Jack stared at Belle, all the clutter in Pops's garage faded into the background till it was just him and the car.

The silent christening was broken, and reality rushed back in, when a bell's *ding*

interrupted the moment somewhere in the distance.

"Ha! Finally," Pops said as he hopped up and hurried over to his computer.

"What's that?" Jack asked as he stood and finished his beer.

"This, boy, is drivin' tunes. A playlist that perfectly reflects my mood and will inspire

me while behind the wheel." Pops handed the CD to Jack, who had never seen one before.

"CD-R 79 minutes play time. That's it? It only has seventy-nine minutes' worth of music?" Jack asked in disbelief.

"Yep, that's plenty! Trust me." Pops took the CD back and opened the driver-side

door. "Hit the garage door, will you?" he asked.

Jack didn't move. "Hit… what?"

Pops rolled his eyes and shook his head.

"He means this," Kyle said as he pushed a physical button on the wall next to the

garage entryway door. "Listen, I'm going to get back to your mom. You kids enjoy your playdate and stay out of trouble." Kyle put his hand on Jack's shoulder. "Bye, Dad. I'll see you later," Kyle called out as he exited through the raised garage door.

"Byyye! Good job, son!" Pops called out, knowing that Kyle knew what he meant. "Come on, Jacky, let's take her out!"

A thrill ran through Jack as he eased into the passenger seat.

CHAPTER TWENTY-NINE

Eyebit Immersion 53%

WARNING! NEARING HALF IMMERSION...

Vrrooommm. Pops turned the ignition, and the Mustang roared to life. As Pops pulled the car out of the garage for the first time, Jack couldn't help but notice how the trinkets strewn about the garage rattled in response to the sheer power of the engine.

"Hey, do you have your eye-swatch-it?" Pops asked.

Jack pulled his gaze away from the vibrating tchotchkes. "What do you want the Eyebit for?"

"I want to try something," Pops said as he drove the car down the street and away from his house. When he was reasonably sure they were far enough away, Pops shut the car off and climbed out. "Come on, boy." He indicated that Jack needed to get out as well. "Okay, stand here, put it on, look at the car, and no matter what happens, do not look at me. Understand?"

Jack reached up, placed the Eyebit on his face, and pushed the button. The lenses lowered to rest on the bridge of his nose. Flash! Jack was connected. "Holy shit!"

"Don't look at me!" Pops said. "Are you looking at the car? What do you see?" Pops clenched his jaw as he waited for Jack to respond.

Jack didn't move at first. Then he started to make gestures as if he were wandering around a cave without a flashlight. He took slow and labored steps and held his arms and hands out, fumbling for something tangible.

Pops smiled. "What do you see?" he asked again.

Jack could only think of one word. "Nothing."

"Ha! Yes! Hot damn!" Pops shouted as he jumped. "Okay. Now, *don't* disengage but slowly slide the Eyebit down your nose and tell me when the car reappears."

As Jack did as Pops instructed, the top of the car appeared just over the edge of his Eyebit. As he continued to slowly lower the Eyebit, the window and door appeared. The image was bizarre to behold. The car was half visible and half invisible, separated only by the edge of the Eyebit.

Jack could feel the invisible part of the car just the same as he could the visible part. So the car was there. But looking at it through the Eyebit, all Jack saw was his hand and arm against the yard that was beyond the car. Almost like the car was a mirage.

"Okay, you can shut that thing off now," Pops said.

Jack disengaged and looked at Pops with wide eyes, wanting an explanation.

"Let me see that," Pops said as he held out his hand. Jack gave him the Eyebit. As Pops held it close to his face in examination, he asked, "Ever wonder why two people wearing these, when they look at each other, they don't see the Eyebit?"

Jack had never considered it before.

"Well, according to the thirteen layers of bullshit provided by Bit Corp, it boils down to one thing." Pops handed the Eyebit back to Jack. "Every Eyebit is coated with this clear goo that other Eyebits detect. All Eyebits contain software that extrapolates the surrounding area along with stored images and presents a completed image to the wearer minus the Eyebit itself."

"Goo?" Jack asked, clearly confused.

"Well, goo is my word. The technical term is liquid metamaterial technology, which simply bends the light of anything it's applied to."

"Keep going." Jack squinted at Pops.

"Basically, this special goo makes the Eyebits invisible to other Eyebits. I took some of that goo and mixed it with the paint we put on the car. So now the car is invisible to Eyebits!"

Pops stood proudly before Jack, who was flabbergasted. "I even put the goo on the lug nuts, wheels, and windows. Now, we gonna stand round here yakking all night, or are we going for a real drive?"

"Okay," Jack responded.

"Me first!" Pops proclaimed and jumped childishly into the driver's seat. Jack rolled his eyes and walked around to the passenger side.

"Okay, first things first. Seat belts." Pops whispered, "Oh yeah, that's a satisfying sound," as he clicked the belt into place. "Okay, second things second." He held up the CD he had made earlier in the evening. "Talk to me, sweetness." He manually inserted the disc into a device Jack thought was huge. Pops could feel Jack's judgment. "Yeah... my granddad had an 8-track, and I used to think the same thing, but he loved it."

With the engine running, Pops eased off the clutch, and the car lurched forward. As they turned down the first side street, Pops gassed it. The transmission began to whine, and Pops pushed the clutch in and swiftly switched gears. He let the clutch out at exactly the same time he gassed it. Jack felt himself sink deeper into his seat as the tires let out a small bark.

"Think of everything we've accomplished, boy!" Pops said as he turned the knob on CD player to the left, decreasing the music volume.

"What? Us driving?"

"Yeah, but it's more than that. Think about everything we went through to get here. Look at all the work we did. Look at the rewards of that work. Look at what we created."

"Seems like it might have been easier to just buy a transport and fix it the way you wanted it."

"Yeah, but you're missing the point. That's part of what's wrong with the world today. Everything is a direct highway enema of solutions, and nobody really works for anything anymore. Let's say we had done that. Do you realize what you would have missed doing that as opposed to taking the long way round?"

"We would have gotten there sooner and saved time."

"Yeah, but think about all the cool shit you would have missed. Learning about cars and gold, meeting Bones, pizza, your girl."

Jack hadn't thought about it like that. "So what you're saying is it's less about the destination and more about the journey?"

"That's a bit cliché and on the nose, but sure. It's like *The Lord of the Rings*! Seriously, Gandalf couldn't have called the eagles to fly everybody to Mordor at the beginning of the damn story? Well, sure, but it wouldn't have been much of a story if he had, now would it?"

"I'm not familiar with that story."

Pops rolled his eyes. "Look, all I'm saying is, in life, any chance you get, always take the long way, take the side streets, take the back roads.

You'll be better for it, trust me." He then rotated the volume knob back to the right, turning the music up again.

The first track was ending. "Oh, that's a good one! 2Pac is talking about nobody being able to see the *P* because of his window tinting," Pops explained, pointing to himself when he said the letter *P*.

"What is this music?" Jack asked as Pops turned his attention back to the road.

Pops bobbed his head to the side as he answered perfectly in sync with the beat. "It's 2Pac."

Jack could barely hear him because the music was so loud. "A two-pack of what?"

Jack's question interrupted Pops's rhythm. Slightly irritated, he reached over and

turned the knob to the left again. As the volume decreased this time, Jack was momentarily distracted by the action.

"2Pac was a rapper in the late 1990s. He was extremely popular but ultimately was gunned down by a rival."

Jack didn't know what a rapper was but quickly ascertained what kind of music they made.

"See, in this song he is singing about extreme window tinting preventing people from seeing inside his car. Or at least that's my interpretation." Pops pushed the left arrow button, and the song started over. "Here. Listen to it again and compare it to what we've done to this car. Can't see me!"

The song ended, and Jack had a new appreciation of timing music to actions. The next song was just as interesting although completely different from the first.

"This one's called 'If You Want Blood.' It's performed by a rock group called AC/DC."

Rock and roll didn't flow the way rap did. It was louder and more aggressive. Pops seemed to really like it though. Jack could tell because he turned the CD player knob to the right and pushed the gas pedal harder.

"Here's a good one," Pops said as the third song started. "It's called 'Judy Is a Punk,' by the Ramones."

Jack listened to the music as he watched the world go by. The neighborhood Pops lived in was mostly abandoned and isolated. According to Kyle, Pops owned a lot of it, but Jack hadn't wondered why before.

Pops tore through the neighborhood, testing the car. He'd speed up then back off. Then he'd jerk the wheel before slamming on the brakes and skidding the car to a stop. He was playing. Pops drove to the end of a cul-de-sac and started doing donuts.

That was then Jack could fully tell the difference between driving a real car versus a simulated one.

"All right, boy, you wanna drive?" Pops asked as he pulled the emergency brake. Before Jack could answer, Pops said, "Of course you do. Do me a favor. Put your Eyebit on, and look at the headlights when you walk past. I'm curious how light will show up once it passes through the goo I coated the car with."

Worried that Jack would accidently look in his direction, Pops walked around the back of the car as Jack walked around the front. Once back inside the car, Jack disengaged the Eyebit.

"Well?" Pops asked.

"It was strange. I couldn't see the headlights or the light from them at all. They were invisible, just like the rest of the car, but where the light landed was brighter. The ground and my hand both appeared as if they were giving the light off themselves. Like self-illuminated, I guess."

Pops smiled and shook his head. "Hot damn! That's better than I had expected."

As Jack familiarized himself with the driver's side of the car, Pops fiddled with the radio. "Here's a good one," he said as he leaned back in his seat.

By this point, the music was more background noise to Jack. After making sure that he was in first gear, he popped the clutch, felt the tires spin, and was off. A smooth shift to second gear encouraged an aggressive shift to third.

Jack didn't realize it, but his heart rate was up, he was breathing heavily, and he had a death grip on the wheel. It couldn't be explained, but he was tapping into something primal. He wasn't driving; he was discovering something ancient. Disconnecting from the Eyebit world was one thing, but driving this car that was completely subservient to his decisions brought him a greater sense of power than any modern technology ever had.

At that moment, Jack had an epiphany about the endless possibilities that were laid before him. Freedom! Complete, total, possible, real freedom was no longer an abstract thought his teachers told him he had; it was here. He had found it.

Entering a straightaway in the neighborhood, Jack shifted to fourth. Slamming the gas down and feeling the engine respond, Jack became overwhelmed and let out a howl from the depths of his soul.

Pops's only response to his screaming grandson was to smile. The touch of life experience that Jack had just had was one that Pops was all too familiar with.

The two spent the next several hours taking turns driving around the neighborhood listening to Pops's old music. Jack was beginning to understand its appeal and why it paired so well with the physical act of driving. At the end of Belle's first street test, Jack decided to back her into the garage, but when he thrust the shifter into reverse, he was surprised that the knob broke off in his hand.

"Damn, son! You been working out?" Pops asked as he took the shifter out of the hands of a stunned Jack. Turning the shifter knob over, Pops simultaneously turned down the blaring John Cougar Mellencamp song "Fight Authority." He needed to think. "Yep, looks like it was rusted the whole way through. Okay, back her in, and we'll take a look at her."

In the garage, Pops stood examining the problem. He cupped his chin with his right hand and stood with his left on his hip. He muttered under his breath for a few minutes before looking up.

"Ah, that might work," he said as his head shot up and his gaze found Jack's. "Gimme a hand, boy. We're looking for a foot-long, tubular piece of scrap metal. It's got a little red and a little yellow paint on it."

Pops set about throwing stuff around the garage. Jack used a much more sedate approach and picked one item up at a time and placed it to the side. Not finding it immediately, Jack stood back and took a visual survey of the garage.

Thinking about how Pops described the piece, Jack considered that it would most likely roll if it were laid on its side. Jack decided to check the four corners of the garage, and to his pleasure found what he thought was it, in the second corner.

"Is this it?" he asked as he walked toward Pops, grasping the pole.

"Ahh, yeah. That's it. You know what you're holding there, son?" Pops asked as he held out his hand to take the pole from Jack. "It's the only surviving piece of the last roller coaster." Jack listened as Pops's eyes glazed over. "I was there when it was demolished and damn near broke my hand punching a garbage bot." He nodded in satisfaction.

"What's a roller coaster?"

Pops wasn't surprised to hear Jack ask this question as roller coasters had already been falling out of popularity when Pops was young. "It used to be a ride that people would get on to get a thrill. They were very popular at fairs and amusement parks."

Jack pondered for a moment. "How's a ride thrilling?" He wondered how something known to be thrilling could still be exciting at the same time.

"Well, they carried with them a hint of danger, and that always gets people... especially the chicks!" Pops held the rusted shifter shaft and knob next to the roller coaster pole and asked Jack, "Well, whaddya think? Those're pretty damn close, ain't they?"

"Yeah, pretty damn."

"Kinda fitting, too, the last piece of an old thrill ride ending up in a different rediscovered thrill ride... I like that! It's romantic and shit!" Pops gazed at the steel rod. "Come on, boy, we got work to do," he said as he set the two pieces of metal down on the workbench.

Turning around with a screwdriver, Pops took to pulling apart the shaft housing. "So where were we with Charlie and Wilds?" he asked, assuming Jack wanted to hear it.

"Wilds was going to leave the city," Jack answered excitedly.

"Oh right, right..."

CHAPTER THIRTY

Tall Tales with Pops

THE MAN: CHAPTER 4

"Where is my horse?" Charlie asked a second time. He was sitting on one side of a desk that separated him from the manager of the carriage company to whom he had leased his horse.

The manager made little fuss as he ruffled through his papers. "Oh, I see. Yes. Your horse was too wild for service and was sold at auction." Charlie felt his face flush when he heard the manager's words. It took all his faculties to remain calm, but the fire in his eyes was lit, and the manager saw it.

Through gritted teeth, Charlie produced the lease agreement and spoke heavily as he leaned over the desk so close to the manager's face that their noses almost touched. "We have an agreement. Where. Is. My. Horse?"

Having decided to remain steadfast in the face of adversity, the manager didn't relent. "I am not at liberty to give you that information," he said with a slight hint of authority.

At that point, Charlie abandoned diplomacy and let rage take over. He balled his fist in the manager's shirt and yanked downward, slamming his face into the desk. The manager slumped back into his chair, cupping his face and trying to stop the blood from dripping onto his clothes.

Charlie took the manager's ledger from his desk and turned away. Standing with his back to the manager, he thumbed through the transaction ledger. He was horrified at what he found. Two days prior his horse had been sold to none other than the monstrous Eleventh Street Glue Works.

"I should call the police!" the manager shouted through his hands.

Charlie slammed the ledger shut, turned, and threw it at the manager, striking him in the forehead. Charlie shot him a look as if to say, "I dare you" and issued his own threat. "I now have evidence you violated our contract. If I get my horse back, I might not sue you."

———————

Motivated by the looping thought of his horse suffering, he ran the entire fifteen blocks. Standing outside the Eleventh Street Glue Works, Charlie took a moment to compose himself. It had only been two days since the purchase, and Charlie was hoping that nothing had happened yet. He straightened his necktie, braced himself for the worst, walked in, and asked for the manager.

Charlie found this manager only slightly more accommodating. While refusing to resell the horse back to Charlie, the manager did agree to let Charlie see the horse. Formulating a different strategy to get his way, Charlie carefully committed every detail of his surroundings to memory.

Upon seeing his old friend again, Charlie was careful to contain his emotions as best he could. Spying the clipboard posted by the stables, Charlie learned that the entire row was due for slaughter the next morning. *It has to be tonight,* he thought.

Giving into his emotions, if only slightly, Charlie allowed himself to rub his friend's neck. Charlie could tell his horse was glad to see him as his mood was drastically different from when they'd last encountered each other in the street.

Sensing the horse's thoughts, Charlie knew his friend was expecting Charlie to take him away that instant. Whispering in the horse's ear, he said, "Soon, but don't make a fuss. You have to keep yourself in this spot." Charlie reassured his friend that he would not die in that awful place.

"If I wanted to see him again before tomorrow, how long do I have left today?" Charlie asked the desk clerk on his way out.

"We close at dark, and the guards on patrol don't let visitors in. Better get back before then," the guard told him. Charlie tipped his hat and bid him good day. Looking at his watch, he saw he only had six hours before sunset, and there was much to do.

As fate would have it, a coffeehouse stood directly across the street from the Glue Factory. Having situated himself in front of the window facing the factory, Charlie busied himself with the organization of his last few affairs. Signing this, initialing that, Charlie did more for his personal freedom in those few hours than he had done in all the years he spent acquiring wealth. When it was well after dark and Charlie was sure the factory was empty, he put his plans into motion.

After giving his finished correspondences to the barkeep for mailing, Charlie set about his next to last act of business in the city. As he neared the threshold of the coffee house, he paused for a moment's reflection on what he was about to do. The last conversation with his employer was still fresh in his mind. *Walk out that door, and you'll never work in this town again!*

I truly hope so, Charlie thought, cracking a half smile.

Charlie was calm in his approach to the factory. He walked around to the back of the building and simply hopped the fence. Having spent the last hour memorizing the guard's patrol, he knew they were on the far side of the compound. Which put him exactly where he wanted to be.

The holding stables were just around the corner, and he was able to slip in undetected. Sneaking around to the stable entrance, Charlie was careful not to make too much noise for fear the horses would spook. Completely focused on his task, he almost didn't feel the hand clasp his left shoulder. Instant panic set in as Charlie thought, *Ah shit, I'm caught.*

"What are you doin', son?" To Charlie's relief, it wasn't a security guard who had ahold of him—it was his father!

"What? What the hell? Dad, what are you doing here? Are you following me?" Charlie demanded.

"Lower your voice, damn it! I'm here to stop you from making a mistake."

Charlie cut his eyes at his father. "Are you drunk?" he asked skeptically.

"No! I wanna help you, boy. You're making a mistake." His father was almost pleading with him.

Charlie was committed. "I don't have time for this! You wanna help me, then fuck off." Charlie jimmied the stable door open and slipped in without making a sound. His eyes hadn't yet adjusted, but he didn't need them to find where his friend was.

By the time he was leading the horse out of the stable, Charlie's eyes had gotten accustomed to the lack of light. Setting his sights on the door, he was stopped by the silhouette of his father. The horse instantly recognized him and reacted by snorting and jumping backward.

"Whoa, boy, whoa, easy now, he's not gonna hurt you," Charlie said barely above a whisper, calming the beast. Charlie started to lead the horse toward the door, but he stopped again. This time it wasn't Charlie's father that gave him pause but something else.

"Come on, boy... come on." The horse refused to budge. Pulling back on his lead rope, the horse gave himself some slack and reached over to the clipboard on the wall. Taking it in his mouth, the horse gave it to Charlie.

Astonished, Charlie looked at the clipboard, the same one he'd seen earlier in the day, the one that informed him of tomorrow's pending slaughter. "It's okay. I'm taking you away. This won't happen to you," Charlie reassured his friend.

Giving the rope another tug, Charlie attempted to move the horse along, but he refused, backed up, and touched noses with the horse that occupied the stable next to his. He then moved to the next stable, and the next, and the next.

In a flash of comprehension, Charlie understood. "Buddy, we can't take them all," he said as he gave the lead rope another gentle tug.

A moment of silence passed between them before Charlie's father spoke up. "No, that's not a bad idea. If only that horse is stolen, they will know it was you, but if we let all of them out..."

It was a good idea, but Charlie was skeptical. "Why are you doing this?" he asked, his voice laced with accusations.

Charlie's father couldn't look him in the eye when he answered. "I... I... um... I'm trying to make amends." He paused for a moment, swallowed hard, and continued. "I wasn't there for you as a boy. The least I can do is try to help you as a man."

Charlie rolled his eyes. "My forgiveness isn't for sale." Charlie set about opening the stables.

"Damn it, boy, I don't wanna buy it! I wanna earn it." His father was practically pleading.

Charlie pushed his way past him toward the main stable door with twenty horses behind him.

His father quickened his step to be by Charlie's side. Then, peeking around the door, he spotted a security guard. "Okay, there's a guard. I'll distract him by goin' thisaway while you goes thataway."

Charlie squinted at his father and nodded that he understood. With all his strength Charlie's father burst the doors open and ran straight at the security guard, screaming.

"Run, horsies! Run away! Be free!" He flailed his arms, jumped, and ran in circles. The horses bolted out of the stable at full gallop, and Charlie waited till over half were out before he slipped round the corner with his friend in tow.

Before he turned the corner, Charlie looked back at his father. Just as he did so, he saw the security guard with his arm extended, holding a gun. *Bang!* He pulled the trigger, and Charlie's father fell to the ground. *Bang!* Another shot. This one was followed by an unmistakable death cry.

"Gooo! Riiide!"

Bang! A third shot silenced his father forever.

The scene quieted as Charlie witnessed his father breathe his last breath. The world telescoped around him, and he, for a moment, felt the loss as if something had been pulled out of him. It was intangible. Something like his soul had been ripped out, and Charlie was left with just the resulting hole to comfort him. Things had always been unfinished with his father, and now, they would forever remain that way.

The gunshots only aided all the horses' motivation to run. With no saddle, Charlie jumped on his horse as best he could. He nearly fell off when his horse jumped the fence of the glue factory. *Out! But not free yet,* Charlie thought.

The place where Charlie had arranged for the covered wagon to be waiting was only a few blocks away. He tore through the streets faster than he had gone since moving to the city. He was so enthralled with the thrill of his actions and riding fast again that he didn't notice that one of the horses he had freed was following them.

"Yeh didn't tell me yeh had two horses, just the one," said the man who had prepped the wagon.

"Well, it's two now, so I guess I'll need another harness... unless, of course, you don't want my money?" Charlie retorted.

"It's short notice, see. It'll cost yeh extry," the man said, looking at the ground as he spoke.

"Fine." Then Charlie added, "This one is for my... wife." Charlie thought a moment about what he had just said. *My wife... if she'll still have me.* As the man mounted up the horse that had followed them, Charlie allowed his thoughts to turn toward the memory of his father.

The garage fell silent. The wrench stopped cranking, and Pops had stopped speaking. Jack looked over to see Pops staring off in the distance. A deepness was in his eyes.

Jack knew what was about to happen as Pops began to pontificate.

"Forgiveness springs from the heart of the merciful. It can't be taken or claimed. It can't be stolen or liberated. It can only be bestowed. The merciful have the power to change someone's world, to set them free, and allow them peace. Maybe if forgiveness were easier to give away, the world would be a happier place," Pops said and then paused for a moment of silent reflection.

"Anyway." Pops shook his head, shrugged, and refocused his attention. The wrench cranked back up, and Jack was drawn back into the story.

Charlie understood *why* his father wanted forgiveness; what he didn't understand was what prompted him to seek it out. *Now I never will.* Charlie's thoughts lingered on the memories of his father. Finding a few good ones for comfort, he returned his full attention to the task at hand.

"Yeh all set here, partner," the man said. Charlie put his hat back on and paid him. He slapped the reins and pulled the covered wagon into the night. The scariest thing he had ever attempted lay ahead.

For a long moment, he sat outside the apartment he and Wilds had shared. Fear was consuming him. He had never needed anybody before he met her. If she said no, he would be lost. He didn't have a backup plan.

Breathing deeply and checking his clothes, having changed from his business suit to his former persona, Charlie hopped down from the wagon and donned his cowboy hat. He paused a moment outside the door to consider what he would say. He decided it was best to call upon that skill which had always served him well, saying the first thing that came to mind.

He knocked. An eternity passed before the door slowly creaked open.

He met Wilds's stare and said, "You won't have Charlie the investment banker. How about Charlie the horse thief?"

His entire future hung on that one pivotal moment. The silence seemed to drag on for an eternity, and then she smiled.

He had her. "There's an old friend outside with a wagon who will take you home if you want to go." Wilds dashed to the window to look out. Recognizing the horse, she smiled again. Charlie called back to her from the threshold. "If you want to go, we need to leave soon. When can you be ready?"

Wilds pushed herself into his arms and kissed him long. "I'm ready now," she said. As they left, they weren't even bothered to close the door of the apartment. Neither of them looked back at the trappings of the life they were leaving behind. They simply walked away, together.

As they mounted the wagon, dawn was breaking. The streets were beginning to fill as the knocker-ups had been plying their trade, banging on the windows of their customers to rouse them from sleep. As Charlie and Wilds neared the edge of the city, a newsie caught Charlie's attention.

"Read all about it! Murder at the glue factory, horses run through city!" the boy was shouting.

Charlie stopped the wagon. "I'll take one of those."

The headline was bold and struck Charlie deeper than he had expected. Animal Rights Activist Shot Dead at Eleventh Street Glue Works. Horses Roam City.

Charlie was silent for a long moment. "Okay, Dad... Okay."

As the two left the city for good, Charlie took one last look over his shoulder before turning toward home. He didn't *know* they would never go back to the city, but he had a feeling. Moreover, he didn't want to. No longer concerned with the city, Charlie decided not to finish reading the second article about bandits raiding the rails and tossed the paper in the wagon.

CHAPTER THIRTY-ONE

Eyebit Immersion 51%

ALERT! ALERT! NEARING HALF IMMERSION...

"Had Charlie paid attention to the rest of the newspaper, he might have been more prepared for what happened next," Pops said as he stood up, put his hands on his lower back, and pushed his stomach out. "Oooh, okay, the hard part is done." He let out a groan.

"What time is it?" he asked as he shuffled around the garage looking for a clock.

"It's... Oh shit!" Jack said as he shot Pops a worried glance. "Eleven o'clock. Shit! Shit! I gotta go. Kyle is gonna be pissed."

"Okay. You better take off. Listen, you're already late. It's best to just own it at this point. Part of being a man is admitting when you screw up," Pops said as he looked Jack in the eye.

"Kyle is gonna ground me for sure, regardless of what I say."

"Yeah, he probably is. But you are in the wrong here. Just be honest and apologize. Say something like, 'Hey, sorry I'm late. Time just got away from us,' and leave it at that, come what may. Okay? Don't worry about the car. I can finish from here. Now go on, git."

"Okay. Thanks," Jack said as he hurried out of the garage.

Jack connected his Eyebit and stepped into the transport. Immediately upon reconnecting, there was a priority message from Kyle. Jack breathed deeply and opened it. ***One week! Home and school only. No Pops! I hope it was worth it.*** Jack was relieved; he had expected worse. *Totally worth it,* he thought as he sped away.

Pops sat behind the wheel of Belle. His left hand gripped the steering wheel while his right shifted through the gears. He had finished fixing the shifter. As he sat in the car parked in the garage, he rested his hand on the shifter and stared at it as he let his mind wander back to the day he'd found the part he used to fix it.

It felt like a million years ago now. It was a beautiful summer day nearly forty years ago, at the beginning of the end. The world was no longer getting its thrills from strapping people into machines designed especially to scare the shit out of them. *The world is becoming a bunch of masturbating hermit crabs,* Pops thought as he stood as close as he could get to the rollercoaster.

He had already crossed one safety barricade of the condemned amusement park. Being on the border of two states, this park was hot real estate. Bit by bit the lines were becoming clearer and more defined. Fewer and fewer people were interested in the things that were mixed.

Pops tipped his hat to the forgotten machine and watched as the charges at the base lit up one by one in a left-to-right pattern working their way up. *Boom. Boom. Boom. Boom.* And it was gone, like it had never been there. Pops waited for the dust to settle and committed the image of the battered and broken machine to memory.

As the garbage drones began plying their trade, Pops looked away, refusing to watch this magnificent machine being thrown away like some useless piece of trash. Casting his eyes downward, he saw a single steel rod at his feet. Pops crouched down and grasped the metal, which was still warm from the explosion. He resolved to keep it.

As he turned to leave, a garbage drone spotted the piece and tried reclaiming it from Pops. The instant the garbage drone touched the metal, Pops used it as a weapon and struck the drone on the claw.

"Fuck you!" Pops screamed in hate.

―――――――――――

His mind's eye returned to the present. Seated in the driver's seat of Belle, Pops released the death grip he had on the shifter. Looking down, he grasped it again and gave it the classic back-and-forth neutral shake check. "Yeah, fuck you," he said as he climbed out of the car.

He hadn't seen Jack in several days. *Must have gotten him in a good bit of trouble,* Pops thought, blaming himself, as he turned off the light in the garage and closed the door.

―――――――――――

Jack couldn't help but stare at her. From across the cafeteria, he was out of her sight, mostly because he wasn't connected. The world was amazingly boring without the Eyebit. Everyone wore gray, and nobody went out of their way to stand out in any regard.

Sure, the Eyebit projected the wearer's most attractive image, but as Pops had explained, nobody committed to a single style anymore. They just let the machine pick for them. But none of that mattered to Jack as he looked at her. *She'd look amazing in anything.* The world faded out around her, and he took in her every movement. The curvature of her lips, the almond shape of her eyes—but it was her hair that was the most captivating to him.

He had never seen hair quite that color. The fire red excited in him a lust he had never experienced before. Even though she wore it in a ponytail, as was standard for every single girl, he couldn't help but imagine how good it would look if she wore it down, less like a girl and more like a woman.

Reality had its drawbacks, though, and Jack was forced to deal with the reality of the situation. As it crept its way in, Jack broke his gaze and looked down at his folded-up Eyebit. *She has a boyfriend,* he thought.

As quickly as the thought entered his head, Jack heard Pops's voice in retaliation: *That don't mean shit!* Jack sat back in his chair and folded his arms across his chest. *Your grandma had a boyfriend too. You gotta figure out how to get her attention is all.* Pops's words ran in a loop in his head. Jack stared at his Eyebit. *How do I do that?*

Jack picked up his Eyebit and held it close to his face. "You are the problem." He paused a moment and examined it further, as if his stare might scare it into giving up its secrets. "Why will you not introduce me to her?" He paused and mulled over the question. "What do you do?" he asked aloud while squinting at it. "How do you work?"

Pondering the question "how do you work," Jack continued to talk to himself out loud. "Okay, you're a difference engine. You search for commonalities." He paused and thought harder on *commonalities.*

"I can't turn the Find Commonalities function off. It's why you exist... and... well, I tried. How do I make you work for me?" he wondered aloud, talking himself through the problem. "Commonalities... commonalities... commonalities..." A smile spread across his face. Jack clasped the Eyebit and all but leaped from his seat. He had to get ready.

———————————

Pops rode up to the house on his bicycle. "Whatcha doin' here, son?" he asked, surprised to see Kyle waiting in his driveway.

"Is he here?" Kyle demanded.

"Well, hello to you too. Is who here?"

"Cut the shit, Dad! You know who! Jack didn't come home from school, and he's still grounded."

Pops cocked a smile. "Grounded, you say? And he ignored you? The hell you say! Sound like anyone you know?"

Kyle only stared Pops down.

"Look, son, I haven't seen Jack since the last time he was here about a week ago."

Kyle gritted his teeth. "Yeah, it's about to be two weeks!"

Pops shook his head, expressing his disapproval at the repeated groundings. "Well, there's no other transport here, so if he is here, he must have spent his own money to get a ride. Come on in, though. If he's not at home, he's probably in here with Belle." He gestured for Kyle to enter.

Pops slowly opened the garage door and fumbled for the light switch. Incandescent light bathed the garage and all its contents, minus one fully restored Ford Mustang. Pops's eyes went wide with shock, then slowly closed till they were half-lidded as he smiled a little, suddenly understanding what had happened.

"He's not here, Dad... and where's your car?" Kyle asked, not yet having figured out that Jack had taken it.

Pops slowly turned to face his son but avoided eye contact. "Um, I forgot, it's in the shop. No, it's... ah..."

Pops didn't get a chance to finish before Kyle erupted in complete fury. "Son of a bitch! I'm gonna kill him." He stormed for the garage door.

"Now hold on, son!" Pops called after him. Kyle didn't stop. Pops redoubled his efforts. "God damn it, son, *stop*! He's just gone to see about that girl!"

Kyle stopped as if he had run smack into a wall. He turned around to face Pops. "Girl? What girl?" He gestured with his hands as if he were holding a great weight.

"He met a girl at school, but that shit you people put on your faces won't let him connect to her, so it looks like he's taking it old school," Pops said with a dash of sarcasm.

Kyle couldn't see past his anger. "I'm still gonna kill him. He knows better than this kinda shit!"

Pops glanced down and noticed Kyle was clenching his fists so hard his hands were shaking. "No, I don't think you will," Pops said, with a defeated tone in his voice.

"Oh, you don't, do you?"

"No, I don't." Pops hung his head.

"Why the hell not, Dad?"

"Because you're a better father than I was." Silence fell between the two men. In that instant, Kyle deflated as the hatred left his body. Pops's sudden admission captured his full attention. Kyle listened intently, knowing, longing, needing to see his father ask for forgiveness in the only way he knew how.

"Me hitting you didn't stop you any more than you hitting Jack would." Pops was silent for a moment after that as he let Kyle process what he was apologizing for. Kyle relaxed his hands.

"I'm very proud of you, son," Pops said, and his voice cracked. Clearing his throat and slapping genuine emotions back down, Pops composed himself. "Now come on, boy, that anger and rage has got to go somewhere." He adjusted his hat and raised his arm to show Kyle the way.

Chapter Thirty-Two

Eyebit Immersion 46%

Congratulations! You've earned a free upgrade!

The Vista-Blue Mustang roared to a stop on the street in front of the girl's house. Jack climbed out and started the march up the yard toward the front door. His heart was racing, and his feet were as heavy as lead.

Nearing the door, he felt momentarily sick. *Just a girl,* he reassured himself. *Talk to them every day.* His hands shook a bit as he placed the Eyebit on his face and pushed the button. The lenses closed on his eyes and flashed the bit to life.

He wasn't assaulted with the normal mainstream projections he used to have up all the time. He had stripped the Eyebit programs away so that it was just the basic operating software. All he saw was the word **Searching** in red lettering.

Blink. *Searching...* Blink. *Searching...* Blink. ***Commonality found. Commonality found.*** The girl's profile illuminated across Jack's screen, and he smiled. His gamble that the Eyebit would recognize the two of them as only having the school in common had worked!

"Jackpot."

The front door jerked open, and to Jack's surprise, he was met by a tall, overbearing man with the same red hair as the girl he was there to see. The two stood staring at each other for a moment, which was the custom in the Eyebit world. People simply let the two devices do the introduction.

Jack's eyes were fixed on the man's. He recognized the characteristic eye swipes, followed by the forming of actual words. "Jennifer, there's someone from your school here." Then he said calmly at Jack, but not to Jack, "She'll be right down."

Jack waited patiently just outside the door. Jennifer's father had not invited him to step inside. *Deep breaths, Jack, deep breaths*, he told himself as he waited.

At the fourth inhale, she appeared before him. He didn't time it well and let out a little squeak as he clamped down on his lungs. The two stared at each other for just a moment.

"Hi, Jack." Having no other commonality other than their accident, Jennifer could only ask about that. "Is your head okay?"

Jack mimicked Pops's cool half smile and shook his head slightly. "No, not at all. In fact, I've not been the same since we ran into each other." Jack heard Pops's voice in his head. *Easy, son, don't lay it on too thick now.*

Jennifer looked confused. "What do you mean?"

"Well, it's really strange, but I'm seeing things that haven't been seen in many years, and I was wondering if you are seeing them too?"

Almost before he'd finished his sentence, she said, "Is your Eyebit broken? I don't see you participating in anything. I'm just getting your profile."

That was the answer Jack was looking for. "Right. Come on, and I'll show you." Jennifer offered no resistance and followed his lead toward the street where the Mustang was parked. Jack was surprised at how *easy* it was to get her to follow him.

As the two approached the end of the driveway, Jack had to remind himself that the car was parked there. Bringing the two of them to a stop at the curb, he proudly proclaimed, "There it is!"

Jennifer squinted. "Are you talking about the street?"

Jack responded by reaching up and disengaging his Eyebit.

"Why did you do that?" Jennifer asked in earnest.

"It's the only way you can see it."

"Riiight."

Jack gingerly took her by the hand. "Here, I'll prove it to you. Open your hand." As he led her hand to the edge of the car, Jack's heart rate went up. He was *affectionately touching her,* he thought as he slowed the pace of their reach.

The instant her skin felt the cool steel, she recoiled. "Whoa!" she said. She then put both hands out and touched the car, longer this time. "Wow, what is this?" She looked at Jack.

"You have to take your Eyebit off to see it. It's the only way," he said, a sympathetic look on his face.

Jennifer was hesitant. She couldn't recall the last time someone had seen her without her Eyebit. The insecurity of it, the implied nakedness, gave her pause.

"It's okay. I'm not wearing mine, and when we're done, if you don't wanna see any more, you can put it back on," Jack reassured her.

Jennifer thought about it for a long moment. In truth, she had forgotten how to disengage. "I-I don't know how... I sleep in it," she said almost guiltily.

Jack smiled and raised his index finger to the edge of her bit. "Push here." Their hands briefly brushed as she mirrored his movements, and his heart skipped again.

Jennifer breathed deeply and quickly jerked her arm up to disengage the bit. Flash! The lenses raised to the sides. She held her eyes closed and fought to keep her balance.

Jack watched as her eyes squinted tighter and then shot open.

A look of fear came across her face, and she turned away, hunched over, and thought she might throw up. After a few seconds, she was able to right herself. The sensation of suddenly being disconnected had consumed her enough that she hadn't realized Jack was now by her side.

Her eyes widened when she cast her gaze toward the car. "Wow! I've only ever seen pictures. I think my grandpa used to have something like this."

Jack smiled. "Yeah, I call mine Pops. Is yours as cranky and backward as mine?" Jack seized on any commonality he could find.

Jennifer hung her head and shook it lightly. "No, he went to the place we don't talk about when I was a little girl."

"I see." Jack desperately tried to think of a way to recover. Clearly her grandfather's death was painful to her.

The silence between them was brief, as Jennifer's attention had returned to the car.

"So, what do you do with this?" She circled the ancient automobile.

Yes! Jack thought. "Well, it's better if I show you," he said as he opened the passenger door for her to get in.

Jennifer examined the car and thought to herself for a second. *Who is this person? Is this safe? I want to do this. Should I do this? What will Jeff and Julia say? Will I get in trouble? If I don't get caught, no one will know. Get caught doing what? Are there rules against this sorta thing? I want to do this.*

Jack could sense her hesitation and sought to put her at ease. "It's a lot of fun, and I promise it will be unlike anything you've ever experienced before."

Coming off the Eyebit's chemical influence, Jennifer found herself flooded with thoughts, feelings, and emotions she was unaccustomed to. "Um, sure, okay," she answered, and with a quick jut of her left hip she slinked into the passenger seat.

Jack was so mesmerized by her curves he had forgotten he had to close the door.

"You good?" Jennifer asked, peering around the door.

Jack reclaimed his senses. "Yes, watch your fingers," he said as he closed the door. Walking around to the driver's side, he muttered to himself, "Shit! Shit! Shit! Be cool. Shit! Be cool, be cool."

Jack fumbled with the driver's door and whacked his head on the door jamb when he sat down. Pain shot through his head, but that pain was nothing compared to the momentary bruising his pride took. He hoped she didn't notice, as he carried on as if nothing had happened. "Okay, so this is the wildest thing about this... transport. You have to use your hands!"

Jennifer's eyebrows shot up. "Really? How do you do that?"

Jack thought for a moment. "Well, the easiest way I know how to explain it is, this car reacts to everything I do. If I want it to turn left, I have to turn the wheel left, and the car will turn left."

Jennifer leaned over and examined the steering wheel. "I don't understand." She cocked her head slightly.

"Okay, no problem. Let's go for a drive. Put your belt on."

Jennifer sat in her seat, in silence, not moving.

"You have to use your hands," Jack said.

Jennifer gave him a look. "I don't know how."

Jack, picking up on her discomfort, was quick to attempt to put her at ease. "Oh right, sorry. It took me a really long time to get the hang of this. Here." He leaned down on the armrest and reached across with his left hand to grab the seat belt.

Once he grabbed the seat belt, Jack began to nervously draw it across her chest. Jennifer, not feeling entirely comfortable in her seat, squirmed, just enough for Jack's hand to brush her breast. As if the moment wasn't awkward enough, in this position their lips were mere inches from one another.

With her breast on his mind and his nose too near to her mouth, the two froze in a moment of terror. Jennifer turned away, fearful of her breath, and Jack finished buckling her belt.

Doing his best to play it off as if nothing had happened, Jack verbalized the next step. "Okay, next we have to start the car." He pushed the clutch in confidently with his left foot and turned the ignition. *Vrrrooommm,* the Mustang roared.

Jennifer held her hands on the dash, feeling the vibrations. "It's really noisy." Her voice was elevated. "What's an airbag?" she asked, looking at the dash.

"Something I hope never to need. You ready?" Before Jennifer could answer, Jack dropped the emergency brake, slipped the clutch, and laid on the gas. The tires barked, and the Mustang lurched forward.

Jennifer was thrust back in her seat; her hips sank deeper into the seat as Jack shifted to second gear. Unable to contain her anxiety at having no control, Jennifer howled, "Aaahhh!"

Jack allowed himself a slight smile as the Mustang slid into the night.

CHAPTER THIRTY-THREE

Eyebit Immersion 35%

PLEASE CONNECT... PLEASE...

"All right, boy, what you wanna do is strike it right here," Pops said as he placed the iron wedge in the center of the log.

"Yeah, Dad, I remember how to do this," Kyle said as he rolled up his sleeves.

"Ah, maybe, but do you remember how to do it *well*?" Pops's tone was sarcastic.

"I always did it well."

"Hmph. Well, let me move my hand before you show me how *well* you remember." Pops chuckled as he laid the wedge on its side and stepped away.

Kyle picked up the wedge and held it in the center of the log. Choking up on the neck of the sledgehammer, he tapped the wedge in place. He took a few steps back and eyed the distance of his reach against the head of the sledgehammer and the top of the wedge. Kyle inhaled deeply and brought the sledgehammer down, striking just to one side of the wedge. *Ping! Thud.* The wedge flew off the log into the dark.

"Well," Pops said, not flinching as the wedge just missed his arm. "Easy there, Thor!" Pops joked, while at the same time wondering if Kyle would remember who Thor was. But Kyle did and snorted as he stifled a laugh.

"It's okay, boy. Good to see that you can still do that," Pops said with a grin.

Kyle looked at him, confused. "What's that, Dad?"

"You know, laugh." Pops cocked a smile and shook his head.

"I laugh all the time, I'll have you know!" Kyle said, almost defensively.

"Coulda fooled me. You seem so angry nowadays. I understand you don't like me, but what's your problem with Jack?" Pops asked, piercing Kyle's defenses with ease.

Ting. The sledge hit the center of the wedge and sunk into the log.

"Jeez, Dad, I don't know... Kids these days aren't like when I was a kid." Kyle swung the sledge down. *Ting.* The wedge sunk even farther into the log.

"How so?" Pops asked.

Ting. The log split and fell into two pieces.

"They just sit there, staring off into nothing," Kyle said as he rested on the sledgehammer and stared at the split wood.

"Oh, I see. So it's totally different than staring at a cell phone or video game. Yes, you're absolutely right," Pops retorted, outlining Kyle's behavior when he was the same age.

"Stop it, Dad. I at least used my thumbs!"

"So you think he's lazy?"

"Maybe that's part of it. Or at least it was till I brought him here. Now he doesn't listen, he's combative, and he's pissing me off!" Kyle's voice was rising. *Ting*. Another split. "Where's your maul?"

"Here," Pops said as he handed the axe to Kyle. "So he's independent, rebellious, determined to do what he wants to do. Sounds like someone I know." Pops sat back down.

"Yeah, Dad, he's just like you."

"Oh, I didn't mean me," Pops said as he gave Kyle an accusatory look. "I recall having this exact conversation with my father about you."

Kyle brought the log splitter down and dropped his shoulders. It had never really occurred to him that Pops didn't always know how to be a dad. "You had to get advice?" Kyle asked with a wide-eyed look of disbelief.

"Well, yeah. Why does that surprise you?"

"You always seemed so confident, so sure. You never changed your mind! Not once." Kyle turned away from the wood and toward Pops.

"Yeah... Well, I should have." Pops paused a moment. "I have a great deal of regret,

son."

Kyle was shocked. "Dad! You're blowing my mind here! What do *you* regret?"

Pops cast his eyes downward. "Plenty, son, plenty. I regret not telling your mother I loved her more. I regret not being a better dad. I disciplined with force because it was all I knew. I regret not being man enough to break the cycle. I regret every single time I wished you were anything other than who you are, just so it would make my life temporarily easier."

Kyle had stopped chopping firewood and stood staring at Pops, tears welling in his eyes. "Dad, I had no idea... I thought... Well, I always felt like you didn't like me very much."

Pops, still avoiding eye contact, said, "I know, son. I put up this wall and tried to be what I thought I should be and not what you needed me to be."

Kyle had been squeezing the log splitter handle as Pops spoke. The nervous energy took over, and his arm started to twitch. Desperate to break the tension, Kyle let out a half-laugh, half-cry of an exasperated sigh. "Well, you were kind of a dick."

Pops couldn't help but chuckle. "Yeah, that's a word for it, I guess." He nodded.

Kyle returned his attention to the logs. The only sounds were the swish and thud of the maul hitting the wood. It seemed easier now, as if the load wasn't as heavy, as if maybe the wood wasn't as difficult. Regardless, Kyle raised the maul and brought it down with confidence and grace.

Slipping deeper into the memories of his own childhood difficulties, Kyle lost himself in the past. Finding more bad memories than good ones, when anger and rage resurfaced and threatened to boil over, he simply swung harder. With each split of a log, a little more of the hate died.

No words were spoken. Kyle's complete focus was on the splitting of the firewood. Pops was busy in the background, trying to stay out of the way, gathering the split pieces, and pulling new logs around for Kyle. Kyle didn't notice any of this activity, only that new logs appeared. Neither of the men was interested in the positions of the hands on the wall clock.

Kyle let out a sigh of relief and slowly brought the axe down from over his head. He used the handle as a crutch, breathing heavily. He hung his head and closed his eyes.

"Feel better?" Pops asked, cradling several pieces of split wood.

"Yeah, I think so... Wow," Kyle answered through a gasp.

"Good... You got a lot of hate out with that bout," Pops replied, sincerity in his voice.

Kyle didn't answer but took Pops's words to heart. He did feel better. He also felt tired.

Pops couldn't resist. "Come on, boy, no time for rest. You split all this shit, now you gotta carry it to the rack."

Kyle's half smile of satisfaction melted away. *Damn it.* "Yes, sir."

———————————————

"You all right over there?" Jack asked as he looked at Jennifer.

"Don't look at me! You have to use your hands with this thing. You need to look that way," Jennifer scolded.

Jack couldn't help but feel a start. *Shit, she's right*, he thought as he grabbed the shifter and downshifted.

"What is that you keep moving?" Jennifer pointed to the gear shift.

"What?" Jack asked, keeping his eyes forward.

"This?"

Jack knew she was pointing to the shifter but decided not to look in that direction. "I'm sorry, I have strict orders to not look away from the forward position." Jack cocked a half smile at his own smart-ass remark. "Here, take my hand and put it on what you are talking about," Jack said as he held his right hand up for Jennifer to take.

His little plan worked. Jennifer took his hand and guided it down to the shifter.

"Oh, that's the shifter. It allows me to control the gears, which allows me to regulate the speed." Jack didn't give her a chance to pull her hand away. Thinking quickly, Jack slipped his hand off the knob and covered hers as it fell on the shifter.

"Here. I'll show you. Make a fist around the knob. Okay, now I'm going to give it more gas. When you hear the engine get louder, I'll push in the clutch, and we will shift to a higher gear." Jack covered Jennifer's hand and performed the shifting motions. A charge shot through his entire body and not because of the car or the speed. This was a rush of a different kind.

All of Jack's surroundings, problems, and concerns faded away, and he was completely focused on Jennifer's hand in his. He had been enthralled with things in the past, he was sure, but couldn't recall them now. No matter what happened in life, in the future, however things turned out, right here, right now, they were together. This moment in the present was for *them*, and nothing could ever change that.

Realizing the power of the present moment, he pulled the car over. Jennifer wasn't looking at the shifter anymore and met Jack's eyes.

With his hand still on hers, he leaned over slightly and all but whispered to her, "You handled that like a pro. Trade seats with me."

A smile spread across Jennifer's face. Once they'd changed seats, she popped the clutch, and the tires barked. Surprisingly, she didn't kill it her first time trying. Jack could see the change in her happening. Just like he'd experienced. He was watching Jennifer come alive.

The car sliced into the night, with Jennifer commanding the machine. Jack kept his hand on hers, stacked on the shifter. He held his hand strong enough to influence her movements, but gentle enough not to crush it. In this moment, Jack understood the delicate interactions of man-woman relations and how fragile those relations could be.

———————————

Kyle swore under his breath as he stumbled toward the brick patio behind Pops's house.

"Boy, all I would ever need to find you is to follow the trail of firewood," Pops said as he come along behind Kyle, picking up the dropped pieces.

"Yeah, I know, but what's it matter anyway, Dad? It's not like you can burn any of this." Kyle relaxed his arms and dumped more wood on the pile next to the ancient fire pit.

"The hell you say!" Pops exclaimed as he started wadding up paper and cardboard. "A shame to let all that work you did go to waste, ain't it?"

"You're serious?" Kyle looked at Pops, concerned. "How do you avoid the hydro-drones?" he asked, referring to the AI-controlled drones that sought out fires and dumped water on them by pulling and focusing moisture from the air.

Pops pointed up and gave Kyle a smile that stretched from ear to ear. Kyle turned his eyes skyward. Above his head were two triangular sails spanning thirty feet. One corner of each sail was attached to the house, and the other two were tethered to fence posts standing in the yard.

"Relax, boy, we're covered," Pops said as he lit a match and sprayed an aerosol can of hairspray at the pile of paper and cardboard in the center of the firepit. Kyle watched in worried fascination as the smoke began to rise and escape between the two sails.

"So let me get this straight. You know the hydro-drones' fly-by schedule?" Kyle asked, swigging his home brew.

"Yep."

"Okay, and you sewed these sails yourself out of old firefighting gear?"

"Yep." Pops swigged then nodded.

"Dad! Wow! You're kind of an evil genius. Where did you get that idea?"

Pops shrugged. "Well, it stands to reason that if those coats could keep fire and heat out, then why not keep it in? Or at least concealed." Pops took another swig before continuing. "See, the hydro-drones look for infrared heat signatures. Once spotted, they evaluate temperature, movement, and fuel sources. So by limiting the heat signature, there is no reason for them to come over here."

Kyle shook his head in understanding. "So the fireman-gear idea?"

Pops snorted lightly. "Yeah, I got doused a couple of times before I figured out to double-layer them." Thinking back on what he'd originally been using the fireman jackets for, he continued. "I was using them for protection while welding when the idea hit me." A moment of silence passed between the two men as Pops lapsed into a memory.

"I was there, you know?" Pops said as he stared into the fire.

"Yeah, where?"

"When they closed the last fire station. It was awful. They set fire to it and let the drones put it out. Those things really are genius contraptions, pulling moisture from the air the way they do. Anyway, after the show, I managed to pull this gear out of the rubble..." Pops's story was broken as his and Kyle's attention was called to the unmistakable throaty roar of the Ford V8 pulling into the driveway.

Kyle felt the anger returning. "I'm gonna kill him. I'm going to put a stop to this kind of shit so it doesn't ever happen again." He balled his fist.

Pops, seizing on the moment, said, "Wait!" and grabbed Kyle's arm. "Listen! I know what you're thinking! 'Stop him from seeing that girl.' Well, that didn't work for me, and it sure as shit won't work for you!"

Kyle retorted, "This is different, Dad!"

Pops raised his eyebrows, let go of Kyle's arm, and straightened up. "Oh really? How's that? What happened with that girl anyway?"

Kyle looked away. "I married her."

Pops nodded. "Look. Your son is trying to become a man. And if you try to come between him and this girl, it will drive a wedge between the two of you. Punish him, sure. He needs to know what he did wasn't okay, but do it in a way that doesn't make him hate you!"

Kyle still wasn't fully convinced. "Come on, Dad! I was better for what you did."

Pops's demeanor deflated. "No, son, you weren't. I was wrong." The two men read each other's eyes, and in that moment of silence, Pops knew that he had reached him. "Be a better man than I was. Be a better dad," he said with a final plea.

Jack entered the back porch area glowing with a man's pride, but he was also a little scared. Kyle stood quietly for a moment, examining his son, who was beaming with victory.

Letting his anger go, Kyle smiled. "Well, I hope it was worth it. Cause you're in trouble."

Thinking back on what Pops had told him about owning and admitting his errors, Jack faced his father with confidence. He didn't shrug. He didn't hang his head or even divert his eyes. He looked Kyle straight in the eye and, like a man, said, "I understand."

Kyle raised his eyebrows. "Oh, you do?" All was still, and the night sounds had gone silent. The tension was at a fever pitch. Pops inflated his chest, ready to jump between the two men if necessary. Jack braced for impact. Then, the extraordinary happened.

"Well, okay, then. Hopefully Pops takes it easier on you than he would have on me. It's his car, so it's his decision," Kyle said as he gestured with his thumb to Pops. In that moment, Kyle broke the cycle of abuse that had hung over the family for generations. But even more exciting, Kyle had just given Pops a second chance.

Pops was flabbergasted. He couldn't believe it and was completely unprepared for what had just happened. He fumbled with his words. "Um, yeah, well... Belle needs a wash... and a wax..." He managed to get that out before finding his composure. "And there's some other stuff I need help with around here too!"

Jack was unfazed by Pops's punishment. "Okay" was all he said, but his smile was beaming.

"Okay? Just okay? Seriously? *Okay* then, you jumped-up little shit, two coats of wax!" Pops huffed as Jack handed the keys back to him. The two men stared at each other for a moment, then Pops gave him a quick wink.

"All right, all right. You're going to have to show me how to do that," Jack said as he turned to go. Kyle was calling from inside the house that they needed to get home.

"Only if you tell me how it went!" Pops called after him.

Watching the two men disappear into the house, Pops's heart swelled with admiration and pride. In that one sliver of a moment, that one decision, his son had done what he never could. His eyes welled with tears, and an all-too-familiar pain shot through his arm.

Leaning back in a lawn chair, watching the fire die out, Pops drifted off to sleep. Despite being alone and outside, he found himself with an inner peace he couldn't recall the last time he had experienced.

CHAPTER THIRTY-FOUR

Eyebit Immersion 30%

CONFORMITY REQUIRED...
CONFORMITY REQUIRED...

The transport slid along the digital track, speeding toward their home.

"Well, I don't have to ask if you scored, cause you obviously did," Kyle said, looking over at Jack, who only smiled and looked away, rubbing his forehead as he did so.

Because Jennifer wasn't anywhere in Jack's Eyebit network, Kyle was forced to talk to Jack about her. "So, what's she like... this girl you're willing to risk unimaginable punishment to spend just a few hours with?"

"She's perfect." Jack grinned as he turned away from Kyle, letting his mind slip back to the evening that had just transpired.

————————————

The Mustang roared to a stop outside of Jennifer's home.

"That's it! Now, when you're coming to a complete stop, push the clutch in at the same time you push in the brake."

Jennifer followed Jack's instructions to the letter.

"See, you're a natural. Now we're stopped and you're planning on sitting somewhere for a few minutes and you don't want to hold the clutch and the brake, so you shift to neutral and pull the emergency brake."

Jennifer thought for a moment. "Neutral?" She flipped her hair as she turned to face him.

"Right. Pull the emergency brake, let your foot off the brake, and grab the shifter." Placing his hand on hers, Jack eased the shifter out of first gear and shook it vigorously. "This is neutral. If it helps, think of neutral as between the gears—you know, not committed." He hoped speaking in metaphor would plant a seed.

Picking up on Jack's hint, Jennifer cut her eyes at him. "Well, I should go back in. I've been disconnected for too long." She looked down and tucked her hair behind her ear.

Not wanting the evening to end but knowing it had to, Jack smiled at her. "Yeah, I should get back too," he said as he pulled the door handle, popping the door open.

———————————

As Jack got out of the car, Jennifer eased back into the driver's seat. A memory had sparked to life inside her. She was young again, maybe six or seven, and she was sitting on her grandfather's lap. They were driving somewhere. She was working the wheel, and he was controlling the pedals. She began to smile as his voice played in her head. *Remember, sweetie, you're in complete control.*

She lingered for a moment, gripping the wheel, feeling the pedals, touching the shifter. She soaked it in, not knowing when she might have another opportunity to feel this rush. But she knew she could again, if only she could bring herself to act.

Jack was coolly leaning on the passenger-side front fender with his arms crossed. Jennifer slowly walked around to the front of the car, running her hand along the edges as she did so. She didn't take her eyes off Jack.

They both wanted the same thing. Hormones unregulated by Eye-bits combined with the thrill of driving meant their teenage angst was boiling over. She was standing an arm's length away, twirling her hair and shifting her body weight. She was about to say goodnight, but Jack didn't give her the chance.

It's now or never, Jack thought and acted on impulse. He reached out and grabbed her arm, and she willingly fell into him. Unfortunately, youthful inexperience manifested. He had pulled too hard, she fell too easily, their lips missed, and their foreheads connected.

As they both reeled in pain, Jennifer looked at Jack and asked, "Isn't that the exact same spot we hit last time?" They both stood looking at each other with their palms cradling their foreheads.

"Yep, think so," he said. He could tell she was embarrassed.

"I'm so sorry." She approached him, fearful the moment had passed.

"It's okay... but you can make it up to me," Jack said as he reached out and took her by the hand. He smiled at her as he pulled her in more slowly this time. Their lips softly met...

"And then what happened?" Kyle asked, hanging on Jack's every word.

His question jarred Jack back to the present moment. "Then nothing. I watched her go inside." He ran his fingers through his hair. Jack turned his attention back toward the window and let his mind wander to what she might have done after she got back inside and reconnected to the Eyebit world. *Hopefully dumped her boyfriend,* he thought.

————————————

The front door closed as Jennifer leaned her back against it. Looking down at her Eyebit, she toyed with it a moment, but she opted not to put it on. Instead, she set it on the coffee table and called out to her mother. "June?"

No answer.

She called again and began to wander about the house. "June?" She found her mother and father sitting at the kitchen table, engrossed in their Eyebits. "June?"

At hearing her name, June perked up. "Oh, yes, dear? Where's your Eyebit?" she asked, straining to see her daughter through her stream of images.

"Huh? Oh, it's over there," Jennifer said, dismissing her mother's concern. She cast her eye on it and paused for a moment, trying to remember the last time she had been disconnected that long. "I want to ask you something." She craned her neck to make eye contact with her mother, whose attention had already strayed.

"Hmmm, yes, dear, of course." Her mother sounded slightly annoyed that she was being pulled into Eyebit-less communication.

Jennifer's thoughts turned back to Jack, and she relaxed. "How did you meet Jeff? And how did you know he was the one you were going to marry?"

June's eyes instantly met Jennifer's, and she read the change in them. June understood the longing for knowledge manifesting in her daughter. Jennifer wasn't connected to the Eyebit, and June knew she had to disconnect from it herself in order to truly connect with her daughter.

————————————

The next morning Jack rose early. He wanted to get to Pops's and get whatever a wax was over with.

"Oooh yeah, have fun with that. Too bad I can't join you."

"Why would you want to do that?" Jack asked.

"Sarcasm, son. Sarcasm. I hated waxing cars; it was a major pain in the ass."

"Great," Jack said.

"Oh, it's a punishment for sure. I can think of a thousand better ways to spend a Sunday. Be sure you're home for dinner. It's a school night."

Jack found Pops in the garage, sitting on a lawn chair, breathing heavily, almost gasping for air. "You okay, Pops?" Jack asked as he came to his side.

"Yeah, boy, I'm aight. Just got winded." Pops reached out his hand for Jack to help pull him up. To Pops's surprise, Jack easily lifted him out of his chair. Jack had developed confidence behind his strength, and it was beginning to show. Jack stood eye to eye with Pops. The two men looked each other in the face for a brief moment before Jack smiled and slapped Pops's shoulder.

"All right, old man, show me what wax is," Jack said as he turned to Belle.

The pain Pops had been ignoring in his arm returned worse when he stood up. "Well, first, Daniel-san, you have to wash her, then you wax," Pops said with a smile as he rubbed his arm.

Jack stood holding a garden hose and bucket as Pops dragged his lawn chair out into the driveway. "Damn fine day," he said, handing Jack a home brew. "Ahh," Pops said as he adjusted his hat and slumped down in the chair. "Now start at the top, and work your way down."

A few minutes of silence passed before Jack spoke. "So, what happens next with Charlie and Wilds? They were just leaving the city headed for the homestead." Pops didn't answer. Jack looked over and noticed he had dozed off.

The proverbial devil and angel appeared on Jack's shoulders. The devil won out, and Jack squirted a sleeping Pops with the garden hose. He aimed it perfectly, and a splash of water went directly into Pops's gapping mouth.

"Awghahahgya!" Pops yelled incoherently as he sprang from his seat with his arms flailing. "What the hell, boy?"

With a smile, Jack asked again. "What happens with Charlie and Wilds?"

Pops glared at him. "They shot the horse for being a little shit. The end!" He stooped over and picked up his hat and his home brew, which he'd dropped when he'd startled. "And then they kicked the dead horse for spilling da beer! The end again." Pops sat back down with a huff, trying to hide his smile.

Pops took the last little sip and began the story...

CHAPTER THIRTY-FIVE

Tall Tales with Pops

THE MAN: CHAPTER 5

The first half of the first day on the trail home was slowed by the steady downpour of cold spring rain. They should have made a solid twenty miles in that first day but only managed ten. As night fell, the clouds parted, and the rains stopped. This pleased Charlie. Not only was he able to keep the fire going, but this meant the horses didn't have to sleep in the rain. The next morning, they rose with the sun and continued onward.

The second day was wide open, clear, and smooth. By midmorning Charlie had finally put his finger on the weird feeling ailing him. Solitude. He couldn't remember the last time he had been so alone. He didn't have to wonder if Wilds was feeling the same.

"It's the quiet," she said as she came to sit beside him. "That constant hum of the city is gone. The noise of the people and their meaningless ramble, the intrusive train whistle, the false light, all gone. It's nice, isn't it?"

Charlie hadn't realized how much he had missed it till just then.

As the end of the second day approached, they happened upon a wagon company. Charlie opted to steer clear of the wagon train. Nevertheless, a single rider broke off and started in their direction. "Ah, shit," Charlie muttered under his breath. "Get the shotgun, get in the back, and shoot anything that tries to come through without giving you the signal."

Wilds nodded and obeyed Charlie's command. As the rider approached, Charlie brought the wagon to a stop and hopped off. Walking toward the rider, he very deliberately put his hand on his holstered gun.

"Whoa there, stranger, I just want to talk," the rider said as he put his hands up.

"So talk," Charlie stated flatly.

"We're pilgrims on the way to our promised land. You're the first person we've seen since starting out. Our leader would like to speak with you about some supply trade if you are so inclined," the stranger said.

Charlie was a businessman at heart and couldn't resist improving his situation. "Lead on," he said as he took his hat off and tossed it into the wagon. The pilgrim was visibly taken aback when an Indian with a gun emerged from the wagon. Wilds put the gun down but stared at the pilgrim.

The stranger looked over his shoulder more than once as they made their way to the lead wagon. It was clear to Charlie that he was nervous about Wild's presence. While the stranger may not have meant it, Charlie was insulted, nonetheless. When they reached the wagon, Charlie made sure to allow Wilds to go in ahead of him.

"This here is Mr. Young," the stranger said as he introduced Charlie to the leader of the wagon train. Charlie's manners dictated that he shake his hand, and he was thusly inclined, though only because it was polite, not because he wanted to.

"You look like a good God-fearing man. Have you heard the news of Mormon?" the leader asked, making it sound like a command.

Charlie wasn't interested. "No, but before you go any further, allow me to introduce my wife, Wild Like Beast."

A look of disgust drew across the leader's face, and Charlie was quite satisfied with himself. Charlie knew that Mormons didn't like Indians, or Nephites as was one the names they referred to them as.

As Charlie and Wilds rode away from the wagon train, Wilds shook her head at Charlie. "Why are you so fond of irritating others?"

Charlie couldn't help but grin. As they steered the wagon southward, the sun was beginning its descent in the western sky. He eyed it for a moment before speaking his thoughts aloud.

"You know, the sun doesn't actually set. As the earth turns, it gives us the illusion it goes down. But it's the earth that is moving."

Wilds was quick with a response. "That sounds like fire-time talk."

"So, we're camping here then?" Charlie asked, already knowing the answer.

As night drew in, the two sat wrapped in a blanket by the fire. Silence was in short supply, as they talked the night away. They discussed their big plans and their small ones. They told each other of how they each spent the last few months in the city and how grateful they were to be leaving. Then finally, when all conversation ran out, they made up names for the stars.

The next morning, Charlie was up with the sun. He packed the wagon for—if they were able to keep to the schedule—the last time. Wilds was dousing the smoldering coals when Charlie announced they were ready. Excitedly, Wilds hopped up on the seat beside Charlie. As the two rode closer toward home, Wilds was happier than she had been in many months. If fortune favored them, they could be home… home by nightfall.

Wilds was inside the wagon when she felt it come to a stop. Looking toward the front, she was met with a very serious Charlie.

"Don't move! Stay in the back! Take this, and shoot anybody that comes in here! Ya hear?" Charlie said as he handed her the shotgun. "Watch for the signal. Ya hear?"

Wilds knew something was wrong. Charlie hated that phrase. She had only heard him use it twice before, and both times it was accompanied by the same ill-content that had possessed his father.

Five men on horseback galloped up to Charlie, who stood a good ten feet to the right of the wagon. Charlie positioned himself with his feet shoulder-width apart, right hand on his revolver and his head tilted so that his eyes were cut in half by the brim of his hat.

The man in the middle of the five steadied a shotgun on Charlie's chest. The horse, sensing the tension in the air, snorted, shook his head, and half jumped.

"Whoa, boy," Charlie said, not taking his eyes off the center man. "Nice posse you got here," Charlie said, his expression grim.

The men all dismounted at once, and the center man approached Charlie slowly. "Drop your pistol, friend. I'd prefer not to kill ya," the man said, faking sincerity so poorly a child wouldn't be fooled.

Charlie didn't move, keeping his hand on his revolver.

"Ya ain't that fast," the man said as he pressed the shotgun barrel into Charlie's chest. "We only want your stuff." He pushed the gun in harder, as if that would help make his point. "Go on now, check the wagon," the man commanded his cohort.

That's it, check the wagon, Charlie thought as he gently and ever so slightly lifted his pistol. Expertly slipping his finger over the trigger, Charlie knew he couldn't cock it. When the moment came, he would have to squeeze the trigger as he raised the gun.

———————————

Inside the wagon, Wilds only heard muttering. When she was young, she'd studied the warriors of her tribe even though it was forbidden. She knew silence, stealth, and quick strikes made the difference in battle. She made no mistake. This was battle. Charlie was well past the mark for giving her the signal if all was okay. She knew they were in trouble.

She crouched with the shotgun trained at the wagon entrance. She inhaled as a shadow was cast into the wagon. No hat! Wilds gave herself a split second longer just to get a look at the intruder's face... Just in case...

Booom!

Not even the embalmer can make it so you'll ever wear a hat again, Wilds thought as she readied the gun for another shot.

———————————

The sound momentarily distracted the remaining four bandits, giving Charlie just enough time to swing his left arm into the barrel of the shotgun pressed against his chest while at the same time bringing his pistol up and firing it. Charlie's pistol shot caught the only man on his left square in the throat.

Charlie hit the shotgun so hard that the bandit nearly lost his grip on it. In attempting to regain it, he squeezed the trigger too tightly and discharged the weapon. Lucky for Charlie, it landed a gutshot in the bandit immediately to the left of the wielder. *Three down.* The entire business took less than two seconds.

As Charlie looked in the direction of the remaining bandits, he was met with the smooth, slightly warm steel of the bandit's shotgun barrel. In the haste of the moment, the bandit had turned the shotgun into a bat and swung it directly at Charlie's head. Darkness.

"Leave them! Get her!" one of the remaining two bandits shouted. The fading screams of Wilds were the last thing Charlie heard as he sank deeper into the blackness.

———————

"Okay, now you rotate the pad like this, applying the wax," Pops said as he demonstrated to Jack. "It's best to do it in sections. Like, do the entire roof, let it sit for a second, then wipe it off." Pops handed the pad to Jack and watched as he mimicked the movements.

"Why is this necessary? Doesn't the clear coat protect the paint?" Jack asked.

"It does, but the wax is the sacrificial layer. You can't replace a clear coat without replacing the paint. So, we wax. Trust me, it will pay you back in dividends."

"But..."

"No buts, boy!" Pops cut him off passionately. "You take care of things you care about! You cherish them! You honor them! You work for them! And sometimes, if it's necessary, you fight for them. Make no mistake, we're fighting right now, against the sun, the heat, the lack of beer." Pops held his beer bottle upside down.

"But," Jack said loudly. "I think you mean 'so, *I* wax.' Not 'we.'"

Pops glared at him. "Okay, smart-ass!" he said as he sat down with a fresh, cold home brew. "None for you," he concluded with a huff.

"Anyway!" both men said at the same time, indicating a desire to return to the story.

———————

A single flicker sparked in the darkness. Then another and another, then fire. As the flames cast off light, the darkened chamber came into focus. Charlie found himself sitting Indian style on the floor, two feet from the fire.

To his left lay the chief. Charlie tried to rouse him but found he was unresponsive.

"He's dead, son."

Charlie turned to the right side of the fire to find his father. "How are you... I'm dreaming," Charlie said, deflated.

"Hmph, the chief would call it a vision," Charlie's father answered wisely.

"Why am I here? Why are you here? Why is the chief dead?" Charlie spouted off in confusion. He then paused a moment, collecting his thoughts. Looking down at his hands, retracing his thoughts, he suddenly remembered. "Wilds!" he said, and he quickly looked up at his father.

"Yes, there isn't much time." Charlie's father rose to his feet. He thrust his open hand into the fire and clasped it shut before bringing it out. He slowly stepped over to Charlie, who had gotten to his feet.

His father extended his hand and opened it. There, dancing in his palm, was a small piece of the fire. It was a different color from the whole. "The chief isn't truly dead. His body died, but his soul has returned to that which he worshipped—the land. We've been sitting together for a while now, and I understand what I must give you." Charlie's father paused, and the flame flickered.

"The chief taught you love. Love of the land, love of his people, and love for yourself. It is because of that love that he will never be gone." His father paused again.

Charlie couldn't help but notice the flame diminished more and more every time his father said the word "love."

"It is to my great regret that I have come to realize all I ever gave you was hatred, rage, revenge, and sadness."

As he spoke, Charlie watched the flame increase as his father uttered the hurtful words. The part of the fire his father held was being fueled by the negativity.

His father brought the flame up to Charlie's face. "I tried, hoped, and did everything I could to drive you away from me so that I wouldn't give you this. What I should have done was teach you how to use and control it." Through the ever-growing flame, Charlie could see the pain in his father's eyes.

"Will it bring me peace?" Charlie asked, wide-eyed.

"No, son, there is no peace in this." He drew closer to Charlie.

Charlie instinctively took a step backward. "How do I stop it?"

"Look upon that which you love," his father answered, taking another step toward him.

"Dad... wait," Charlie said.

His father smiled upon hearing his son call him dad. He had earned forgiveness and in so doing found redemption.

"You have to wake up! Now!" his father yelled as he thrust the flame into Charlie's chest.

Charlie's eyes shot open. The throbbing in his head was momentary. *Wilds,* he thought as he staggered to his feet. He took a moment to get his bearings and locate his gun. Finding it easily, he turned his attention to the man wailing a few feet away. He'd suffered a gutshot and left for dead.

Rage!

Charlie grabbed the man by the shirt and raised him to eye level. "Which way?" he commanded.

The bandit spit in his face. Charlie released the man, who hit the ground with a thud and a wince. Charlie knelt down and put his revolver in his face. The bandit scoffed, "I've been gutshot, ya hear? I'm already dead."

Charlie grabbed the man by the bandana around his neck and dragged him to the wagon. Being fueled by rage made the task easy. After dropping the man near the back wheel, Charlie retreated into the wagon and shortly emerged with a barrel.

Placing it in the path of the wagon wheel, Charlie then dragged the bandit's head between the barrel and the wheel.

Hatred!

"Now, I'm going to park this wagon on your neck! You may already be dead, but the question is how much pain do you want to die in?" *Fear!* Charlie saw it as clear as day in the bandit's eyes. "Which way?"

The bandit was all too accommodating and swiftly pointed out the direction in which his cohorts had retreated. "There's a cave, in them hills straight that way. We been camping in it." The bandit coughed as he brought his hand back to hold his guts.

Charlie believed him. *Bang!* Charlie fired the gun in the air and read the sheer panic and betrayal on the bandit's face as the horses lurched forward. He kicked like fury when the wagon wheel came to rest on his neck. By the time Charlie had unhitched his horse, the bandit had stopped squirming.

"I'm counting on you, friend," Charlie said to the horse as he held him by the bit. Charlie jumped on. "Hee-yaw!" he screamed, and the two were off. The horse ran as if he had been touched with the same fury that consumed Charlie.

They rode as if their lives depended on it. Charlie's mind was consumed with the thoughts of what might be happening to Wilds. *Was she in pain?* The next thought was worse. *Was she alive or being tortured?* And worse still: *Raped?*

Charlie well understood that man's capacity for cruelty was unmatched, and he resolved to be equally cruel. With each passing thought, he slipped further into the darkness that was swiftly consuming him. Hatred almost owned his soul.

Spying the cave entrance, Charlie steered the horse in that direction. It was the right place. Two horses were tied up outside. As Charlie dismounted, he heard the most blood-curdling screams echoing out of the cave. They gave him a moment's pause, not because it was Wilds screaming, but because they were the screams of men. Charlie drew his gun and took the first step to run headlong into the cave when Wilds emerged into the light.

Her hands were holding something out in front of her, the top of her dress was ripped, and she had a bit of blood in the corner of her mouth.

Charlie dropped his gun and grabbed her shoulders. "Are you..."

She only smiled at him, slyly.

As Charlie looked her over, he stopped at her hands, in which she held two scalps and a well-sharpened blade. She was safe, and the rage left him in an instant.

"Where did you get the knife?" Charlie asked as he took it out of her hands and cut the rope hanging from her wrist.

Once the rope was cut, she tossed the scalps aside and lifted her dress to the middle of her thigh, revealing a garter with a knife holster.

A look of genuine surprise came over Charlie's face. "Do you always..." He raised his eyebrows.

"Okay, hold that thought," Jack said. He put the towel down, having just finished wiping the second coat of wax away. "Bathroom break."

Jack stood washing his hands at the sink. He was intrigued by how the water felt different after handling car wax. As he dried his hands, his elbow accidentally hit the shower curtain. A gap opened, and out of the corner of his eye, he caught something very odd.

"What the shit is that in the bathroom shower?" Jack called as he returned to the car.

"Eh?" Pops looked at Jack.

"In the shower in the guest bathroom. What is that?"

"Oh. You didn't go peepin' on Suzie, did you?"

"What?" Jack exclaimed.

———————————

The two men stood in the bathroom with their arms crossed, looking down at the monstrosity in the shower. Jack broke the silence. "Now. Huh? Explain that again."

"Okay, boy. Sexy Suzie is a sex doll that was rated the most lifelike ever. That's a first-generation Eyebit she's wearing, and it's turned on. Now, Suzy is so lifelike, and the first-gen Eyebits are so shitty, it thinks she is a real person. Because she is in the shower, it thinks she is taking a shower. Because of that, it turns on the privacy block."

"Right, I got that. But how does that translate into tricking other people's Eyebits into thinking the entire house is a person in the shower?" Jack asked, still confused.

"So that's where the pipes come in. Because she is in congress with the pipes, the Eyebit can't distinguish where she ends and the house begins. So it defaults to the largest mass detected. Presto! An entire house hidden from the Eyebit." Pops puffed his chest out proudly.

"So the pipes are like veins? Like water instead of blood, but the Eyebit can't tell the difference?" Jack asked.

"Yep."

"And the wiring is like the electric currents in a central nervous system. And the temperature changes with the weather and day and night," Jack said as he slowly began to understand.

"That's right, boy. Second-gen Eyebits won't work. Only first gen can be tricked."

"Pops, that's genius! How did you ever figure that out?"

"Know your enemy, boy. Know your enemy," Pops said and turned to leave the bathroom, rubbing his shoulder.

CHAPTER THIRTY-SIX

Eyebit immersion 15%

DON'T LEAVE US. PLEASE.

The colors of the flowers were brighter than Jack remembered. Crouching in the school memorial garden, he wondered which color was Jennifer's favorite. He ended up settling on uniqueness instead of brilliance.

It wasn't the color that "made" this flower, although that was a factor. The defining feature was the shape of the petals. Jack wasn't very good with the names of flowers. He knew it wasn't a tulip or a rose. But he also knew Jennifer would like it, which was enough to justify his picking it illegally.

As he reached out to take it, a landscaping drone buzzed over and attempted to stop him. Jack didn't think; he reacted. *Wham!*

"Fuck you!" he yelled as he punched the device to the ground.

Snapping up the flower, he quickly sprinted out of the garden. As he ran past the plaque that guarded the entrance to the garden, he gently ran his fingers along it.

"I'm awake," he said as he dashed toward the school and toward her. He found her easily enough.

———————————

He was almost on top of her before she realized he was there. She was lost in the Eyebit world. From her point of view, Jack slowly emerged into the data stream that faded into the background when she shifted her eyes to his. She liked his smile.

As he raised his hand into her field of view, her gaze shifted to the flower. Her Eyebit flashed onto the flower and pulled up a photo of it with an identification marker.

"Pretty orchid," she said as she accepted the present.

"Where did you get it?" she asked.

Hmph. So it's an orchid. "Outside in the garden," Jack said as he turned his gaze back to the flower.

"There's a garden here?" Jennifer asked with a hint of surprise in her voice.

Jack smiled. "Yep, sure is. Come on I'll show you." He took her by the hand and turned to lead her outside.

She didn't move. "Jack, listen, I had a really good…" She was cut off as another voice overpowered hers.

"Is this him?" Jennifer's boyfriend stood taller than Jack, looking down at him. He must have been fairly popular because he was flanked by two equally sized boys on either side.

"Him who?" Jack asked sarcastically.

That seemed to make the boyfriend angrier. Jack had never been in a fight with anyone other than his father before. This felt different. With Kyle, there was always a sense of being inferior, but also a feeling of safety. Jack knew that Kyle wouldn't really hurt him, and Jack always held back, just a little.

Neither of those two stipulations applied here. Jack recognized what he was feeling. He had been experiencing it more and more lately. Adrenaline pumped into his veins. Anxiety, fear, and anger found their way into Jack's hands as he mentally prepared himself. Jennifer's boyfriend lurched at him and grabbed his shirt. Jack braced for an impact that never came.

Jennifer, her boyfriend, and his friends had stopped and stood like statues around Jack. Every person in the immediate vicinity stood as rigid as soldiers. Jack didn't notice right away, but all seven encircled him. With their Eyebits flashing red, the seven students locked arms and formed an unbreakable circle around Jack. Unable to escape or break free, he was forced to move with them as they marched. To where, he didn't know.

They reached the front of the school near the main office and stopped. After they'd waited for a few minutes, the principal emerged from his office and stood within one foot of every student encircling Jack. After the principal's Eyebit interacted with the students', the red light on their individual Eyebits stopped flashing, and they seemed to come out of the trance.

Now freed from one trance, the students quickly trapped themselves again in the Eyebit world and sat, as instructed by the principal.

Jack stood alone, face-to-face with the principal.

"So, you're the cause of today's disruptions," the principal said.

Jack, not interested in anything except Jennifer, looked over his shoulder in her direction before looking back at the principal. "Oh, just today? What a shame."

"Congratulations. Public Violence Riot Prevention Control Mode hasn't been activated in over fifteen years. Step into my office, Jack." The principal extended his arm, showing Jack the way.

Jack sat across from the principal; the office was beige with no pictures. Nothing sat on the desk. Not one single item was in the room to distinguish it. The complete lack of anything caused Jack to ponder the purpose of the desk.

"You know, this would be a lot easier if you would just put on your Eyebit," the principal said.

Jack didn't break eye contact. "Nope."

The principal looked genuinely confused. "But we need to communicate."

"Nope," Jack said, unwavering.

The principal exhaled loudly. "All right, fine. You know you're about to lose your conformity credit."

Jack had been waiting for that threat. "Oh really? And what's the penalty for that?" he sneered.

The principal boldly proclaimed, "You won't get to graduate!"

Jack grinned devilishly. "Oh really? Say, can you point to that rule for me? Where exactly is that documented?"

The haze lifted, and Jennifer found herself seated on a bench across from the principal's office. Through the open door, she could see the back of Jack's head and the face of a very frustrated principal. As she reoriented herself, she felt something in her hand.

Luckily, whatever had taken over her body hadn't forced her to crush the flower Jack had given her. As she stared at it, she disengaged her Eyebit, and she was able to get an unencumbered look. The visual stimulation had an accompaniment—the flower also had a smell.

It's sweet, she thought. Wanting to share this discovery, she naturally reached for her boyfriend.

She turned to him. "Hey, look at this."

Her boyfriend didn't respond. She put her hand on his arm to get his attention. "Hey, look at..." She didn't get to finish her sentence before her boyfriend showed his annoyance at her disengagement. He quickly jerked his arm out of her grasp.

"I'm not looking at that," he snapped.

"Why?"

"Do you really have to ask? You aren't wearing your Eyebit."

"So you can't show me the rule?" Jack asked again.

The flustered principal had never had so much trouble with a student before. "Conformity is key to society; without it, we would fall back into anarchy. If you don't conform, you don't move on."

Jack stacked his fists on the principal's desk and rested his chin on them. Leaning over the desk, he said, "Sooo, what then? I stay here with you?"

The principal squinted at Jack. "I've contacted Kyle. You need to wait in the hall."

"I just want to show you this," Jennifer said as she put the flower directly into her boyfriend's line of sight. Even more annoyed, he slapped her hand away from his face, hard enough that she dropped the flower.

"Yeah, okay. We need to talk," she said as she rose to her feet. Her soon-to-be-ex-boyfriend sat pouting with his arms crossed. "I said, we need to talk," Jennifer commanded as she stood with her hands on her hips.

"I'm not doing anything till you put your Eyebit on."

Jennifer didn't move.

"I said put it on, Jennifer!"

She didn't budge. Before she knew what was happening, he had ahold of both her arms just below her shoulders. "Put it on! Put it *on*! Put it on now!" He was screaming in her face as he shook her violently.

"Ssstooop it, you're hurting me."

––––––––––––––

"And when he gets here, we will all sit down and figure out how to make you conform," the principal said as he opened the door to the hallway, where everyone who had brought Jack there was still waiting. Jack didn't look up as he walked through.

Jack had his Eyebit the entire time but wanted to see what would happen when he forced someone with authority to talk to him on his terms. Looking down at it in his hands, he contemplated if he could never put it on again. Hearing Jennifer's voice in distress caused him to look up. When he saw what was happening, all his thoughts were whisked away.

There, not ten feet away, was Jennifer in danger from her boyfriend. Jack's hands opened, and his Eyebit was gone. His nostrils flared, and his pupils dilated as something primal unleashed itself within his body.

He stepped forward and unshackled himself from the insecurity and fears of boyhood. The first step felt like it took an eternity to complete. He couldn't get there fast enough. Tunnel vision had narrowed his focus. No longer thinking of himself, he lunged at the pair. He bounded effortlessly, the first stride covering five feet, and then with the next one, he was on top of them. *Faster, Jack! Too slow!*

"Hey!" Jack screamed as he grabbed her boyfriend's arm and turned him to face him. A split second after the two made eye contact, Jack's fist struck his nose. The boyfriend's face disappeared into a haze of crimson and shattered Eyebit pieces. He didn't fall, but he did let go of Jennifer.

Before he got a chance to bring his hands up to instinctively cover his face, Jack managed another two punches in rapid succession. Enveloped in blinding rage, Jack continued swinging and advancing. Motivated by more than the threat to Jennifer, Jack let loose all the frustrations that had been mounting over the last months.

By the seventh swing, Jack felt a bone in his hand pop. Allowing himself to pause, he looked at his hand. It was covered in blood, but it wasn't his. He uncurled his fingers and watched as the space under his pinky began to swell.

Jack's attention turned back to the boyfriend, who by this point was on his knees, wailing. Not because of pain—he was weeping over his shattered Eyebit. "You broke it! You broke it... I'm broken... I'm broken..." The boyfriend was scrambling along the floor, attempting to pick up the shards of glass as if he could repair them somehow.

Jack's attention then turned to the principal, who had rushed to the boyfriend's side. Opening a case that read First Aid, he quickly produced an Eyebit, opened it, and placed it on the boyfriend's face. His wailing immediately stopped, and a look of euphoria washed over his face. The principal looked up at Jack and handed him a first-aid bit. Jack ignored him.

Jack was surprised to see a group of onlookers had formed. As most of them were friends of the boyfriend, Jack prepared himself for more fighting. He put himself between them and Jennifer. They all took notice of Jack's fist, and they all backed off when he looked at them.

"Oh good, you're here! I need to see both of you in my office, now!" the principal said to Kyle, who had come to stand beside Jack without him noticing.

Kyle looked his son in the eye, not as man to boy but as man to man. "Are you hurt?" he asked.

Jack broke eye contact with Kyle and looked at his hands. "Oh yeah. It's not my blood." His expression did not betray a single thread of emotion.

"That's not what I meant. Are you all right?"

Jack thought a moment, and despite the pain he was beginning to feel in his hand, he said, "Yeah, I think I will be."

Jack and Kyle sat across from the principal, and for some reason that he could not articulate, Kyle felt nervous. There was no explanation for his anxiety. Was he worried for his son or for himself?

"There hasn't been violence inside this establishment since long before I came here. I didn't even know how to use this kit!" the principal said.

Jack and Kyle sat in silence.

"This is absurd! This behavior will not be tolerated. Jack will conform! He will wear his Eyebit! He will show up every day and graduate with full conformity credits!"

A moment of silence passed in the room before Jack stood. "I will graduate, but I'm not doing it with that thing," he said. Then he turned and headed for the door.

Kyle remained seated and contemplated for a moment how to best handle this situation. The principal had irked him, and he didn't like it. The two men sat looking at each other in silence.

"Well, you're the parent. Do something!" the principal commanded.

Kyle breathed deeply; he had no intention of making Jack do anything. "You heard the man. You and I both know that conformity credits are no more real than the permanent record." Kyle watched the principal blink in disbelief.

"But... But... the rules state that...." The principal trailed off as he struggled with his words.

"Here's what I'm going to do. I'm going to give you an opportunity to avoid the fiasco that will ensue if you don't graduate him. I have no problem pursuing legal action. I may not have a rat's-ass chance of beating the system, but I can sure as shit bring this whole institution to light." Kyle stood and left the office, leaving the principal in slack-jawed bewilderment.

Kyle jogged to try and catch up with Jack. When he reached him, he couldn't help but notice a very pretty redhead sitting and waiting for her parents while holding a crushed orchid. Kyle didn't have to ask; he knew who she was.

Lagging behind, Kyle took stock of the girl who was at the center of the day's commotion. Jennifer's eyes leaped from the orchid to meet Jack's when she saw him approaching. Jennifer gave Jack a look—not the kind of look for a stranger or even a close relative. This look was longing in nature. The kind lovers share. Her face was relaxed, her eyebrows slightly elevated, and Kyle could see her pupils dilate from where he was standing. Once Jack was within arm's reach, she put her hands on his shoulders, ran them down both his arms, then instinctively cradled his hand, which was visibly swollen.

Kyle cleared his throat to get their attention. "Son, are you going to introduce me?"

"Oh, right. Jennifer, this is Kyle," Jack said as he gestured to him.

"Jennifer, nice to meet you. I hope my son hasn't caused you too much trouble." Kyle smiled.

Without taking her eyes off Jack, she responded, "No, I don't mind." She gave a slight smile of pleasure. Skimming over the suggestive tone—which Jack wasn't picking up on—Kyle passed on the remainder of the pleasantries.

"Well, Rocky, let's get that hand looked at. Whaddya say?" Kyle said as he slapped a hand on Jack's shoulder. Acting like he thought Jack was right behind him, he stepped away, looking toward the exit, slyly giving the two another moment of semi-privacy.

Not bad, boy. Not too bad at all, Kyle thought as he walked to the transport.

———————

The hospital proved to be just as difficult as the school. Kyle had to do most of the talking because Jack refused to put on an Eyebit. It was only after Kyle held the doctor's hand and moved it over Jack's hand that they were able to get him treated. Applying the splint even required the doctor to take his Eyebit off. The hospital visit took way longer than it should have.

The transport zipped along its path. It took Jack a moment to realize they weren't headed home. "Where are we going?"

Kyle, facing forward, answered coolly. "We're going to have a word with your grandfather."

Jack fidgeted with his hand splint. The pain pulsed with every heartbeat, and he wondered when it would stop.

"You know, the doctor said that will hurt less if you put on your Eyebit," Kyle said with a slight tone of agitation.

"Yeah... right. That doctor was just mad that he had to dust off... What was it called again?" Jack looked at Kyle with a furrowed brow.

With a huff, Kyle begrudgingly answered, "A 3D printer."

"Right, yeah. That thing was really old. I'm surprised it still worked." Jack grinned, knowing he was annoying his father.

Kyle scowled. "Yep, a word with your grandfather."

When they arrived, Kyle burst through the front door of Pops's house and announced, "Dad! We gotta talk!"

"He's probably in the garage," Jack said, following in his wake.

"Dad!" Kyle called out again as he made his way toward the garage.

"Yeah, we're in trouble again, Pops," Jack announced mockingly.

"See? That! That's what we need to talk about. Dad!" Kyle's words trailed off as he opened the garage door. His mood suddenly shifted and swung in the opposite direction. In an instant, just a blink of an eye, Kyle went from angry to concerned to scared. *"Dad?"*

Belle's driver-side door was open, and Pops was at rest on the garage floor with his back leaning against the car. His head hung low, and he was pale. He looked somewhat at ease, as if he were simply taking a rest. The stillness of his chest and the paleness of his skin indicated otherwise.

"Dad!" Kyle called out in defiance against what his eyes were telling him. Then he said, "Pops?" with a doubt and a whisper.

CHAPTER THIRTY-SEVEN

Eyebit Immersion 5%

WE LOVE YOU. NO ONE ELSE WILL...

Charlie rode behind Wilds. The sun was setting in front of them, and as he stared at her, the streaming light perfectly silhouetted her shape, reminding him of her feminine beauty. *I'd chase this woman anywhere,* he thought, as he daydreamed about the rest of their lives.

Wilds looked over her shoulder and caught Charlie staring at her. He knew it was pointless to act like he wasn't ogling and gave her a wink. She smiled. The homestead was close, and they would be home before dark if they hurried.

Jack crowded into Pops's field of vision. He tried to talk to Jack but couldn't summon the strength to form the words. He knew this was the end. With his last exhale he muttered a single word.

"Home..."

"No! No! No! No!" Jack hit his knees in front of Pops. "Kyle, help me!" Jack called out. "Hang on, Pops, we're gonna get you some help." He looked at his father. "Kyle? Help me!"

Kyle was frozen. He hadn't moved since they entered the garage. Shock and disbelief were apparent on his face.

"Kyle! Help!" Jack called again, to no avail.

I have to get him outside. Then Kyle's Eyebit will work, Jack thought as he jumped up and headed for the garage door opener. As he ran past Kyle, he pleaded again, "Kyle, help me, please." Kyle didn't move.

The garage door was mostly up when Jack decided he was going to try and carry Pops outside himself. He clenched Pops's coveralls with both hands. As he squeezed his right hand, pain from the broken metacarpal electrified his arm. He let go of Pops's coveralls and slumped back in pain, cradling his broken hand. He couldn't lift Pops on his own. They were losing time. Panic was setting in, and Jack had to do something.

The pain. The panic. The fear. The denial. These were all culminating inside Jack as he felt more and more helpless. He had to *do something.* All these emotions boiled over, and he called out to Kyle one more time. "Dad!"

It hit like a thunderclap! Hearing his son call him dad for the first time brought Kyle out of his trance. His son needed his help, and the world flooded in. He jumped, and in a flash, he picked up Pops under both arms and dragged him outside.

"I'm sorry, Dad. I have to look," Kyle said as his Eyebit reengaged and started to scan Pops's body.

Human... Male... Person unknown... Deceased... Cause of death: myocardial infarction... Likelihood of resuscitation: 0%... Coroner notified.

The Eyebit information flashed across Kyle's field of vision, and he knew there was nothing he could do. That moment seemed to last forever. Kyle placed his hand on Pops's chest, and for a brief minute fantasized about being able to transfer some of his life force to his father's body if only for a few seconds, and if it would allow him to say goodbye to Jack.

But he couldn't because that wasn't reality, and that reality came crashing down on him as the tears began to stream down his face. Remembering something his mother had always said—*Hearing is the last thing to go*—Kyle leaned closer to Pops's ear.

"Dad, I forgave you a long time ago," he confided as his heart burst open and the last ounce of hate he harbored for his father dissipated.

Kyle knew Pops heard him, just like he knew Pops heard Jack call him dad. He watched as Pops's body appeared to relax more than he had ever witnessed him relax in life, to the point he thought he caught a faint smile on his face. With that, he knew Pops, or the spark that made Pops who he was, was gone.

A few seconds passed as Kyle composed himself for what was about to happen. He had to tell Jack, who had been standing nervously behind him this whole time. He breathed deep, exhaled, and switched off his Eyebit. He stood and faced him.

"Son, I'm sorry," Kyle said as he looked at Jack. He watched as the information registered and Jack's chin began to tremble. Kyle reached out to embrace Jack but was swatted away.

———————————

"No, no, no, no, no, no," Jack said as he rushed to Pops's side, unwilling to believe what Kyle was telling him. "This can't be it. It can't!" Jack turned his attention back to Kyle. "Do something, damn it. Don't just stand there." He turned back to Pops's body. "Look, look, look, I took off my Eyebit. I'm not going to wear it anymore,"

Jack said, trying to bargain. "Please get up." He all but whimpered as his voice trailed off. "Get up... please..."

Grief was setting in, and he was crying now. The tears dripped off his cheeks and landed on Pops's coveralls like small raindrops. Crouched on his knees beside the body, Jack began to sob.

I needed more time, he thought as he balled his left fist around Pops's coveralls. *I could have come to meet you sooner. I should have. Why didn't I? This is my fault...*

Jack breathed deep, sucking the air through his gritted teeth. The anger was mounting, and it had to go somewhere. He turned on Kyle.

Jack sprang to his feet and started toward Kyle, who didn't move. "Do something! You have to do something! I don't know what to do! You can't just let him die!" Jack continued to sob.

With gritted teeth and angry eyes, Jack pounded on Kyle's chest. These weren't blows with the intent to harm. They weren't the kind of hits one sees in a fight. These were the knockings of a desperate man trying to force open a permanently closed door.

Kyle knew Jack wasn't going to hurt him, and for a few moments, he let his son wail on his chest. He also expected Jack to recoil once the pain from his hand registered, but he didn't. Kyle himself was fighting his own tears, not for Pops but for the pain he knew his son was in.

A memory flashed to life in Kyle. Once when Jack was about five, a wasp had stung him on the back of the knee. They had been playing, and Kyle watched Jack's expression change from mild curiosity to sheer panic.

Jack said, "Ouch, what's that?" then reached behind his knee to feel it. When he brought his hand back around, there was a very menacing black and red wasp in it.

Terror set in for Jack, and he began to scream. Kyle couldn't get him to stop. He couldn't reason with him. Everything he said just made Jack wail louder. The trauma was overpowering his Eyebit's ability to manage the situation. It was up to Kyle to comfort his son.

The memory provided the answer. He reached out and pulled Jack into his chest. Jack's arms folded up between them, and he had nowhere to go. Jack tried to squirm and break free, but Kyle just squeezed tighter.

"He's gone, son. He's gone," Kyle said as he felt Jack give up the fight and slump further into his embrace.

For the first time in longer than he could remember, Kyle felt like the gulf between him and Jack was bridgeable. In his last act, Pops had managed to do what generations of men in this family could never accomplish—reach each other. In an exceptional moment of clarity, Kyle understood the gift Pops had given him. He, Kyle, could change everything!

Okay, Dad, okay, he thought as the sound of the coroner drones approached from the distance.

CHAPTER THIRTY-EIGHT

Eyebit Immersion 0%

WELCOME, NEW USER. THE FUTURE AWAITS...

Jack stood in the garage of Pops's house, staring at Belle from the driver's side. The coat of wax he had applied a few days ago could still be felt. Pops's voice echoed in Jack's head as he replayed an earlier conversation.

"It's what I call pivotal freedom, and it's a time in a person's life when they have all the means to live and none of the responsibilities yet. If people are lucky, it lasts a whole summer. You're in it now, Jacky. Your parents still support you, you're about done with school, and everyone you've ever known or cared about is still alive. Enjoy it, revel in it, maximize it, 'cause when it's gone, boy, it's gone for good."

"Jack, you ready to go?" Kyle called to him from the garage door.

Jack was snapped back to the present. "Yeah." He walked out of the garage. "Where are we going again?"

Kyle and Claire were standing hand in hand. "To the lawyer's. We've finished Pops's list, and he has his will. Once we prove we fulfilled everything according to his last wishes, they will read it."

Jack pondered the possible answers for a moment before asking the obvious question. "And why do we have to physically go down there?"

Kyle cocked a smile. "Well, your grandfather was so stubborn that he never digitized anything, so the actual document is located at the lawyer's office and can't be opened until we are all present."

As the transport zipped along its path, the trio rode in silence. All three knew the others' thoughts were of their significant moments with Pops.

———————

"You know what the hardest part about being a father is?" Pops's voice whispered in Kyle's mind. "Watching and letting your children fail. Knowing you have the power and ability to keep whatever thing from happening and still letting it happen. It'll tear you up inside."

The transport pinged as it pulled into the parking garage. Jack climbed out first. Kyle smiled as he watched Jack jitter the same way Pops had every time he got out of a transport. In his mind's eye, he saw an image of Jack as he was before he brought him to Pops's.

No longer was Jack the practically catatonic, Eyebit-addicted conformist he had been almost a year ago. Even his clothes had changed. He was wearing some of Pops's and Kyle's old things, not the Eyebit projection suit. Jack had become an independent man.

"I'm proud of you, son," Kyle said as he clasped his hands on Jack's shoulders and the two made eye contact. Kyle could tell his mind was somewhere else, but that was okay.

"Thanks, Dad," Jack said as he retreated into his thoughts.

———————

Jack was reliving a moment in Pops's garage.

"Wait, seawater? I thought all these old cars ran on gas."

"Not this one. I fixed it. Now listen, you can't use simply salt and tap water. It has to be seawater," Pops instructed him carefully.

"Why is that?" Jack closely examined the jug of seawater.

"Yeah, I know it looks like regular water, but something to do with the bacteria and sea life makes it all work. Like women—so much beneath the surface."

Jack's memory was silenced as the elevator doors closed.

––––––––––––––

The elevator doors squeaked shut, and Claire's mind was filled with her own last encounter with Pops.

"Are you listening to me?" Claire asked forcefully.

"Yeah, I hear you, Claire," Pops said as he cowered in the corner, trying to make himself invisible.

"Good! Now you better damn well listen. Kyle is going to email you, and you will respond. You will play ball, and you will see them." Claire wagged her finger at Pops with her other hand on her hip and her torso pushed forward.

"And if I don't?" Pops asked as he rubbed his shoulder.

"Well, Charles, you remember where I work, right? The Bit Corps of Engineers, and I've already figured out a workaround for your privacy mode. To be blunt, I'll bake in a fix, and it will go to every Eyebit, everywhere," Claire promised as she took a few steps closer to Pops, further cornering him. "You with me, Chuck?" she asked as she stooped to look Pops in the eye.

"Yes, ma'am."

Claire's position with the Eyebit Corps allowed her to override Pops's privacy mode, and her Eyebit functioned inside his garage. She looked him over without his knowledge and gave him what she figured was the closest thing he had had to a medical exam in years.

"You should get your heart checked. It's not looking so good."

She was slapped back to reality as the lawyer's door swiped open.

———————

The lawyer unlocked the metal box and withdrew the sealed envelopes. "Okay, before we begin, have all the final restitutions been completed?"

It was Claire who answered. "Yes, the estate is as he left it. The remains were processed and left in the plot next to his wife."

"Yes, yes, okay, good." The lawyer shifted the papers, searching for one specific item to ask about. "And the... ummm, coffin knockers?" Immediately upon hearing the words "coffin knockers," Claire rolled her eyes and let out a huff. Jack and Kyle chuckled loudly.

The lawyer looked at the family blankly. "I'm sorry. I don't get the joke."

Kyle flicked his eyes and pushed a video file to the lawyer's Eyebit. The screen came up and displayed to the lawyer the image of Pops lying in a coffin with the lid open. From the left of the screen, Kyle walked toward the coffin. In his hands, he held a pair of prosthetic breasts.

These were the most perfectly shaped breasts he had ever seen. The lawyer watched, captivated, as Kyle fixed the breasts to the coffin lid. Once they were secured, Kyle tested the placement. He opened and closed the lid several times. Crouching beside the coffin, Kyle peered through the crack. He had to make sure that Pops's mouth and nose lined up so that one breast fit firmly on each side of his face.

The video ended, and the lawyer caught himself smiling. "So, let me get this right. He was buried that way, with those left on his face?"

"That's the way he wanted it," Kyle answered.

The lawyer cleared his throat. "Are those for sale somewhere?" His cheeks flushed red when no one answered him. "With all the final arrangements met, I will continue with the reading of the will."

The envelope was thick. The lawyer fumbled with the papers, flipping through several loose-leaf pages. "Okay, here we go." He cleared his throat again.

"To my grandson, I leave the estate and all the holdings of the house and the land on which it sits," he read aloud. "There's a note handwritten in the margins of the will. 'Always know your surroundings.'"

There was a moment of silence before the lawyer asked, "Does anybody know what that means?" He cocked an eyebrow.

All three shook their heads.

"Okay, well, looks like the land parcel is sizable. He made the last purchase a few months ago, completing ownership of the area formerly known as the Regent Heights subdivision."

Kyle cut his eyes and tilted his head slightly. "Wait, so he bought the entire neighborhood? I knew he owned most of it."

The lawyer nodded. "Yes, looks that way." He then turned his attention to Jack. "I'm sorry, son. My advice would be to try and sell to a garbage company and make it a landfill." The lawyer then returned to the will. "The deeds have been transferred into Jack's name. However, before ownership can be completed, Jack has to agree to consulting a financial planner and taking classes on precious metals and mechanical engineering."

Claire huffed. "Is that it?"

"Not quite," the lawyer said. "Included in this envelope are these. They look like work orders, receipts, notes, some maps..."

Kyle reached across the desk and began to examine the papers. "Well, it looks like he was trying to track down the leftover dirt from when they built the bank building downtown. Oh wait, looks like he found it here." He separated one piece of paper from the pile. "Well, that's strange. It says the address is in the same neighborhood as his house. Looks like the dirt was used throughout the entire neighbor-hood."

It took a moment for what Kyle had just said to sink in. Kyle and Jack realized the implications at the same time and said, in unison, "Son of a bitch!"

————————

"Wait, I don't understand," Claire said after uncountable moments of quiet as the transport zipped back to Pops's house at top speed.

"What's not to understand, honey? This whole area was the site of the country's first gold rush. When they built the big bank build-ing downtown, the construction company punched into an old gold mine. It had been abandoned for years and was forgotten."

"Yeah, so?" Claire was still confused.

"So after the turn of the millennium, prospectors started reopening old mines and going in with updated technology and metal detectors. Now, they didn't make gigantic finds, but there was enough to make them all rich." Kyle spoke passionately as he fantasized about what was just sitting there, waiting for the taking.

"Okay?" Claire still was not quiet making the connection.

"Okay, so they didn't inspect the dirt from the mine before they hauled it away and brought it to the neighborhood! So Pops owned the whole neighborhood, and that's where he got his gold from! His own backyard! Wheee!" Kyle yelled as he jumped around in his seat.

Pops's voice shouted in Jack's head louder than anything Kyle could produce. "A prospector never gives up his spot, boy!"

"Know your surroundings," Jack said, which brought silence in the transport. No one said a word for the rest of the trip.

The transport stopped outside Pops's house. Jack was the first out, and much to his surprise, he found Jennifer waiting... along with a large group of people.

She immediately embraced Jack, and he whispered in her ear, "Who are these people?"

Jennifer broke her hug and looked at Jack. "I don't know all of them." She tried to look around casually with raised eyebrows. "I took my Eyebit off and came to find you. My parents came with me, but we kept meeting these people wandering around without Eyebits." She shrugged. "They followed us here."

There was a brief moment of silence as Jack looked at the man and woman standing on either side of Jennifer. Realizing who they most likely were, he said, "And these are your parents?"

"Oh, right. Yes. This is Jeff and June."

"Young man, Jennifer told us what happened at school the other day. Thank you for taking care of our daughter," Jeff said.

"We're sorry to hear about your grandfather," June said.

No physical greetings were exchanged. Jack only smiled, nodded, and said, "Yes, of course" to Jeff and "Thank you" to June.

Jack cast his eyes upon the sea of Eyebit-less faces. Most of them just stared at him, but a few were whispering loud enough for him to hear.

"Is that him?" one said.

A different voice followed up the first. "I heard he beat up the principal and took his diploma!"

Jack's eyes darted in the direction of that voice. "Not quite."

"I heard he has an invisible transport," a voice said from the other side of the crowd.

"It's not invisible, exactly…" Jack started to explain but wasn't allowed to finish before being cut off by another random comment.

"I heard he is the terrorist from the mall!"

Jack was quick to answer that one forcefully. "That one wasn't entirely me."

By this point, Jennifer was standing beside Jack, holding his hand. The chorus of voices was rising until one voice shouted out the most basic question that was baffling everyone who stood there.

"How do you survive without your Eyebit?"

Jack jutted his chin out and squeezed Jennifer's hand. "Here we go," he said softly, so only she could hear.

"Come and help me build a fire, and I will tell you," Jack said more loudly as he cut through the dead center of the crowd with Jennifer in tow.

The chorus of voices whispered, "Fire? Real fire?"

The warm orange glow cast light on every face in the crowd. Jack sat leaning forward with his elbows resting on his thighs. He held Pops's cowboy hat in his hands. All eyes were fixed on Jack as he began to speak. "This is the story about a man who refused to conform and his best friend, a Mustang horse named Belle..."

CHAPTER THIRTY-NINE

Conclusion

"And the rest, as they say, is history," Jack said as he addressed the small crowd of museum workers that had gathered to listen to him.

"So, everything else came after your grandfather died?" one of the listeners asked.

"That's right. The grassroots movement, the great switch off, the reemergence, all happened after," Jack said.

"Wow. What a story," one of the workers said.

"And then, of course, you and your dad's engine designs helped reinspire the space programs," another worker said.

"Yes. Also another story." Jack looked down at his granddaughter, who was fidgeting with the set of keys he had given her. It didn't matter what she did, he always found himself smiling when he was around her.

Every now and then he would catch a glimpse of Kyle dance across her face, but it was the tufts of her grandmother Jennifer's red hair that endeared him the most. It wasn't until she was born that he truly understood what it was to be a grandparent. He initially thought it would be like being a dad, but he was wrong. Being a granddad was immensely better.

There's a quality of redemption that comes when you're an involved grandparent. A second chance to do everything right that you got wrong as a parent. All the things you couldn't do for your children, if you're humble, you can do with your grandchildren. And having come full circle, he had a better understanding of Pops, Kyle, and his story. *Still teachin' me stuff,* Jack thought.

"Papaw Jack?" his granddaughter said as she looked up at him.

"Yes, sweetie?"

"This car looks different from the one we're building."

All the museum workers looked at Jack with wide eyes. "You're building another car?" one of them asked.

Before Jack could respond, the supervisor took to dispersing the group. "All right, you all, that's enough. It's closing time. Check your areas and clock out," she said, waving her hands as if she were dusting an invisible shelf. She returned her attention to Jack while backing away from the exhibit of Belle. "You two take as long as you like."

"Papaw Jack?" his granddaughter asked.

"Yes, sweetie?"

"How does the story with Charlie and Wilds and the horsy end?"

"Well, you know, I never got to hear it, but I like to think they made it to the homestead, had a family, and lived out their days. After all, we wouldn't be here if they hadn't, right?" Jack crouched down to look her in the eyes.

She broke eye contact and looked at Belle for a moment. "We think that's right."

"Who's 'we,' sweetie?"

"Me and the old man in the car. He's doing this." She presented Jack with a thumbs-up on her little right hand. "Tee-hee-hee. He has a funny hat," she added as she giggled and looked at the car.

Jack looked over at the car but wasn't surprised to see that it was empty. Of course, he didn't have to see anything to know who was in it. "Well, I'm glad we are all in agreement. Is he doing anything else?"

"No, he's gone. He waved bye." She turned to Jack and demonstrated a wave. Then she turned back to the car and waved at it too. "Byyye."

Jack felt his heart warm as he stood upright. He and his granddaughter stood in the presence of Belle for a few more moments as the overhead lights began to switch off, indicating the museum was closing up for the night.

"Come on, sweetie. If we're late to supper again, your dad and Grandma Jenn are both gonna have our hides, and we don't want that," he said as he took her by the hand and started walking toward the exit.

"Papaw Jack?"

"Yes, sweetie?"

"Can we color my racecar like a rainbow with a unicorn on it?"

"Sure, sweetie, if that's what you want." Jack answered without a moment's hesitation because when it came to little Charline, he'd do anything to make her happy. "Which way do you want the stripes to go?"

"The rainbow way," Charline answered confidently.

Before Jack could ask her what she meant, she said his name again. "Papaw Jack?"

"Yes, sweetie?" He grinned.

"Will you tell me the story again? Charlie and Wilds and the horsy?"

"Sure, sweetie." Jack paused a moment and breathed deeply before continuing. "Okay. A long, long time ago, when our ancestor Charlie was a young man..."